Yana swiped at the sweat on her forehead. "Now will somebody please tell me what happened back there? Starting with whatever that old woman was yelling about."

"Right," Tycho said. "She was talking about a secret. And Iris. What is that?"

"An old spacer's tale from our great-grandfather's day," Carlo said. "And apparently it's what Captain Lumbaba was looking for. There's no platinum in the Hildas, but maybe there's something else."

"What are you talking about?" Yana asked.

"A fortune," Carlo said. "Waiting out there for somebody to claim it."

· BOOK TWO ·

THE JUPITER PIRATES

CURSE OF THE IRIS

BY JASON FRY

HARPER

An Imprint of HarperCollinsPublishers

The Jupiter Pirates: Curse of the *Iris*
Text copyright © 2014 by Jason Fry

Library of Congress Cataloging-in-Publication Data
Fry, Jason, date
  Curse of the Iris / by Jason Fry. — First edition.
    pages cm. — (The Jupiter pirates ; book 2)
  Summary: "As Tycho and his siblings continue to compete for the
captain's chair of the Shadow Comet, they must work together to
hunt for an old pirate treasure—a treasure that is tied to some long-
buried family secrets"— Provided by publisher.
  ISBN 978-0-06-223024-9
  [1. Science fiction. 2. Space ships—Fiction. 3. Pirates—Fiction.
4. Buried treasure—Fiction. 5. Brothers and sisters—Fiction.
6. Conduct of life—Fiction.] I. Title.
PZ7.F9224Cur 2014   2014001895
[Fic]—dc23   CIP
                                                                AC

Typography by Anna Christian
❖
16 17 18 19 20   OPM   10 9 8 7 6 5 4 3 2 1
First paperback edition, 2016

FOR MOM AND DAD,

WHO TAUGHT ME THAT A HOUSE

OVERFLOWING WITH BOOKS

IS A GOOD START

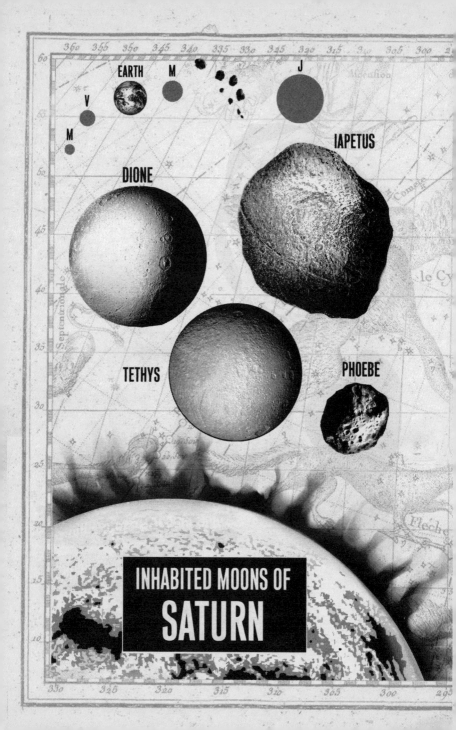

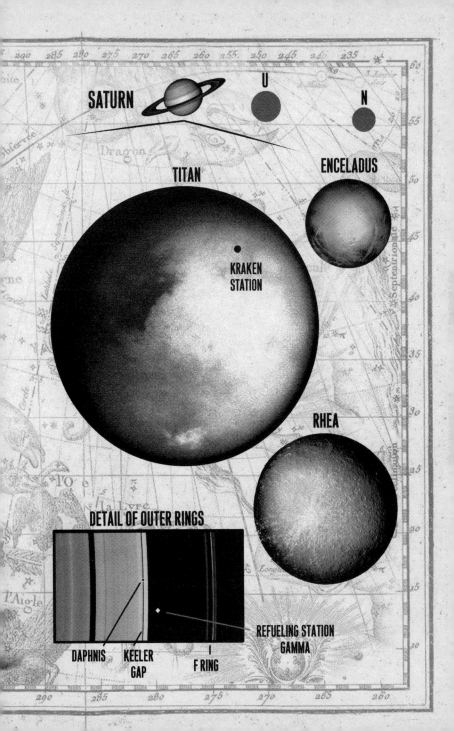

SATURN

U

N

ENCELADUS

TITAN

KRAKEN
STATION

RHEA

DETAIL OF OUTER RINGS

DAPHNIS   KEELER
GAP

I
F RING

REFUELING STATION
GAMMA

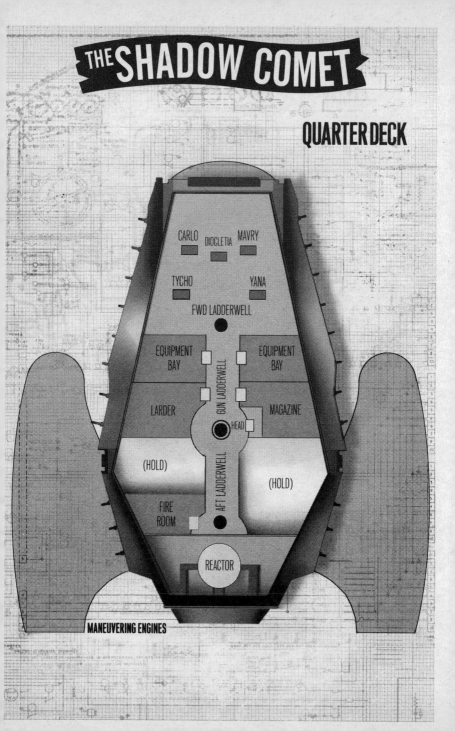

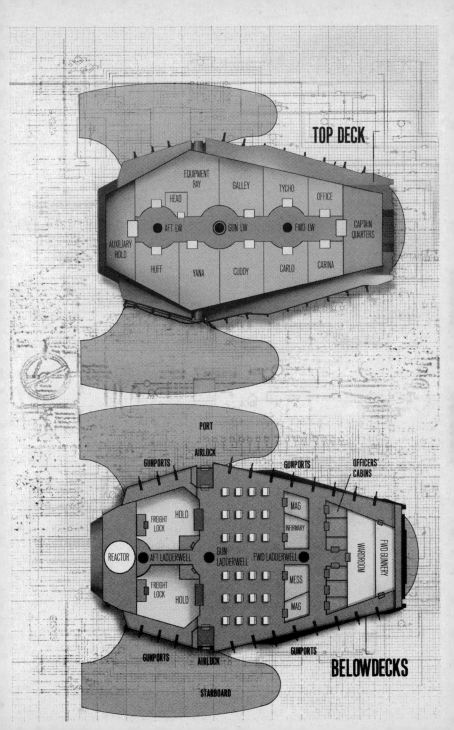

CONTENTS

CHAPTER 1: Asteroid Encounter 1

CHAPTER 2: Death Ship 14

CHAPTER 3: Titan 28

CHAPTER 4: The Tale of the *Iris* 47

CHAPTER 5: Mission to P/2093 K1 63

CHAPTER 6: The Hunted 83

CHAPTER 7: Return to Ceres 88

CHAPTER 8: The Mysterious Message 113

CHAPTER 9: Water and Ore 138

CHAPTER 10: Loris Unger 160

CHAPTER 11: A Princeling of Ganymede 176

CHAPTER 12: Jupiter Invasion 192

CHAPTER 13: Europa and Io 204

CHAPTER 14: The Callisto Depths 223

CHAPTER 15: The *Iris* Cache 243

CHAPTER 16: What Vesuvia Knew 258

CHAPTER 17: Showdown at Saturn 275

CHAPTER 18: The Family Is the Ship 301

CHAPTER 19: At Saint Mary's 312

A SPACER'S LEXICON 321

1

ASTEROID ENCOUNTER

Tycho Hashoone went over the checklist in his head one more time before he stepped back from the cannon in the bow of the *Shadow Comet*.

Projectile loaded into drum. Charge set. Projectile transferred to loading cradle. Cradle status green. Barrel clear. Barrel status green.

"Good to go, Mr. Grigsby," Tycho said.

The *Comet*'s hulking warrant officer nodded, his white dreadlocks bobbing. He looked over at Huff Hashoone, who stood watching them in the gunnery bay. Grigsby raised an eyebrow, and Tycho's grandfather grinned—or at least, a smile split the half of his face that was still flesh and blood. The right half of his head was gleaming chrome, his artificial eye a brilliant spark of white light.

"Ready to fire then, Master Tycho?" Grigsby asked. The tattoos on his powerful arms illuminated in response to some internal timer, sending green, orange, and blue fire snaking across his dark-brown skin.

Tycho looked back at the cannon. The firing console was silent, waiting for the command that would send a shell hurtling across space. He started to go through the checklist again, then shook his head. Huff and Grigsby were just testing him, trying to throw off his confidence.

"Ready," Tycho said. "Fire at will, Mr. Grigsby."

"Pow," said Grigsby as he pantomimed tapping the gun's firing console with his fingertips.

"Yeh only forgot one thing, lad," Huff said. "Too bad it was important."

"What?" Tycho asked. "What did I—"

He stopped and went through the checklist again. Cradle status green, barrel status green, and . . .

Oh.

"I fired the gun with the projectile locked in the cradle instead of chambered in the barrel, didn't I?" he asked in a small voice. "You have to release the cradle and *then* fire. Glad I don't have to explain that one to Mom."

"Wouldn't have been no explainin'," Huff said. "At

2

that power level, the plasma arc would've melted the cradle, the cannon, and a few meters of the hull. Yeh been growin', lad, so you'd be at least a couple of handfuls of ash."

Tycho paled. Grigsby grinned, then tapped the console, cycling back through the firing menus.

"Rest easy, Master Tycho—cannon won't fire with the cradle locked," Grigsby said. "But it would dump the charge, and you'd have to recharge instead of firing. Not a great strategy with enemies about."

Tycho nodded, angry with himself.

"Let's take it from the top then, Master Tycho," Grigsby said. "Starting with the *Comet*'s weapons complement."

Tycho hesitated, knowing he could refuse. Though only fourteen years old, he was a midshipman who served on the *Comet*'s quarterdeck—and he was a Hashoone. That meant he outranked Grigsby and anyone else from the lower decks.

Yes, he'd made a dumb mistake. But did he really need to recite weapons specifications like some eight-year-old who'd just been sent down the ladder to learn the spacer's trade?

Then he noticed his grandfather staring at him, the warning plain on his ruined face. When Tycho was born, Grigsby had already spent decades serving aboard the *Comet*. He knew the privateer's systems better than anyone aboard—maybe even Huff. And Grigsby's father had been a Hashoone retainer before him, as had his grandfather, and so on back for centuries.

"My apologies, Mr. Grigsby," Tycho said. "I was still mad about that blasted cradle release. This gun is called the bow chaser, because—"

Alarms began to blare.

"Bridge crew to quarterdeck, all hands to stations," said the clipped, calm voice of Vesuvia, the artificial intelligence program that the *Comet*'s computer used to communicate with her crew.

The order left no time for polite conversation. Grigsby was already hurrying out of the gunnery bay, gold coins jangling below his holsters. Tycho ducked around his grandfather and ran after him.

The alert had come during one shift's midday meal, and crewers were still wiping their mouths on their sleeves as they rushed out of the wardroom. Scarred, hard-eyed men and women mumbled greetings as Tycho ran down the forward passageway and emerged into the lower deck, dimly lit and thick with smoke. Tycho dodged retainers as they strapped on pistols and swords, spun to avoid gun crews as they wheeled projectile cannons across the deck, and picked up a foot as the ship's cat shot by, seeking shelter.

The bosun whistled out orders on his pipes as Tycho reached the forward ladderwell and scrambled up the rungs. Four meters above, he emerged in a different world—the well-lit quarterdeck, whose broad viewports overlooked the emptiness of space. This was the exclusive province of the bridge crew, all of whom were his family.

His mother, Diocletia, was buckling herself into the captain's chair, closest to the bow. To her left and slightly behind her sat Tycho's eighteen-year-old brother, Carlo, the *Comet*'s pilot, his handsome face creased by a pale scar across his right cheek that he'd received battling pirates two years before. The seat to Diocletia's right was still vacant—it belonged to Tycho's father, Mavry Malone, the ship's first mate.

On the main screen overhead, a cross marked the *Comet*'s position deep in the asteroid cluster known as the Hildas. A flashing triangle indicated an unknown object, with a dotted line mapping out its current course. Tycho studied the rows of numbers on the screen. The object was moving too quickly to be an asteroid, but very slowly for a starship.

"Look out below, Tyke!" someone yelled. He took a quick step forward as his twin sister, Yana, hurtled down the ladderwell with only her hands on the outsides of the ladder, kicking her feet nimbly to land with a thud on the quarterdeck.

"Don't call me Tyke," Tycho protested.

Diocletia gathered her black hair into a loose ponytail and looked over her shoulder with a scowl.

"Yana, must you arrive on my quarterdeck like a supertanker missing its dock?" she asked.

Yana ignored the criticism, peering at the main screen. "Is that a ship?"

"Sensors are your job—strap in and take a look for yourself," Carlo said. "But so far there are no ion emissions or responses to our hails."

The Hashoones were privateers who made their living by seizing cargoes carried by freighters and other civilian craft. Any ship that came their way was a potential prize to be captured—and a payday for the *Comet*'s crew.

But they had to be careful. As privateers the family had to obey the laws of space. They held a letter of marque authorizing them to attack enemy ships on behalf of the Jovian Union, which governed the nearly two dozen inhabited moons of Jupiter, Saturn, and Uranus. Only Earth's ships could be considered enemies; those crewed by neutrals or their fellow Jovians had to be allowed safe passage.

Tycho jumped as someone else crashed to the deck behind him. His father had descended in the same reckless manner as Yana. Tycho turned back, heart still thudding, to find his mother's mouth set in a thin line.

"What?" Mavry asked with a grin. Diocletia just shook her head and sighed. Giggles leaked out from the hand Yana had clamped over her mouth. Tycho felt laughter threatening to rise up in his own throat and hastily looked away.

"Whose starship?" he asked. He wasn't talking about the unknown object out there among the tumbling rocks of the Hildas, either; he was asking who was in charge of the *Comet*.

"Mine," Carlo said. "If you're done gawking like a tourist, why don't you sit down and run communications?"

Tycho bit back an angry reply—he was indeed still

standing beside his station while the rest of his family finished strapping in. He sank into his chair and brought his console to life with practiced keystrokes. He settled his headset over his dark-brown hair and shrugged into the harnesses, buckling them across his chest.

"My boards are green, Vesuvia," Tycho said. "Taking over communications and navigation."

"And I'm up on sensors," Yana said, all business now. "Bogey's eighteen thousand klicks out. Let's try a full-spectrum scan."

"I'll keep navigation, Tyke," Carlo said. "I've already got an intercept course keyed in if we need it."

"Understood," Tycho said. "Vesuvia, open all audio channels. Black transponders."

"Acknowledged," Vesuvia said coolly. "Transmitting no recognition code."

Under normal operations, every starship transmitted a signal indicating its name and allegiance. But in deep space, few freighters or civilian craft broadcast such information unless interrogated by another ship—at which point they could hide behind a false identity in an attempt to avoid trouble. Privateers did the same thing, but for the opposite reason, hoping to draw close to unwary vessels before revealing their true allegiances and intentions.

"Unknown ship, we have you on our scopes," Tycho said, trying to make his voice sound deep and confident. "Identify yourself."

There was no response. Tycho raised the volume as

far as it would go but heard nothing beyond a hiss of static.

"Unknown ship, I repeat, identify yourself," he said. "We have you on our scopes and are preparing to intercept you."

"Scans show no emissions whatever," Yana said. "And no temperature signature. If that's a ship, she's as cold as space."

"Vesuvia, scan visual channels," Tycho said. "Maybe her audio transmitters are down."

"No transmissions detected," Vesuvia said.

Tycho studied his control board, determined not to miss anything. He and his siblings cooperated as a crew, but they were also competing to succeed their mother as captain of the *Comet*, and she noted every decision they made—good and bad—in the electronic record known as the Log.

Carlo drummed his fingers on his console.

"Vesuvia, lock in that intercept course," he said. "Let's take a closer look, shall we?"

"And hope this time we make some money," Yana said with a sigh.

"Belay that," barked Diocletia without turning around, her shoulders rigid.

Yana looked at Tycho and shrugged—she hadn't said anything they hadn't all been thinking. Two years before, the Hashoones had captured Thoadbone Mox's pirate ship, the *Hydra*, and been paid handsomely for rescuing Jovian citizens from one of Earth's corporate factories. The windfall had been enough for the *Comet*'s crewers to indulge in an epic shindy of a shore leave that had ended with six in the infirmary and three more in jail, to the lasting pride of all involved.

But since then, little had gone right. The Jovian Union had claimed the *Hydra* for its own, leading to a bitter battle in the courts that still hadn't been resolved. And for much of the last year, the Hashoones' luck had been stubbornly bad: most of the vessels that strayed into the *Comet*'s path turned out to be Jovian. Those that did fly the flag of Earth were escorted by warships, or they carried cargos that weren't worth the time and effort to seize.

Maybe the ship out there would change their luck.

If it *was* a ship.

"Detach tanks," Carlo said.

"Acknowledged," Vesuvia said. Above their heads, they heard a metallic clank as the *Comet* shook slightly and separated from the cluster of spherical fuel tanks she used for long voyages.

"Tanks detached," Vesuvia said.

"Beginning intercept," Carlo said. "Tyke, Yana, eyes and ears open. Tell me anything I need to know."

Sudden acceleration pushed the Hashoones back into their seats.

"Mind the fuel economy, son," Mavry said mildly. "That stuff you're burning isn't cheap."

Carlo apologized, but he was smiling—and Tycho found himself smiling too. His brother was a naturally gifted pilot, and it had been too long since he'd had a chance to demonstrate his talents.

The *Comet* descended in a smooth arc, her tanks shrinking behind her until they were just another point of light among the stars. Freed of her long-range tanks, the *Comet* was an elongated triangle about sixty meters long, with a trio of maneuvering engines protruding from her stern.

Carlo wiggled his fingers on the yoke and rolled slightly to port to avoid a drift of loose rock and ice, leaving just a few pebbles to rattle against the forward viewports.

"Display colors," Carlo said.

"Displaying," Vesuvia said, switching on the *Comet*'s transponders so they broadcast her true Jovian allegiance.

The *Comet*'s bells clang-clanged four times—it was 1400 hours, the midpoint of the afternoon watch.

"Unknown ship, this is the *Shadow Comet*, operating under letter of marque of the Jovian Union," Tycho said. "Heave to and prepare for boarding."

"Building a sensor profile," Yana said. "Mass and configuration match commercial fuel tanks. Analyzing what's attached to them. Still no detectable levels of emissions."

"Well, at least she's a ship," Carlo said, then activated his own microphone. "Mr. Grigsby, this is the helm."

"Aye, Master Carlo," Grigsby said from his station in the wardroom.

"We are inbound on a bogey—eight thousand klicks to intercept," Carlo said. "We read no ion emissions or transmissions. Tell the gunnery crews to be gentle with the triggers. Right now we're just taking a look."

"Light fingers it is, Master Carlo," Grigsby rumbled.

"Seven thousand klicks," Yana said. "She's about forty meters long. Mass profile is consistent with tanks being half full."

"She's not trying to evade, and she knows we're out here. So why the silence?" Carlo asked.

"Maybe she can't respond," Tycho said.

"The solar system is full of mysteries," Mavry said. "Let's get some facts."

"The solar system is also full of dangers," Diocletia said. "Yana, keep scanning the area. Remember all the pirate attacks we've heard about in recent months. I don't want any surprises."

"Aye-aye," Yana said. Unlike privateers, pirates obeyed no law, preying on any ship they thought they could capture. Sometimes they held crews for ransom. Other times they sold them into slavery—or killed them.

Impacts like hammerblows emerged from the ladderwell, followed by grunts and a series of inventively awful oaths. The Hashoones didn't even turn—they were familiar with the sounds of Huff Hashoone ascending from belowdecks.

"Initial scanner profile complete," Yana said. "She's a Jennet-class transport. Profile match eighty-five percent. Probably an ore boat."

Huff, still grumbling, stepped onto the quarterdeck with a clank of metal feet, clamping one hand onto a rung and standing behind Tycho and Yana.

"Arrr, a Jennet," Huff rumbled. "Is she full?"

"She's too small to get a good estimate, Grandpa," Yana said. "I'd just be guessing."

"Piratin' is half guessin', missy," Huff said. "Whose flag she flyin'?"

"No transmissions," Tycho said. "Best as we can tell, she's dead in space."

"I'm going to circle," Carlo said.

As they approached, the unknown ship grew from a bright dot into a tiny cluster of bulbous tanks. Carlo swung the *Comet* wide of the transport, which was a boxy, unlovely craft. Then Carlo wheeled the ship around to approach from above and behind, careful to keep the Jennet's fuel tanks between the *Comet* and any guns that might be pointed at her.

"Any ideas?" Carlo asked.

"Either there's nobody at the helm or controls are unresponsive," Diocletia said. "Otherwise they'd blink the running lights, or roll the craft, or something."

"So we can salvage her then?" Yana asked.

"Depends how long she's been out here," Mavry said. "And if anyone's looking for her. And how much money we're willing to spend in court."

"And if anybody on board is alive," Tycho said.

"Arrr, that one's easily solved," Huff said. "Put a ventilation hole in 'er, wait a few bells, an' then finders keepers."

"That's piracy, Grandfather," Carlo said. "It would mean the hangman."

"Ain't never been afraid of the noose." Huff snorted.

Diocletia turned to regard her father, one eyebrow cocked.

"And if it turns out she's Jovian, Dad?" she asked. "Or registered on Mars or Ceres and overdue in port? If I ever forfeit our letter of marque, it won't be for a rusty ore boat adrift in the Hildas."

Huff subsided into muttering.

"But Mom, what if that rusty ore boat's full of platinum from the New Potosi asteroid?" Carlo asked with a grin.

"Like that would happen," Tycho said. "What if it's full of flesh-eating viruses?"

The Hashoones considered those possibilities in silence as Carlo came around for another pass, easing off on the throttle and matching the slow drift of the crippled ship. Vesuvia activated the *Comet*'s portside cameras, which revealed nothing to indicate how long the ship had been out here. It could have been a day, a decade, or a century.

"Begin docking procedure," Diocletia decided. "And prepare a boarding party. Follow biohazard procedures—wear full spacesuits and take environmental samples before you go aboard. Carlo, it's your starship, so you'll take lead. Tycho, go with your brother. Platinum or viruses—let's see who was closer."

2

DEATH SHIP

Tycho hated spacesuits. It was hard to see out of them, and no matter how often you cleaned them they still smelled like feet. He asked Yana to check his suit seals, ignoring her complaints about being left behind, then clambered down the ladderwell, his breath loud in the enclosed bowl of his helmet.

Carlo was waiting at the portside airlock with a trio of *Comet* crewers—Grigsby, Richards, and Porco. All were veterans, their spacesuits adorned with swirls of glowing paint, stickers, and scrawled prayers for safety in the void. Carlo had two chrome musketoons—the weapons traditionally wielded by a starship's ranking officer during a boarding action— tucked into his belt.

Carlo nodded at Tycho, then peered through the narrow viewport in the inner airlock door. Joining him, Tycho glimpsed an environmental sampler balanced on a trio of legs, a fan of sensors protruding from its top. Beyond the sampler, a pitch-black corridor led into the derelict ship.

"We wired up the transport's airlock and opened it remotely," Carlo told his brother over his suit radio. "No reaction when we did that."

A beep sounded in their ears. Carlo peered at a small monitor strapped to his wrist.

"Environmental sampling complete," he said. "Temperature a few ticks above absolute zero; carbon dioxide's off the charts. Artificial gravity's out, of course. But there's no sign of Tycho's flesh-eating viruses, or any other abnormal readings at all."

"Did you say *flesh-eatin'*, Master Carlo?" asked a wide-eyed Richards.

"Go ahead and open her up," Diocletia's voice said in their ears. "But I want our airlock sealed while you're aboard."

"Aye-aye," Carlo said. "Mr. Grigsby?"

Grigsby stepped forward and thumbed the airlock controls, closing the *Comet*'s outer airlock and letting the air inside the enclosed lock bleed out into space—along with any dangerous contaminants. He then resealed the lock and opened the inner door. Wind rippled loose stickers on the crewers' suits as air from the *Comet* rushed in to fill the vacuum.

Six bells rang out aboard the *Comet*. Carlo stepped forward, with Grigsby right behind him. Richards and Porco hesitated, turning uneasily toward each other. Grigsby gave them a steely look, and they tramped reluctantly into the lock, with Tycho having to squeeze in behind them so Carlo could close the inner door.

"Quarterdeck, we're opening the outer lock."

Grigsby moved the sampler aside, thumbed the hatch controls, then drew his carbine and clicked the safety off. Tycho did the same. The weight of the blaster felt reassuring in his hands. The *Comet's* thick outer airlock door retracted into her hull.

"Let's go then," Carlo said, activating the lamp on his helmet but leaving the pistols in his belt. He took a step forward into the derelict, with Grigsby by his side. Their feet gently lifted from the deck, leaving the two men floating. Once again Richards and Porco hesitated, peering into the darkness with their carbines raised.

"Honestly, you two," Carlo said. "We're the most dangerous things within a million kilometers. Now come on."

The five moved ahead in a line, using the magnets in their gloves to pull themselves along the corridor. Their lamps revealed no movement, while their earpieces recorded no sounds except the huff of their breath and the dull thunk of magnets on metal.

"Standard layout for a Jennet," Carlo said from his place at the front of the line. "Bridge should be right ahead, and . . ."

He was silent for a moment, then spoke again, in a quiet voice. "I found the crew."

Tycho followed Richards and Porco onto the dark bridge, locating Carlo and Grigsby by their helmet lamps. He turned his head left and right, his lamp sweeping across the bridge.

The members of the bridge crew were still strapped into their chairs, but their faces had collapsed into leathery ruins. The skin was paper-thin across the skulls, the mouths agape and empty, the eye sockets hollowed pits. Tycho let his lamp play over the navigator's station. It was like looking at his own console back on the *Comet*, only transformed by horror.

"What happened to them?" Tycho asked.

"No idea," Carlo said as he drifted by the captain's chair. "We'll need a generator to get the computer up and running. Mr. Grigsby, take a look aft—maybe we'll find our answer in the hold. And check the crew cabins."

"Will do, Master Carlo," Grigsby said, turning to find Richards and Porco flattened against the back wall of the bridge, as far from the bodies as possible.

"What a sorry pair," the warrant officer growled. "Quit hangin' a leg and get to it. Dead men don't bite, but I sure as thunder do."

The hold contained neither platinum nor viruses—it

was empty. The ore boat's cabins, unfortunately, were not. Richards and Porco found the other six members of the crew in their bunks, mummified by time and cold.

With the initial survey of the ore boat complete, Mavry crossed over and joined them with a portable generator. Tycho sighed with relief as the emergency lighting flickered on and the artificial gravity returned, though his suit sensors warned that the air remained unbreathable and perilously cold. He still felt like he was intruding in a tomb, but at least now the bodies were out of sight, covered with tarps in the empty hold.

As the bridge consoles flickered to life, Carlo settled into the captain's chair, with Mavry looking over his shoulder. Tycho admired his brother's easy confidence but found he couldn't bring himself to sit in the navigator's seat. Instead, he chose to lean over the dead man's console and peer at the screen.

"Want me to pull up her logs?" Carlo asked their father, fingers already hovering over the keyboard.

"Not yet," Mavry said. "Prospectors are paranoid— you could trigger a software trap and erase everything. Plus we'll only get a few hours out of our generator. First thing is to see if we can figure out what malfunctioned and fix it."

Carlo pulled up the main diagnostics screen, and Mavry let out a low whistle.

"Look at that—the air scrubbers are off," he said.

"Carlo, see if you can reset them. It'd be nice to able to breathe."

Carlo typed a command, tried again, then shook his head.

"Let's take a peek in the engine room," Mavry said.

Mavry was already on his way aft. Carlo and Tycho hurried down the dim, silent corridors after their father.

"What happened to the others?" Tycho asked.

"I sent them back to the *Comet*," Mavry said, then smiled. "Richards and Porco made the crossing in record time."

Carlo scoffed, the noise a little burst of static in their ears. "I don't understand. They're from belowdecks—it's not like they've never seen dead men before."

"Take it easy on them, Carlo," Mavry said after a moment. "Dying in a fight doesn't scare them—it's the life they chose, just like their parents and grandparents did. But a slow death in deep space, with no one back home ever knowing what became of you? That frightens them, and there's no shame in it. It frightens me too."

"Is that what you think happened, Dad?" Tycho asked as they entered the engine room, now once again vibrating faintly with the thrum of a living ship. "You think they died slowly?"

Mavry's eyes traced the conduits where they ran along the ceiling.

"Slowly at first, then all at once," he said.

"What does that mean?" Carlo asked.

"I'll show you. Power up the engineer's console and

get me an atmosphere reading."

Tycho tapped out the commands, and Mavry shoved a red valve hard to the right, grunting with the effort.

"Dad, the air scrubbers—" Tycho began.

"Are back on," Mavry said. "I know."

"They were working?" Carlo asked. "Then why turn them off? That's suicide!"

"Yes, that's exactly what it was," Mavry said. He crept along on his knees, hands tracing a conduit's route from the main reactor behind them to a boxlike vault about a meter high. He popped open the vault's doors and sat back on his haunches as much as his bulky spacesuit allowed.

"The energy feeds run from the main reactor to the power converters," Mavry said. "Notice anything?"

Tycho and Carlo peered over his shoulders, accidentally bumped their helmets together, and glared at each other. The converters inside the vault should have been gleaming metal but were a dull black instead.

"They're cooked," Tycho said.

"And upside down," Carlo said. "Which is *why* they're cooked."

"So why didn't they install backups?" Tycho asked.

"Good question," Mavry said. "Let's see if we can figure out the answer."

Carlo saw the converters first, lying on the deck beneath the engineer's station. He returned to find Mavry had dug out the scorched ones and used his utility knife to scrape the contacts clean.

"Put them in, Carlo," Mavry said. "Preferably not backwards. Tycho, check the monitor."

Carlo fitted the converters into their sockets.

"Monitor shows no charge," Tycho said.

"That's what I thought," Mavry said. "Their primary converters overloaded, which happens—every reactor suffers from the occasional flux or surge. They had backup converters, like any sane spacer would, but they installed them wrong and cooked them. And then they had nothing."

"But it's crazy to only have one backup set of converters," Tycho said. "We probably have a dozen on the *Comet*."

"Prospectors do things differently," Mavry said. "Their crews are smaller, and they spend their money on chemical sniffers and buying old ship logs instead of on maintenance."

"And they install power converters upside down," Carlo said with a snort.

"It was dark and they were scared," Mavry said quietly.

"But they must have called for help," Tycho said, imagining the engine room filling with smoke, then the ship left in silent darkness, with the chill of space beginning to creep into the deck.

"Probably not at first," Mavry said, digging the dead converters out of the vault and getting to his feet. "A distress call might have tipped off other prospectors to their position. They probably thought they had another set of converters somewhere, or that they could fix the main pair. And by the time they realized they were wrong, there was too little power left to send a distress call far enough."

"And then they were dead in space," Carlo said. "It was freeze to death or starve."

"Or shut off the air scrubbers and let the carbon dioxide levels rise," Mavry said. "If they were lucky, it was like falling asleep."

"Do you think they were lucky, Dad?" Tycho asked.

Mavry looked down at the dead converters.

"No," he said. "I don't think they were."

"She's called the *Lucia*," Mavry said. "Registered to a Captain Lumbaba, out of Titan, and last seen twenty-four years ago."

He took a sip of coffee and looked around at the other Hashoones where they sat in the cuddy aboard the *Comet*, warming their hands with their own drinks.

"So the next step is to find out if anyone has an insurance claim on her," Diocletia said.

Yana looked up from her mediapad with a smile.

"I checked—she's clean. Insurance money was paid out ten years after she disappeared, to Eurydice Lumbaba and her son, Japhet. They live on Titan, at Kraken Station—that's a refinery run by the Huygens-Cassini Corporation. The ship's up for grabs as salvage."

"An' what a prize she is," muttered Huff, standing in the doorway. "One rusty ore boat, tanks half empty, hold clean as a new middie's mind. Arrr, truly these be the glory days of piratin'."

"Privateering," Diocletia corrected him. "It may not be much, but it's more than we've run across in months. Nice work, Yana. Mavry, what have you found in the logs?"

"Multiple entries are protected, as you'd expect with prospectors," Mavry said. "But mostly they did runs in and out of the Themistians and the Cybeles. Captain Lumbaba was a platinum hunter—all the *Lucia*'s gear is calibrated for that chemical signature."

"Platinum hunter?" Huff rumbled in surprise. "Then what was he doin' out here?"

"Looking for Carlo's lost New Potosi hoard, obviously," Yana said with a grin.

Eight bells clang-clanged the time—it was 2000 hours, the end of the second dog watch.

"Ain't no platinum left in the Hildas worth huntin'," Huff said. "After the New Potosi claim, every rock hound in the solar system scoured these asteroids for a generation. They were played out during my grandfather's time."

"Maybe Captain Lumbaba heard differently," Tycho said. "Or maybe he had a tip that there was something else out here worth finding—something interesting enough to make a platinum hunter try a new region of space."

"Or maybe he was as crazy as an outhouse rat, like most prospectors," Huff said. "Half of 'em are geology professors what can't fly a ship, an' half would rather talk to rocks than people, an' half of 'em will fly to the Oort cloud chasin' a rumor."

"That's three halves," Carlo pointed out.

"Don't get mathematical with me, boy," Huff growled.

Diocletia rolled her empty coffee cup back and forth in her hands, brows knit. Tycho found himself listening to the hum of the *Comet*'s air scrubbers. He'd barely noticed the sound before today; now he swore he'd cherish it forever.

"Carlo, transmit a salvage claim on the *Lucia*," Diocletia said. "She ought to fetch enough at auction to pay for this cruise, at least. Tycho, set course for Saturn— we'll sell her at Enceladus."

"Enceladus?" Carlo asked. "That's a lot farther than Jupiter. The fuel costs—"

"I'm familiar with the geography of the solar system, Carlo," Diocletia said. "Enceladus is the best secondhand ship market in the Jovian Union, and it's a jumping-off point for prospectors heading for Uranus and beyond. Plus we should visit Titan and tell Captain Lumbaba's family what happened to him."

"Now don't go developin' a conscience, Dio—it's unbecoming in a pirate," Huff said.

"We'd want the same done for us," Diocletia said. Then the corners of her mouth twitched. "Besides, while one of you is consoling the widow Lumbaba, conversation might be made. Topics might be discussed."

Mavry grinned. "Such as lesser-known points of

interest for platinum hunters in the Hildas?"

"It could come up," Diocletia said innocently. Then her smile faded, and she was all business again. "All right then. Tomorrow morning we'll do a final checkout of the *Lucia*. I'll figure out the prize crew later, but assuming she's green to fly, I want engines lit by 1030. Anything else?"

"There is something, actually," Mavry said. "It's the crewers. They're scared of the ship—think finding her was a bad omen and opening her up was worse. They say we've invited ghosts aboard the *Comet*."

"They'd never put up with this in the Defense Force," Carlo said. "Orders are orders. If they don't like it, cashier them."

"And if we get in the habit of doing that, how many of our crewers will put up with a run of bad luck like ours?" Diocletia asked. "Let alone risk their lives for us in battle?"

"All of them," Carlo said stubbornly. "Or at least all the ones we want serving with us."

Diocletia shook her head. "I'd rather not take that chance. Where are the bodies of the *Lucia*'s crewers?"

"Still in her hold," Tycho said.

"Make shrouds for them," Diocletia said. "And do it right—no slapdash work. Then we'll bury them in space. You remember the Spacer's Farewell, Dad?"

Huff grunted. "Ain't I said them words a hundred times before?"

"At least," Diocletia said. "We'll have the ceremony

as soon as we can, then. At the risk of being accused of developing a conscience again, it's the decent thing to do."

Tycho had expected only the most superstitious crewers to turn out for the hastily arranged funeral, but he was wrong. Best as he could tell, the entire complement of sixty-six was assembled in the *Comet*'s hold, arranged in lines that would have infuriated a military officer but were pretty respectable for a bunch of roughnecks and vaguely reformed pirates.

The Comets elbowed one another and pointed to the open hatch of the freight lock, where ten shrouded forms lay on the deck. Standing beside Yana in his formal clothes, Tycho heard the crewers murmur approvingly at the handiwork of the shrouds and the arranging of the bodies.

Then the crewers parted, with an admirable lack of collisions and vile language, as Huff entered the hold, wearing his best bright-yellow tie and carrying a worn book in his hand.

Huff bowed briefly in the direction of the lock, then turned, fixing the crewers with the white spark of his artificial eye. The Comets bowed their heads, a few stragglers belatedly snatching off their own hats or those of their less attentive neighbors.

Huff touched the book to the flesh-and-blood half of his forehead, then began to speak with a care Tycho had rarely heard him use:

"From star stuff were we sprung, to star stuff we
return;
As space was your birthright, so shall it be your bier.
To the brotherhood of spacers you have belonged,
And so drift free forever of surly dirt and air,
Your tomb the bejewelèd vault of our Creator fair.
May you see His face in the glimmering of distant suns,
May you know His mind in the blowing of solar
winds.
To the brotherhood of spacers you have belonged;
From star stuff were we sprung, to star stuff we
return."

The Comets muttered amens. Huff turned and nodded to Carlo, who walked slowly to the back of the hold
and closed the freight lock. All bowed their heads again,
and then Carlo hit the release that opened the outer lock
door, releasing the shrouded bodies into eternity.

3

TITAN

Titan's a lot busier than the last time I was here," Carlo said, peering through the viewports of the *Comet*'s gig as it approached the pale orange atmosphere of Saturn's largest moon.

Space stations ringed the moon, and kilometer-long feeder lines connected enormous refineries with giant tankers. Navigation buoys blinked red and green, marking traffic lanes for the gigs, jolly boats, pocket freighters, avisos, ore boats, and sloops coming and going from the icy surface.

"Feels like everything around Saturn's gotten busier," Yana said from the pilot's seat. They'd left their parents and Huff at Enceladus for the auction, taking the *Comet*'s gig for the ninety-minute voyage to Titan. Carlo had reluctantly ceded the controls to his sister, then spent the whole trip telling her how to fly.

"Try not to bump into anything," he said.

That earned him a scowl from Yana. Tycho, determined to ignore their bickering, tried to count the tankers around them and gave up.

"Ever get the feeling we're in the wrong business?" he asked, fussing with the collar of his spacesuit.

"Depends how you look at it," Carlo said. "Refining corporations like Huygens-Cassini are mostly partnerships between Earth's government and the Jovian Union."

"And what does that have to do with anything?" Tycho asked.

"Listen and I'll tell you," Carlo said. "The Union gets a bigger share of the refinery profits because Titan belongs to us. If that weren't true—if Union ships like ours didn't stand up to Earth—we'd get a smaller share. Or nothing. So we're really in the same business."

"Except the folks in this part of the business don't get shot at," Tycho muttered.

"Where's the fun in that?" Yana asked, then held up her hand for silence, listening to the traffic controller's instructions in her earpiece. She shook her head, exasperated.

"They want us to hold here," she said, tapping the retro rockets. "I don't want to talk about the stupid Jovian Union, though. It just makes me mad."

"Why's that?" Carlo asked.

"The *Hydra*. It's outrageous that the Union won't give her to us—if it weren't for us, Mox would still be out there grabbing ships."

"You're *still* upset about that?" Carlo asked. "Let it go already, Yana—it's just bureaucrats doing bureaucrat things. Like I keep telling you, we intercepted the *Hydra* during a Jovian military mission, so someone in the Defense Force thinks she should belong to the military. Plus the Securitat is worried about who'd buy her— imagine if another pirate got hold of her."

"I won't let it go," Yana insisted. "Besides, what if we didn't sell the *Hydra* at all?"

Tycho and Carlo looked at each other, then back at their sister.

"There are three of us competing for one ship," Yana said. "But what if there were two ships? Or three? Then we could all be captains and take more prizes."

"It doesn't work that way," Tycho said. "The family is the captain, and the captain is the ship, and—"

"—and the ship is the family," Yana said. "I know that old saying by heart, you know. But *why* is it that way? Think about it. Every generation, one Hashoone becomes captain of the *Comet*, and the others wind up twiddling their thumbs dirtside. That's a total waste. Why are we limited to one ship as a family, when we could do so much more with a fleet of them?"

"Okay, but what happens when you and Tycho both intercept a fat prize in the Cybeles?" Carlo asked. "Do you take turns? Flip a currency chip, maybe? Or do you wind up shooting at each other?"

Yana looked surprised.

"Tyke's my brother," she said. "He's annoying, but I wouldn't shoot him."

"I love you too, sis," Tycho said.

"What if that other Hashoone isn't your brother, but your cousin?" Carlo asked. "Or your sister-in-law's sister? Or your third cousin once removed? And once Hashoones start shooting each other in the Cybeles, what happens back home? Are we shooting each other in Port Town? In Darklands?"

"We wouldn't—wait, Traffic Control's talking to me. Finally. We're cleared to descend. Get ready to vent the atmosphere."

They donned their helmets and carefully checked one another's seals. Air would burn if it mixed with Titan's nitrogen-rich atmosphere, so ships without airlocks were required to vent their interiors to space before descending to the surface.

"I get why what you say was true in pirate days, Carlo," Tycho said. "But we're privateers now—we work for the Jovian Union. Couldn't the Defense Force use a fleet of Hashoone ships, instead of just one?"

Carlo hesitated.

"I guess they could," he said. "But these are *our*

traditions—we're the ones who have wanted it done this way. Maybe the Union could use a Hashoone fleet, but who says we want them to have one?"

The gig began to shake as it entered the outer envelope of Titan's atmosphere.

"If this is about what *we* want, why is the *Hydra* still in dry dock?" Tycho asked.

"The one has nothing to do with the other," Carlo said.

"I'm not so sure," Yana said. "Just like I'm not so sure the Union is really on our side. Remember back before you made bridge crew, when you were down the ladder learning the spacer's trade?"

"I'd rather not think about it, but yes," Carlo said.

"Well, you played cards with the belowdecks crewers, right?" Yana asked.

"Never," Carlo said.

Yana and Tycho glanced at each other. They'd both loved playing cutthroat games of poker, whist, and cát tê with off-duty crewers in the mess or the wardroom.

"Maybe you should have," Yana said. "Belowdecks, they say every game has a sucker—and if you can't figure out who it is, it's you."

Kraken Station was a cluster of habitation domes sprawled on the shores of the Kraken Mare, not far from Titan's north pole. Yana set the gig down on the landing field with a bump that bounced them in their seats and caused Carlo to raise an eyebrow.

"Oh, like all your touchdowns are perfect," she retorted. "I forgot to correct for the thicker atmospheric pressure, is all."

"Today's bump, tomorrow's crash," Carlo said, looking down at his mediapad. "You're just lucky Mom wasn't here to note it for the Log."

"Sorry to disappoint you," Yana said, peering at the diagnostics readouts. "It's 200 below outside, so they ought to have a cold jump-pop. I'm dying for one. And maybe some fruit."

"It's not a sightseeing trip," Carlo chided his sister as Tycho headed down the gangway. "Keep your eyes open—there have been reports of pirate activity around these outposts."

"Good. I could use a little excitement," Yana said, marching down the gangway and nearly plowing into Tycho where he stood at the foot of the ramp, staring up at the sky.

"What are you doing?" she demanded.

"I've never been outside and not been able to see stars," Tycho said. "It's weird."

Yana looked up into the thick orange haze above their heads.

"It is strange," she admitted. "Wait a minute . . . TYCHO! Get back in the ship!"

"What's wrong?" Tycho asked. Then he felt it too—a spatter of liquid on his helmet's faceplate, followed by another, and then several more. He retreated hastily to the shelter of the gig's hull, where Yana was scrubbing at her helmet and checking her suit seals.

"My suit's fine," she said. "But I can't figure out what's leaking. A fuel line? Coolant?"

Laughter crackled over their suit radios, and Carlo brushed past them, a carryall over his shoulder. Before either of them could stop him, he strode down the gangplank and out onto the landing pad.

"The *sky* is what's leaking," Carlo said, turning with a grin. He spread his arms as thick droplets bounced off his helmet and suit and splashed on the landing pad. "It's just methane—it won't hurt you. I forgot you two hayseeds have never seen rain."

The main airlock for Kraken Station cycled every half hour. First sirens and flashing lights alerted the Huygens-Cassini workers on the landing pad that it was time to grab a place inside the lock. A minute later, the huge outer door shut and pumps vented away Titan's atmosphere, leaving a vacuum inside. Then air was pumped into the lock and the inner door opened, allowing the workers to remove their helmets and enter the station. Fifteen minutes later, the process was reversed.

The second Tycho took off his helmet, he wished he hadn't: the interior of Kraken Station smelled like a nose-wrinkling combination of fuel and sewage.

Japhet Lumbaba, the son of the *Lucia*'s captain, was waiting for them by Huygens-Cassini's offices. He was dark and slim, almost fragile looking, and dressed in a faded red coverall, with a helmet and thick work

34

gloves slung over one shoulder. He shook hands gravely with Carlo and Tycho, bowed slightly to Yana, and led them deeper into the warren of shops and shelters. They threaded their way through crowds of burly, bearded men in similar coveralls, suits ornamented with a bewildering assortment of meters and probes and graspers and wands. Mixed in with them were more men and women in clothes more suited for working at a desk.

Refinery workers and pixel pushers, Tycho guessed. Both groups had hard eyes and looked like they were in a hurry.

But then the Hashoones passed a tavern whose holographic sign had decayed into a smudge of light. A knot of men standing outside caught Tycho's eye. They dripped with tattoos and earrings and wore carbines on their belts, with bandoliers crisscrossed across their chests. Several had the same patchs on the shoulders of their jumpsuits: the stylized face of a wolf, white on a black background.

Lumbaba tugged at Tycho's elbow.

"Bad men. Do not attract their attention."

"So you work in the refinery, Mr. Lumbaba?" Yana asked.

"Yes," Lumbaba said. "I analyze complex compounds. It is not so different from my father's prospecting. Except I do not have to leave Titan."

"How old were you when your father left?" Tycho asked as they entered an elevator and descended below the surface.

"Two," Lumbaba said. "I do not remember him. My mother swore he would return, that he always had before."

"Does your mother know the news?" Tycho asked.

"Yes," Lumbaba said. "She had the courts declare him dead years ago, because the insurance claim would allow me to attend school. But she never believed it. Not until we received your message."

Tycho nodded, not sure what to say. The elevator doors opened, and Lumbaba inclined his head, indicating they should go first.

"When I was a boy, I believed her stories," he said quietly. "Every day I told myself that this would be the day my father made contact, to say he was coming home. But eventually I realized it wasn't true. . . . Our home is right this way."

A dull metal door slid aside with a groan, and the Hashoones stepped into a little room with bare metal walls. A cabinet and a cooking unit with a single burner sat in the corner. There were plastic stools scattered around a low table and a couch against the wall, between two closed doors. A green-and-gold blanket covered most of the couch. Those were the only colors in the room except for the dull orange glow of a portable heater.

Tycho realized a figure sat huddled on the couch, a lined face peering out from a dark mass of robes.

"My mother," Japhet Lumbaba said, thumbing the door shut behind them.

The woman struggled to her feet and bowed, then

indicated they should sit on the couch. Carlo plopped himself down, discarding his helmet on the table in front of him. Yana and Tycho looked at each other, then settled themselves carefully beside their brother. Captain Lumbaba's widow shuffled over to the cabinet and returned with a tray and three small cups with steam curling above them.

"Thank you," Yana said, sipping immediately. Tycho did the same. The tea was strong and bitter, but he managed not to grimace.

"Excellent," he said with a smile. "Thank you, ma'am."

"Is it coffee?" Carlo asked, hand poised above the tray.

"Tea," Japhet said.

"I'm fine then," Carlo said.

They waited for Mrs. Lumbaba to return and take a seat beside her son on one of the stools.

Carlo unfastened his carryall and extracted a small bundle wrapped in rough cloth. He turned to Lumbaba, who inclined his head toward his mother. Carlo got up awkwardly, the spacesuit hampering his movements, and held out the bundle to the old woman. She looked up at him for a moment, baffled, then slowly raised her arms.

"We thought you would want Captain Lumbaba's personal effects," Carlo said, placing the bundle in her hands.

Mrs. Lumbaba stared at the bundle in her lap. A bump sounded from behind one of the closed doors.

Tycho looked questioningly at Japhet.

"My grandmother," he said. "She is not well."

He leaned over and spoke softly to his mother, then gently opened the bundle for her, revealing a stack of his father's shirts. Sitting atop the stack was an ancient silver chronometer, engraved with the initials O.L.

Mrs. Lumbaba picked up the chronometer, her hand wavering. Then she shut her eyes and pressed the time-piece to her lips.

She was making a small sound, Tycho realized, as Japhet leaned in close.

"She is asking if he suffered," Japhet said.

Carlo started to speak, but Tycho beat him to it.

"The air scrubbers failed, ma'am," he said. "It would have been like falling asleep."

The widow lowered the chronometer and nodded faintly.

"It was good of you to deliver these things," Japhet said. "Are the flight logs from the *Lucia* among them?"

"Under salvage law, the logs are considered components of the ship," Carlo said.

"I see," Japhet said, his eyes hard.

Carlo turned to smile at Mrs. Lumbaba.

"Ma'am, your husband mostly searched for platinum, isn't that right?" he asked.

The widow opened her eyes and murmured something.

"What did she say?" Carlo asked, leaning forward eagerly.

Yana kicked Carlo in the ankle, but he only gave her

a puzzled glance, then turned to find Japhet glaring at him.

"My father never spoke of such things with his family," Japhet said. "You have kept the flight logs for yourself—find your own answers."

"Forgive us, Mr. Lumbaba," Tycho said. "We didn't mean—"

"My mother is tired," Japhet said, getting to his feet. "Thank you for returning my father's things. I will take you back to the landing pad now."

Carlo looked like he wanted to protest, but Yana and Tycho were already getting to their feet. He nodded glumly, gathered up his helmet and gloves, and joined his sister and Japhet at the door.

Tycho, though, stopped where Captain Lumbaba's widow sat slumped on her stool, cradling the chronometer. He lowered himself to one knee, and her hollowed eyes turned to meet his.

"I'm very sorry for your loss, ma'am," Tycho said quietly. "I hope your husband is at peace."

The widow Lumbaba nodded at him. Tycho stood and offered her a low bow. Japhet Lumbaba stood in the doorway, watching him.

They rode the elevator in silence, eyes fixed straight ahead. It wasn't until they reached the customs house that Japhet spoke.

"Master Hashoone," he said.

All three siblings looked at him, but he was looking at Tycho.

"We have air scrubbers at Kraken Station too," he

said. "If they failed, I do not think it would be like falling asleep."

"I'm afraid that's true," Tycho said.

Japhet nodded.

"Thank you for not saying this," he said. "Some truths are better not shared."

Tycho started to reply, but before he could, someone shrieked and heads turned throughout the dome. He looked over Japhet's shoulder and saw a thin old woman in a baggy robe staggering through the crowd, one finger outthrust accusingly.

For a moment he thought it was the widow Lumbaba, but this woman was far older, and her eyes were wild and staring.

"Grandmother!" Japhet said, pushing through the curious onlookers.

"THIEVES!" screamed the old woman, spit flying from her mouth. "THIEVES AND MURDERERS!"

Her bony finger was pointing straight at them.

Japhet tried to calm the old woman, but she flailed at him with surprising strength, her fury still directed at the Hashoones. The Huygens-Cassini workers around were staring, as were the rough-looking spacers.

"My son spent his life searching for the secret of the *Iris*!" she screamed. "And when he found it, these filthy outsiders murdered him for it!"

"We need to go," said Carlo, his voice low but urgent. "Head for the airlock. Do it *now*."

Japhet dragged the old woman away, still screaming,

as the Hashoones began to walk quickly in the other direction. Most of the people around them simply went back to what they'd been doing, shrugging or laughing. But Tycho saw a few curious glances lingering—and one of the bearded spacers with the wolf patch on his jumpsuit was speaking urgently into his headset.

His sister and brother saw it too.

"Are we running?" Yana asked, trying to extract her gloves from the bowl of her helmet.

"We're walking," Carlo said. "But we're walking *fast*."

They turned the corner and saw the inner door of the airlock open. Lights were flashing inside, illuminating a crowd of men and women in spacesuits. Sirens sounded, signaling that the lock was about to close.

"Never mind—we're running!" Carlo said.

They broke into an awkward trot, helmets clutched to their chests. Tycho heard someone yell. He pushed past a brawny refinery worker, who barked indignantly at him. They were ten meters from the lock when the sirens stopped.

"Go faster!" Carlo urged.

The gap between the airlock's heavy doors began to narrow. Carlo dashed inside, with Tycho right behind him. He turned and saw Yana still a couple of meters away.

"Yana!" yelled Tycho, looking for a way to stop the doors.

"Idiot kids," grumbled someone behind them. "If I get docked for being late, it's coming out of your hides."

Yana turned sideways and slipped through the closing doors, yanking her helmet in after her. The doors banged shut, and she shook her head, gasping.

"Helmets," Carlo said, fitting his over his head and locking the collar. The airlock's venting mechanism began to hiss.

Tycho locked on his helmet and pulled on his left glove, fumbling with the seal. Wind tore at his right hand as the lock's pumps began sucking out the air. Yana struggled with her helmet, still panting. She had only one glove on.

The workers around them were yelling.

"Seal it up, you stupid dirtsiders! Seal it up!"

Tycho cinched his right glove shut. Yana looked frantically around the lock. Tycho saw her other glove lying on the deck. He dropped to his knees and handed the glove to her. The wind whipping past them began to subside as the pumps did their work.

"Tyke, we need to check seals," Carlo said urgently, over the angry commotion around them. "If anything's open, we'll all burn."

Tycho's instincts screamed to help his sister, but he knew Carlo was right. He forced himself to look at the readouts on Carlo's chest.

"You're green," he said.

"So are you," Carlo said.

They turned and found Yana fumbling with her wrist seal. Sweat was pouring down her face, and they could hear her breath thundering over their suit radios. The workers around them had backed away, but there wasn't enough room in the lock to protect them in case of an open seal, and their frightened gazes showed that they knew it.

The sirens began to blare again. Yana yanked at her wrist seal so hard Tycho feared she might tear it open. He forced himself to focus and examine the readout on the front of her suit.

"Yana," he said, "stop. You're green. It's all right."

Wind ruffled around them as hidden machinery pumped the nitrogen-rich atmosphere of Titan into the lock. The workers turned away, muttering in mingled anger and relief. A moment later, the outer doors split in the center, revealing the landing pad beneath a feature-less orange sky.

"That was fun," Yana gasped. "What was that crazy old woman so mad about?"

"Quiet," Carlo said as the lock began to clear. "We're not safe yet—we need to get on the ship right now."

"What's wrong?" Yana asked. "Nobody followed us—I was the last one in."

"I'm not worried about who's back there," Carlo said. "I'm worried about who's out here."

They moved across the pad at a brisk walk, eyeing the spacesuited workers busy at various tasks. To their right stretched the broad expanse of the Kraken Mare. Undisturbed by wind or ripples, its surface formed a per-fect mirror of the featureless sky. Glancing at it left Tycho momentarily confused between up and down, and he forced himself to look away.

"There's no point hurrying," Yana said. "It'll take at least an hour to get a flight plan filed and approved."

"We're making our own flight plan," Carlo said. "If those guys don't stop us first."

Tycho followed his brother's eyes and saw a pack of spacers emerging from a squat structure near the shore of the lake. They wore mismatched spacesuits—all of them decorated with the white wolf against the black background.

Yana, behind her brothers, couldn't see where Carlo was looking.

"What guys?" she asked. "We can't just blast out of here, you know. It's a big fine—"

"They can bill me," Carlo said.

The lead spacer was pointing at them.

"Carlo—" Tycho warned.

"I see it! Run!"

They jogged for the gig, struggling in the bulky suits, breath booming in one another's ears. Carlo tapped out a command on his wrist control as he ran. The gig's gangplank began to descend.

"I'm flying," he said as they rushed up the gangway. "Tyke, you handle the atmosphere exchange. Yana, sensors. Forget preflight."

Tycho peered out the viewports as the gangplank sealed itself behind them. The spacers raced toward the siblings, carbines in their hands. Some came to a halt in front of the gig, while others ducked beneath it, out of sight. Something clanked against the hull.

"They're breaking in!" Yana warned.

"Not with hand tools, they're not," Carlo said. "And they don't have time to burn through. Just get the atmosphere exchanged and strap yourselves in."

"You realize they're all around us," Tycho said.

Carlo grinned, the scar on his face flexing. "They'll move."

He slammed a bank of levers into the upright position, and lights winked on across the pilot's console. A recording started to warn them about proper flight procedures. Carlo silenced it with a slap of his hand and pulled back on the control yokes. The engines whined, and the gig rose a meter above the landing pad.

"We are going to be in *so* much trouble," Yana said. "Those aren't pirates out there, you know. They're port security, and—"

"I'm not sure there's much difference out here," Carlo said. He whipped the gig's nose around in a full circle, and the spacers dodged, arms held protectively over their heads.

"We're at vacuum," Tycho said. "Opening the air tanks."

A rattle told them the gig's landing gear had retracted. Carlo nudged the gig forward on its maneuvering jets. Several spacers still stood ahead of them. One raised a carbine uncertainly, then lowered it in disgust, retreating as the whine of the gig's engines rose to a roar and Carlo pointed the craft's nose toward space.

"Don't cook anybody," Tycho warned.

"Not my style," Carlo said. The gig rose smoothly into the orange sky, and within a few seconds the landing pad was a tiny rectangle far below them.

A chime sounded on Tycho's board. "Atmospheric cycling complete," he said, tugging off his helmet gratefully as his siblings did the same.

Yana swiped at the sweat on her forehead. "Now will somebody please tell me what happened back there? Starting with whatever that old woman was yelling about."

"Right," Tycho said. "She was talking about a secret. And Iris. What is that?"

"An old spacer's tale from our great-grandfather's day," Carlo said. "And apparently it's what Captain Lumbaba was looking for. There's no platinum in the Hildas, but maybe there's something else."

"What are you talking about?" Yana asked.

"A fortune," Carlo said. "Waiting out there for somebody to claim it."

4

THE TALE OF THE *IRIS*

The *Shadow Comet* sat nestled in a docking cradle, one of dozens of starships moored in orbit above the gleaming white sphere of Enceladus. Workers in spacesuits swarmed over her hull, attaching fuel lines, cleaning fouled conduits, and patching damage from bits of space debris.

Yana was busy with her mediapad, leaving Tycho to watch as Carlo shut down the gig's engines, then tapped the maneuvering jets so the craft rose smoothly and latched into its socket in the larger ship's belly.

As he shut down his console, Carlo noticed Tycho's envious look.

"All in the touch, little brother," he said with a waggle of his fingers. "Well, that and a few thousand hours of practice."

They climbed up the ladderwell to the *Comet*'s ventral airlock and found the lower deck silent and still—the crewers were away, enjoying a brief shore leave. But their parents were on the quarterdeck with their jumpsuits unzipped and bunched around their waists, revealing ratty T-shirts.

"Ah, able hands and eager young minds," Mavry said. "Exactly what we need to finish recalibrating the fuel injectors!"

Tycho and Yana groaned—that was a tedious job, even as shipboard chores went.

"You might want to hear something first," Carlo said.

Diocletia frowned at the account of their getaway from the refinery and the men with the wolf insignia, then asked them to go over what Japhet's grandmother had said again.

"Dad, you're going to want to come up here," she said into her headset.

"Does this mean someone will finally tell me who Iris is?" Yana asked.

"Not a who—a what," Diocletia said. "The *Iris* was a mailboat that made runs between Earth and its corporate outposts in the outer solar system. She mostly

carried documents and bulk freight, but luxury retail-
ers started using her for moving more expensive goods
around. Somebody told somebody who told somebody
else, and so about eighty-odd years ago, a flotilla of pirate
ships ambushed her between Jupiter and Saturn. They
cleaned out her hold, then scattered with the Defense
Force on their heels."

"The *Iris*?" said Huff, stomping onto the quarterdeck
from the passageway that led aft to the engine room.
"Arrr, that's a name I ain't heard in a long time. Father
came to regret that particular escapade."

"You mean your father? Johannes?" Tycho asked as
six bells rang out.

"Aye, ol' Johannes Hashoone. He was one of the Jupiter pirates what hit the *Iris*. Some said he was the leader,
though soon enough nobody much wanted that honor.
Like yer mother said, they scattered in all directions after
the raid. Wasn't the Defense Force chasin' their tails,
though—it was the Securitat."

"The secret police?" Yana asked. "Why would they
care? Seems like a pretty routine bit of piracy to me."

"Nobody ever figured out why," Huff said. "There
were rumors, of course—there's always rumors. The *Iris*
was carryin' the ancestral jewels of the heiress to the
Amalgamated Social Graph corporate fortune, things
like that. Whatever the reason, Earth raised enough
of a ruckus with the Union that the Securitat was sent
after the raiders. The dumb pirates shot it out with them
and died, while the smart ones went to the brig—Father

spent four years locked up on 1172 Aeneas. The *Iris* cache was never found, but good riddance to it. They say it's cursed, an' from the history I don't doubt it."

"Cursed?" Yana asked. "Cursed how?"

"Generations of fools 'ave hunted that treasure, and plenty of 'em 'ave come to bad ends," Huff said. "We knew better than to discuss the cache around ol' Johannes—said he never wanted to hear about it again."

Huff trailed off, his flesh-and-blood eye narrowing in suspicion.

"But why all this ancient history? What are you not tellin' me?"

Tycho watched his grandfather as Carlo explained what had happened. The living half of Huff's face registered shock, then dismissal. But in between, Tycho saw a flash of the last emotion he would have expected: fear.

"What a load of bilge," Huff said. "Listen, boy, there's two kinds of people what never tell the truth, and that's Earthmen and prospectors."

"But we have the *Lucia*'s flight log," Tycho said. "We know where she was headed. The old woman said Lumbaba searched his whole life for the treasure—what if he was following a lead when the accident happened?"

"Ain't you been listenin', boy?" Huff demanded. "I told you the *Iris* cache is cursed, and what happened to that ore boat proves it."

"Come on, Grandfather—that's just superstition," Carlo said. "How can the contents of a mailboat be cursed?"

"I bet Cap'n Lumbaba believed they was, there at the end. There in the dark."

For a moment, all on the quarterdeck were silent.

"I don't believe in curses," Mavry said. "But I also don't believe in wasting valuable time and fuel on prospectors' fantasies."

"But Dad—" Yana began.

"That's enough, all of you," Diocletia said. "We don't have enough information to make a decision—but we can change that. And Dad, your power indicators are red."

Huff glowered down at the lights in his chest, which were warning that his cybernetic parts needed to be recharged. Still grumbling, he clanked laboriously up the ladderwell to the crew quarters on the top deck.

"Well, then," Diocletia said, "get your consoles up and running. Mavry's loading the navigational data from the *Lucia*. Let's see if we can figure out where she was going."

"We *know* that," Yana said with a sigh. "It's the end point of her flight plan."

"This should be easy, then," Diocletia said. "Vesuvia, are you monitoring? We're going to plot some potential flight plans."

"Acknowledged," the ship's AI said. "Awaiting input."

"Vesuvia, plot these points," Yana said. "Here are the coordinates where we intercepted the *Lucia*, and here are the coordinates of her destination."

"Plotting onscreen," Vesuvia said.

The main screen lit up with the ellipses of planetary

orbits and a pair of blinking crosses.

"There's nothing there," Yana said. "Deep space."

"That's not a surprise," Diocletia said. "Who can tell me what it means?"

Tycho swallowed. They were being tested again, and even though they were in orbit above Enceladus and not in combat, their success or failure would become another note in the Log.

"What if someone found the *Iris* cache, put it aboard a gig or in a message capsule, and launched it in the direction of Sirius?" he asked. "Didn't the old pirates used to do that? They'd memorize the heading instead of writing it down, right?"

"Right," Mavry said. "And then half of them would forget it after the next shindy."

"If that's the case, the treasure's gone forever," Carlo said.

"Wait a minute," Yana said. "You said it wasn't a surprise that there's nothing at those coordinates."

"Yes, I did," Diocletia said, then waited.

Carlo's hand shot up.

"We don't care what's at those coordinates *now*," he said. "We care about what was there twenty-four years ago. Basic law of piloting: you don't fly to where things are, but to where they will be."

"Or in this case, to where they were," Mavry said.

"Correct," Diocletia said. "What we've got here is the kind of navigational problem every captain encounters. Wait a minute, Carlo. Tycho, how do we find the coordinates we want to fly to now?"

"You . . . you *can't*," Tycho said. "We can determine where the *Lucia* was heading twenty-four years ago, but that doesn't help us, because we don't have the heading of what she was trying to intercept—the ship or message drone or whatever it was. The number of possibilities is basically infinite."

Diocletia said nothing for a moment. Then, to Tycho's dismay, she nodded at Carlo.

"This is ridiculous, Mom," Yana complained. "It's a piloting question. Of course he's going to know it."

"Incorrect, as you might have realized if you'd been thinking instead of sulking," Diocletia said. "It's a navigational question."

That stung both twins, who sank deeper into their chairs as seven bells sounded.

"Tycho's assuming the *Lucia* was on an intercept," Carlo said. "But what if she were going to a celestial body—one with a natural orbit?"

"That's a big assumption," Tycho objected.

"Right, but you've got to start somewhere," Yana burst out. "It's like Grandfather said the other day: pirating is half guessing."

"Sometimes a lot more than half," Mavry said.

"Let's plot those twenty-four-year-old coordinates against the orbits of charted celestial bodies," Carlo said. "Pick an eighty-five percent confidence interval to start."

"Three potential matches," said Vesuvia.

An X appeared on the diagram of the solar system,

connected by a curved line to the coordinates the *Lucia* had never reached. "The first is a centaur, designation 356925 Powhatan. Records indicate it was the site of an Earth scientific facility that was decommissioned in 2874."

"That's after contact was lost with the *Lucia*," Tycho said before anybody else could. "No one would hide a treasure on a rock that had an inhabited science lab sitting on it."

"I'm inclined to agree," Diocletia said. "What's the second potential match, Vesuvia?"

"P/2093 K1 is a short-period comet inbound toward the inner solar system," Vesuvia said, displaying a new X and a different loop on the screen.

"That's out beyond Ceres," Mavry said. "Any data about P-whatever-it-is?"

"I have 6.2 terabytes of compiled observational data about P/2093 K1," Vesuvia said. "Along with compositional—"

"Any *interesting* data?" Mavry asked.

"I do not know how to define 'interesting,'" Vesuvia said.

"I'll consider that a no," Mavry said. "And the third object?"

"The third object is an asteroid, designation 2144 ND1. Orbit is eccentric."

"To say the least," Carlo observed, peering at the screen. "Any interesting data?"

Vesuvia paused, no doubt assessing that troublesome

word again. Tycho and Yana grinned at each other.

"No data reach sufficient confidence levels for presentation to crew," the AI concluded primly.

"All right then," Diocletia said. "Good work, Carlo."

The Hashoones regarded the orbits on the screen.

"So what are you thinking, Dio?" Mavry asked after a few moments.

"I'm thinking that we're privateers, not treasure hunters," she replied.

As his children groaned, Mavry raised an eyebrow.

"I take it you disagree?" Diocletia asked him sharply.

Mavry spread his hands peaceably. "My dear Captain Hashoone, the way I see it, we're whatever the solar system tells us it's profitable to be."

"And you think it would be profitable to go chasing all over creation to take a peek at rocks and ice balls?"

"No. I think the science lab isn't worth investigating, and that rogue asteroid is awfully far away. But we're due on Ceres soon anyway, and taking a look at that comet would only add a few days to the journey."

"We're going to Ceres?" Tycho asked. "Why?"

"There's been a spike in pirate attacks on outbound shipping in the asteroid corridors," Mavry said. "The consulate is calling in privateers who operate in the area for discussions."

"Does that mean Earth is up to its old tricks again?" Yana asked.

"No, the Securitat thinks it's something else," Mavry said. "Exactly what, nobody knows."

"Could the men at Titan have something to do with it?" Tycho asked.

"Like I said, nobody knows," Mavry said. "That's what we're there to talk about."

Tycho nodded and turned back to his mother, who was gazing at the main screen, fingers steepled.

Yana broke down first.

"Mom, please," she implored.

"This isn't a jaunt to Port Town, Yana. Let me think."

Mavry put a finger to his lips, his eyes bright with amusement.

"Very well," Diocletia said. "We'll do it your way. Vesuvia, issue a recall order. I want crewers back by 1800 and engines lit by 2000. Yana, prepare the articles for a cruise to Ceres and from there back to Jupiter."

"Aye, Captain," Yana said, suppressing a sigh at the pixel work she'd been given. Articles were documents prepared before each voyage and signed by all hands, setting out the rules of the journey and how any prize money would be divided.

Then Yana furrowed her brow. "What should I say about the *Iris* cache?"

"Nothing," Diocletia said. "There's enough superstitious whispering these days without throwing around *that* name."

"But if they find out what we're doing en route—" Yana objected.

"Then someone on my quarterdeck talked," Diocletia said. "And that's not going to happen, is it?"

"Of course not," Yana said.

"We're checking out a lead from a flight log," Diocletia said. "That's something we've done hundreds of times and would have done even if you'd never met Captain Lumbaba's mother. If anyone has a problem with that—on whatever deck—they can find another ship."

The *Comet*'s crewers returned to the ship with a minimum of complaints, which Tycho knew meant they'd had little money to spend on shore leave and were impatient to be elsewhere.

Meanwhile, five crewers didn't return at all, and four of those had taken their belongings with them—clearly they hadn't intended to come back. When Carlo asked if Diocletia wanted to remain in port to recruit new hands, she shook her head emphatically.

"I don't like the look of the spacers around here," she said. "There are pirates enough in these parts—I don't need them belowdecks."

But once the *Comet* extracted herself from her docking cradle and drifted gently away from Enceladus, Diocletia seemed to relax. They all did. The *clang-clang* of the bells, the squeal of the bosun's pipes, and the familiar tumult of shouted orders from belowdecks meant normal life had resumed and the ship was herself again.

"Green across the boards, Captain," Carlo said. "Take her up to the fuel tanks?"

"Not yet, Carlo," Diocletia said. "Let's loop through the planetary rings. Pilots assume it's like flying through asteroid debris, but they're wrong—there's all sorts of magnetic anomalies that will throw off your steering. If you ever have to do it, you'll be glad you practiced."

Carlo grinned, clearly eager to show off his skills. As one bell sounded, he engaged the throttles and aimed the *Comet* at the vast pale-yellow globe of Saturn.

Tycho knew the rings were mostly tiny bits of ice and dust, rotating clouds of particles held in place by Saturn's gravity. But it was hard not to believe they were solid— as the *Comet* accelerated away from Enceladus, it looked like she was on a collision course with a massive grooved circle, its colors shifting from white through tan to black and back again as the angle of their approach changed.

"We're past the F ring already," Carlo said. "Now approaching the A ring."

"Take her in until you start recording magnetic fields," Diocletia said. "Then hand her off to Yana, who will pass the helm to Tycho."

The edge of the A ring expanded until it became a wall, and then the *Comet* was inside it, surrounded by motes of ice, dust, and rock that gleamed and flashed in the sunlight reflected by Saturn.

"It's beautiful in here," Tycho breathed.

"Watch your scopes," Diocletia said. "There are ribbons of ring material that are quite dense, with debris big enough to wreck the ship."

Huff clanked down from the top deck and stood in his usual spot behind Tycho and Yana as Carlo banked smoothly through tumbling snow-white chunks of ice.

"Magnetic readings increasing," Carlo said. "Ready to take the sticks, Yana?"

"Absolutely," Yana said. "Vesuvia, I've got the helm."

"Acknowledged."

The control yokes beneath Yana's console emerged with a whine, telescoping out to her waiting hands.

"The magnetism throws off the yaw and pitch indicators," Carlo said. "Trust your eyes and hands, not your scopes."

Yana rolled the *Comet* to starboard as a ball of snow five meters across shot past them. Dust and ice crackled against the privateer's hull, leaving a shimmering tail behind the ship for a few moments before the whirling of the rings erased it.

"I see what you mean," Yana muttered, staring at her instruments. "It's hard to keep her level."

"Arrr, this is old-fashioned flying—gotta look out the window," Huff said, gesturing at the viewports with the blaster cannon built into the stump of his left arm.

"Vaporizing the viewscreen is not advisable," Vesuvia said.

"All I'm doin' is pointin', you demented abacus."

Yana lifted her eyes from the scopes and gazed into the dazzle ahead of her, biting her lip.

"You're right, that's better," she said. "But I can still feel the yokes pulling all over the place."

"It's a tangle of magnetic fields in here," Mavry said. "Physicists have been trying to figure it out for centuries."

"They need to try harder," Yana muttered, yanking

back on the yokes to ease the *Comet* above a flurry of stones and gleaming dust.

"We're coming up on Daphnis, another of Saturn's moons," Diocletia said. "Tycho, take the controls. Bring us around Daphnis, then up and out of the rings."

"Aye-aye," Tycho said, trying to sound confident. "Vesuvia, I'm taking the helm."

"Acknowledged."

Tycho took hold of the control yokes with clammy palms. He had never felt at ease piloting the *Comet*, even when there weren't dangerous magnetic ripples and whirlpools all around him.

The yokes shimmied briefly in Tycho's hands, warning him they were active. He felt the *Comet* pulling in all directions, her automated flight systems trying to make sense of data distorted by the forces around her. Blinking away sweat, Tycho glanced back and forth between the scopes and the viewport.

"We're fifteen thousand klicks from Daphnis," he reported. "Should be entering the Keeler Gap in just a moment."

A minute later the *Comet* passed through a scree of dust and emerged in empty space—a brief gap in the rings carved out by the gravity of Daphnis. Once the ship was clear of the ring material, the controls settled down and Tycho exhaled gratefully. The *Comet* still felt huge and unwieldy, but at least she wasn't fighting her own yokes.

Daphnis gleamed ahead of them, a chunk of icy rock

perhaps eight kilometers long. Tycho stepped on the throttle, eager to finish the exercise, and the moon grew rapidly on the viewscreen, surrounded by a halo of ice crystals.

"Easy, Tycho," Mavry warned. "Daphnis is heavily magnetized—"

Suddenly Tycho's scopes spun, and the yokes felt like they were trying to fly out of his hands. He thrust them forward, struggling to regain control, and the *Comet* tumbled forward in a roll, spinning bow over stern. Shouts came from below, and Tycho felt his vision going gray. Vesuvia intoned a warning, but Tycho couldn't hear it over the roaring in his ears.

He eased back on the yokes, breathing hard, and managed to stop the *Comet*'s tumble and bring her upright again. Still fighting for control, Tycho heeled the ship over to port, aware of Daphnis hurtling overhead. Ignoring the nonsensical readings filling his scopes, he struggled to climb out of the moon's magnetic field.

Then he had control again, the yokes quiet in his hands.

"I'm okay," he said, wondering if that was true. "Are we clear?"

"No," Mavry said. "We're still in soundings—Daphnis is less than a kilometer to stern."

Tycho twitched the yokes to starboard, and the *Comet* rolled that way, as obedient as if this were a basic simulation. Curious, he cut the throttles and gently spun the ship to face the way they'd come, until the surface of the hulking moon filled the viewport.

"Am I going crazy?" Tycho asked. "Instruments register no anomalies whatsoever."

"That's my reading too," Yana said.

"We must be in some kind of lee—a place where the magnetism drops to zero," Mavry said.

Tycho raised the *Comet*'s nose and accelerated away from Daphnis. A moment later, the yokes began to flail against his hands. This time, though, he was expecting that. He kept his eyes on the viewscreen and his hands steady, correcting the *Comet*'s course until the magnetic readings shrank to nothing.

Two bells sounded. Nobody said anything for a moment.

"Well, Tycho," Diocletia said in a small voice, "I'm not sure if that was the worst piloting I've ever seen or the best."

Tycho let his breath out and shut his eyes for a moment. He heard his father chuckle.

"I think maybe it was both," Mavry said.

5

MISSION TO P/2093 K1

All on the quarterdeck were relieved when the *Comet* drew close enough to P/2093 K1 to detach from her long-range tanks. For the Hashoone kids, the voyage had been seventeen endless days of homework and flight simulations interrupted by boring watches. By the time they approached P/2, Tycho was certain Vesuvia had taken a dislike to him: her critiques of his homework struck him as borderline vicious, and she filled his flight simulations with clogged fuel lines, tricky docking maneuvers, and magnetic anomalies.

"Processing data on P/2," Yana said, fingers flying over her keyboard as her scopes filled with information gathered by the *Comet*'s sensors. "Looks like a typical cosmic snowball—just enough ice, loose rock, and organic compounds for gravity to hold together."

"Arrr, we better not 'ave come all this way for nothin'," growled Huff.

"Any anomalous surface features?" asked Mavry, peering at the main screen. It showed nothing but the darkness of space, sprinkled with stars—comets like P/2093 K1 were practically invisible without the bright tails they sprouted when buffeted by the solar winds.

"You'll have to get me closer," Yana said. "At this range I can only resolve surface features larger than a hundred meters."

"Closer it is," Carlo said. "Finalizing intercept course. Captain?"

"Take us in," Diocletia said.

"Aye-aye," Carlo said. He activated his headset microphone and alerted Grigsby as he angled the *Comet* to port and accelerated toward P/2093 K1.

"Building spectrum analysis of organic compounds," Yana said. "Appears to be basic primordial ooze."

"Maybe the treasure is buried inside P/2," Tycho said.

Six bells sounded.

"Hold on a sec," Yana said. "I'm picking up something. Looks like . . . wait. Vesuvia, sensors just went blank. What—"

Something slammed the *Comet* to starboard, the impact driving Tycho's neck and shoulder into the tough leather of his harness. There was a flash of brilliant light and a thunderclap of sound that left the Hashoones instinctively clamping their hands over their ears, spots dancing in their vision. The enormous noise faded into a low, rolling groan, accompanied by the shuddering of the quarterdeck beneath their feet.

"What was that?" yelped Yana.

"Impact," Vesuvia said in her emotionless way. "Port engine support."

"Damage report?" Diocletia demanded.

"Damage assessment initiated," Vesuvia replied. "No data at present time."

"Carlo, evasive action," Diocletia said. "Yana, what have you got?"

"Nothing!" Yana said. "I'm totally blind!"

Carlo yanked the left control yoke back and shoved the right yoke forward. Acceleration pressed the Hashoones back in their chairs as he spun the *Comet* to port, trying to shield the damaged section of her hull from their attacker. Tycho heard the wail of the bosun's pipes belowdecks, ordering the gun crews to their stations.

"Damage consistent with a missile impact," Vesuvia said. "Hull breach contained. Power feeds severed in affected area. No further diagnostics available. Calculating trajectory of enemy projectile and sending data to gun crews for target acquisition."

"Someone was waiting for us," Diocletia said, then activated her headset. "Mr. Grigsby, sensors are down. If you see a target, take the shot."

"Our pleasure, Captain," Grigsby growled. "Nobody takes a piece out of the barky without us having something to say about it."

"Tell the crews to make it count, Mr. Grigsby," Diocletia said grimly. "Yana?"

"Electromagnetic interference across all bands," Yana said. "Someone's jamming us. It's more powerful than anything I've ever seen."

"Fight fair, you scurvy buzzards!" Huff roared, his forearm cannon jerking madly in response to its owner's anger.

"Initiating countermeasures," Yana said. "Looking for where the interference is weakest so we can boost a signal and punch through it."

"How long?" Diocletia asked.

"Can't tell you," Yana said. "I need some time to analyze the interference."

"Fast as you can, then," Diocletia said, her voice brisk and businesslike. "Carlo, take us in so we can get a visual on our attacker. Dad, get below and assist the gun crews. Mavry, go aft and get me a more detailed damage assessment. Tycho, you're on communications."

No one argued—a captain's word was law, especially during combat. Mavry unbuckled his harness and rushed for the passageway leading from the quarterdeck to the fire room, arms out to catch himself in case the ship took another hit. As Huff clomped down the ladderwell, the *Comet*'s cannons began to roar, making the deck tremble beneath Tycho's feet.

Tycho stared at the main screen, on which the enemy ship was little more than a brighter point of light against the stars. At this range and without sensor data, the *Comet*'s gunners had no chance of doing real damage to their foe. Their best hope was to keep the enemy gunners off-balance.

The bright spot on the viewscreen pulsed momentarily brighter.

"Missile launch detected," Vesuvia warned.

Carlo yanked back on the control yokes and stomped on the pedals, lifting the privateer's bow, then rolling her hard to starboard. The stars spun crazily on the main screen, and a streak of light flashed across their view—a projectile fired by the enemy ship.

"Portside controls are sluggish," Carlo grunted. "But it's nothing I can't handle."

"Releasing chaff," Huff growled over the comm. A moment later they heard a faint series of popping noises, and three bursts of light flowered in front of the *Comet*. The light faded, revealing expanding clouds of glittering particles—bits of metal launched into space to confuse the targeting systems of enemy missiles.

"Who do you think they are?" Carlo asked his mother.

"The ones shooting at us," Diocletia said. "That's all that matters right now."

Sitting at his station, Tycho found he had nothing to

do but worry—there were no communications to monitor. His eyes jumped from his sister, hunched over her instruments, searching for a weakness in the jamming, to his brother and his mother, both busy at their stations with their backs straight as ramrods.

Tycho understood his mother's dilemma. Missiles were long-range weapons, and with the *Comet*'s sensors blinded, there was no way to tell what kind of ship had fired them. If the *Comet*'s attacker was small, the best strategy was to engage at close range, where the privateer's cannons would make short work of their opponent. But if the enemy ship was larger and better armed than the *Comet*, drawing nearer could be a fatal mistake.

"I've got it!" Yana said. "Punching through on the PKB band, oscillating within spectral harmonics . . . and sensors are coming back up. Nobody keeps Yana Hashoone blind for long!"

"You can congratulate yourself later. What do you see?" Diocletia said.

"She's a Harrier-class missile boat, maybe twenty-five meters long."

"Not for long, she isn't," Carlo growled. A Harrier was no match for a frigate like the *Comet*—with her sensors restored, the ship's heavier weapons would chew the enemy craft to bits.

"Mr. Grigsby, the pirate that fired on us is a Harrier," Diocletia said into her headset. "Yana's sending the gun crews a target profile now."

"Mom, wait—" Yana said.

"Send it!" Diocletia barked.

"Done," Yana said, spots of color flaring in her cheeks.

"Thank you," Diocletia said. "Now, what is it?"

"There's two more ships behind the Harrier. Still building sensor profiles, but one's about seventy-five meters long, the other maybe twice that. Probably a frigate and some kind of pocket cruiser. They've shed tanks and are on course to intercept."

"Well, that changes things," Diocletia said. "What's the range?"

"Still calculating," Yana said.

Missiles lanced out from the *Comet*, white streaks in the darkness of space. A moment later, there was a flash, and the crewers belowdecks roared in triumph.

"Harrier disabled," Vesuvia said in her flat voice. "Scan indicates ninety-three point eight percent chance enemy power linkages are severed and control systems unresponsive."

"Mr. Grigsby, we have two more bandits out there," Diocletia said into her headset. "Yana, what's the range? Do we need to run?"

"No . . . the frigate is probably half an hour out, the cruiser an hour or more. One more thing: I'm scanning a concentration of metals on the surface of P/2. It's an irregular pattern, but the main mass looks like it's thirty meters by ten."

"That sounds like a ship," Tycho said.

Diocletia nodded. "Any ion emissions or heat signature? I don't need anybody else shooting at us right now."

"Cold as space," Yana said.

"A wreck, then," Carlo said.

"Maybe the *Iris*?" Yana asked.

Diocletia shook her head. "The pirates never took the *Iris*—just what she was carrying. This is something else."

"I have an incoming transmission from the cruiser," Tycho said.

"Put it onscreen," Diocletia said. "Silence on deck."

The main screen flashed, and a face glared out at them from across space. The man was bald, with tattooed tears trailing down his cheeks to his white mustache, which was stiffened with wax so it was wider than his face. Diamonds and silver hoops decorated his right ear, while his left was a blackened stub surrounded by deep white scars. His left eye was missing, replaced by a black telescoping lens.

Tycho felt his heart jump at the sight of the notorious pirate Thoadbone Mox, formerly captain of the *Hydra*. Mox had escaped capture two years ago, after Huff let him go, to the astonishment of the other Hashoones. They knew him as one of Jupiter's most infamous traitors, suspected of having sold out his fellow pirates at the Battle of 624 Hektor. Even thirteen years later, that dark day was close to a forbidden subject among the Hashoones. Huff had nearly been killed, and his injuries had forced him to surrender the captain's chair.

"Look what I've caught," sneered Mox, his telescopic eye whining and whirring as he stared at the viewscreen on his own ship. "It's the Hashoones in that antique bucket they call a ship."

"Well, if it isn't Thoadbone Mox," Diocletia said. "I see someone's lent you a new ship to replace the one we took from you."

"A bigger and better ship!" Mox crowed. "This here's the *Geryon*. I'll give you an up-close look at her in a minute. And then I'll blast that sad little scow of yours into particles."

"You can't afford your own pocket cruiser—whose errand boy are you now, Thoadbone?"

"Errand boy? That's rich coming from a pretend pirate like you," Mox said, then leaned close to the camera on his console, so that his face distorted hideously. "If I were you, I wouldn't be talking—I'd be running. But there's nowhere in the solar system you can hide from me, Hashoones."

"Who's hiding? We're right here, Mox—catch us if you can. Vesuvia, end transmission."

Diocletia drummed her fingers on her console for a moment.

"I don't like that man," she muttered, then activated her headset. "Mavry, how's the damage look?"

"Minor," Mavry said over his comlink from the fire room. "Some severed auxiliary power feeds and melted control linkages. We can fly with it—though if that missile had been two meters to starboard, it would have vaporized an engine."

"Well, I guess we're not totally unlucky these days," Diocletia said. "Though we've got company—that's Mox out there."

"How far off?" Mavry asked.

"Not as far as I'd like," Diocletia said, then gazed up at the main screen. Yana and Tycho exchanged a glance but kept quiet. Once their mother had all the information she needed, her decisions were her own.

"Tycho, get your father," she said. "Take the gig down to P/2 and investigate the wreck. You're going to need to work fast, so get moving."

She activated her headset again. "Mr. Grigsby? Blow that Harrier out of space."

"Gladly, Captain," Grigsby said.

It was definitely a ship—or it had been one until it plowed belly first into the surface of P/2093 K1. The impact had scattered twisted metal for hundreds of meters and buried what remained of the ship's stern in the tarry surface of the comet, with the needle-shaped nose protruding several meters above the surface, aimed at the stars it would never again reach.

Mavry flew a few hundred yards beyond the wreck and set the gig down with a stuttering of landing jets. He and Tycho were descending the gangplank when Diocletia's voice crackled in their ears.

"We're peppering the frigate with missile fire to keep her busy, but she's coming and coming hot—with Mox's cruiser behind her," she warned.

Mavry beckoned for Tycho to hurry. "We have time, Dio. Huff and Grigsby will make them duck."

"If I comm you to get out of there, do it."

"Of course, Captain," Mavry said mildly.

To Tycho's surprise, he couldn't see the wreck—there was nothing ahead of them but a bleak landscape of frozen muck, broken by rocky outcroppings and drifts of ice and snow. He looked in the other direction, thinking they'd gotten turned around somehow.

"This way," Mavry said over his suit radio. "P/2's diameter is so small that the crash site's over the horizon."

"Oh," Tycho said, embarrassed.

P/2's minuscule gravity allowed him and Mavry to move across its surface in bounds, each leap carrying them a good ten meters above the comet's fractured landscape. In different circumstances, it might have been fun.

"Short, controlled jumps," Mavry said. "Let's not achieve escape velocity and fly off into space."

Tycho tried to remember the relevant equations and made a halfhearted attempt at the math.

"I don't think that would happen, Dad," he said.

Mavry laughed.

"You're right, it would be more of a high parabola. Still, let's not risk it."

Above them, a dot of light brightened, marking a missile launch from the *Comet*. A moment later, another bright dot flashed—twice, then three times—as the enemy frigate fired back. Tycho reminded himself to focus on their mission and not on those spots of light. It was hard, though—one of those spots of light had his family on it.

"Almost there," Mavry said. "Look—there's the wreck."

The ship's violent impact with the comet had churned the area around her stern into waves of muck, which had then refrozen into a crazy zigzag landscape. Mavry and Tycho picked their way over the scrambled ground until they stood in front of the port airlock.

"We're going to have to cut our way in," Mavry said, unholstering a cutting torch attached to a power pack on his belt.

Tycho's faceplate automatically darkened as his father activated the torch and began to carve a circle through the airlock. Droplets of liquefied metal dripped onto the surface of the comet, melting through the frozen crust and sending up little puffs of water vapor that instantly froze into streamers of ice. They were tiny, short-lived comet tails, Tycho realized with a smile.

Mavry completed the cut and activated his headset. "We're going in. How's it look up there?"

"Hurry," was all Diocletia said.

Mavry pressed the magnets in his gloves against the hull and kicked at the circle he'd cut in the airlock. On the third try, the chunk of hull plating gave way, rattling briefly in the darkness inside the wreck. Mavry activated his helmet lamp and squeezed through the hole. After one last look at the battle overhead, Tycho followed.

They tramped through the lower deck toward the bow, pushing off the bulkheads to stay balanced on the uneven deck. There were bodies scattered throughout the ship, little more than skeletons wrapped in shrunken gray flesh. Some had flung up their arms in a last vain effort to shield themselves from whatever had killed them. Tycho stepped gingerly over the bodies as he followed his father to the forward ladderwell.

"This isn't just crash damage—she took a beating first," Mavry said as they climbed up to the quarterdeck. "I'm guessing the belly flop on P/2 finished the job."

The quarterdeck was interrupted by a meter-wide gash that had opened from below and to starboard. The edges of the hole were rippled, fringed with metal droplets still hanging where they'd cooled and solidified.

"Missile impact," Mavry said grimly, peering into the hole.

The entire bridge was a shredded, blackened ruin. There were bodies here too, except these were in pieces, surrounded by bits of machinery. Tycho spotted a twisted headset, the half-melted backrest from a chair, and a shattered keyboard, surrounded by spilled keys like loose teeth.

His father turned to look at him, his lamp dazzling Tycho's eyes.

"You all right?" Mavry asked.

"I'm fine," Tycho managed.

"Good," Mavry said, gesturing down at the captain's console. "The computer banks look like they survived the impact, but they're pretty beat up—I'll have to cut the memory core out."

"Mavry," Diocletia said in their ears, "Mox's pocket cruiser is closing faster than we first estimated. I need you two back here."

"Can you give me five minutes?" Mavry asked.

"At most."

"It'll be enough," Mavry said, unholstering his cutting torch again. "Tycho, go aft and look in the hold."

Tycho skirted that terrible hole in the deck and rushed down the aft passageway. Something glittered in the light from his headlamp, and he stopped, holding his breath. Then he scowled: the corridor was littered with gleaming foil packets that had been flung out of the open galley door.

"Coffee," Tycho read, kicking a packet out of his way. Some treasure.

He passed the head, the cuddy, and the cabins reserved for the bridge crew. A few meters beyond the last pair of doors, the passageway vanished in a twisted ruin of crushed hull plates, shattered conduits, and dangling wires.

"I can't reach the hold, Dad," he said over his headset. "Unless you brought mining equipment with you."

"Afraid not," Mavry replied above the crackle and hiss of the torch.

Tycho turned away from the tangled wreckage and poked his head into the captain's stateroom. The ship's starboard beam had been bashed inward as if by a giant fist, leaving the frame of a bunk twisted into an arrowhead shape and its mattress lying on the deck. Tycho looked through a dresser built into the wall, first carefully shifting the shirts and socks, then yanking them roughly out of the drawers and flinging them onto the deck. It wasn't like their owner would ever need them again.

There was nothing.

"We have to go," Mavry said in his ears. "If there was anything in the hold, it's destroyed or buried."

Tycho let his lamp play over the wrecked cabin one last time, then hesitated. He pushed the mattress aside. An iron strongbox about the size of his helmet sat beneath the captain's bunk, attached to the cabin wall by thick metal bands.

His headset crackled again.

"That's five minutes," Diocletia said. "Get moving, Mavry—Mox is almost within range."

"On our way," Mavry said.

"Dad, you need to see this first," Tycho said.

He got down on one knee. There was a dial set in the strongbox's door, with a small readout set above it, displaying a trio of small lights. Tycho recognized the device as a self-destruct rig. If the wrong combination were entered too many times, an explosive charge would incinerate whatever was inside.

His father tromped into the cabin, saw the strongbox, and sighed.

"Your mother's going to kill me," he said, lowering his carryall to the deck. "Dio? We need another minute."

"You don't have it," Diocletia said, and they both heard the roar of the *Comet*'s guns.

"Tycho found the captain's strongbox," Mavry said. "I just need to cut it free."

"We have to be gone by the time Mox's cruiser gets here," Diocletia said.

"We will be," Mavry said. "I promise."

He cut through the first band, then scooted sideways and reignited the torch. The metal securing the strongbox began to glow yellow, then orange. A notch appeared in the top of the band, and molten metal began to drip onto the deck. Tycho tried to urge the torch to work more quickly.

"Mavry—" Diocletia began.

"Already on our way back," Mavry said. Tycho could see sweat dripping down his face inside his helmet.

"Then why can I still hear the torch?" Diocletia demanded.

Mavry shut off the torch and scooped up the strongbox, careful not to touch the still-glowing metal. Tycho grabbed the carryall and slung it over his shoulder, feeling the weight of the computer's memory core inside. They rushed down the ladderwell, and he lowered himself through the hole in the airlock, reaching up to take the strongbox from his father.

Overhead, Mox's pocket cruiser was visible now, too, another point of light in the distance.

Tycho bounded after his father across the surface of P/2, reminding himself that the gig wasn't as far off as his brain insisted it had to be—unlike on Earth, P/2's horizon was only a couple of minutes away. But he still exhaled in relief when he saw the gig. To his surprise, the little ship was wreathed in mist.

"Water vapor," Mavry said. "The landing jets softened up the surface, and then the weight of the ship broke through the crust."

"Oh," Tycho said. "That doesn't mean it's stuck, does it?"

"I sure hope not."

Tycho hurried up the gangplank, relieved to see the landing gear had only sunk a few centimeters into P/2's crust. He stowed the carryall and strongbox in the gig's locker and closed the gangway behind them. His father was already in the pilot's seat, stabbing at switches on the console.

"Strap in," Mavry said. "We're leaving in a hurry."

"Seems to be the way we do it these days," Tycho said, buckling his harness.

"The life of a pirate is always exciting."

The gig's engines rose from a purr to a whine. After a brief shudder, the little craft broke free of the crust and shot away from the surface of P/2.

"Hold tight," Mavry warned. "This could get messy."

Above them, they could see the blue flares of the *Shadow Comet*'s engines, then green light spitting from her top and bottom gun turrets. Tycho followed the pulses to the distant silver triangle of the enemy frigate.

Flashes surrounded the frigate, and lines of green fire lanced out from her hull in their direction. Mavry yanked back on the control yokes, and the gig's engines screamed in protest. Bolts of plasma shot past them, leaving spots on Tycho's vision.

"We see you, Dad," Carlo said over their headsets. "Your approach vector looks good."

"The other guys see us too," Mavry said, juking the craft from side to side with practiced ease. Tycho scowled at the thought that he was the least capable pilot in his family, then shook his head, annoyed with himself. The *Comet* was thickly armored, but the gig wasn't. If his father strayed into the path of one of those cannon blasts, Tycho's anxieties would instantly end—along with his hopes, dreams, and everything else.

Brilliant green light filled the gig's cabin, and the craft shook violently.

"That one melted the paint," Mavry muttered.

"Stay on course, Dad," Carlo said. "We'll help you out. Top turret gunner, maximum elevation on my mark! Give it all you've got!"

The *Comet* rolled smoothly onto her starboard wing, dipping her nose toward P/2 far below. That shielded the gig from fire, but left the top turret as the only weapon the *Comet* could bring to bear on their attacker.

"Just watch the docking maneuver," Carlo said over the comm. "Sideways can be tricky."

Mavry snorted.

"How about a little respect for your elders?" he asked. "I was standing this old crate on its head while you were still piloting toy ships."

Now sheltered by the *Comet*'s hull, Mavry rolled the gig onto one wing, mimicking the larger ship's earlier maneuver and leaving Tycho hanging in his harness.

Then he simultaneously killed the main engines and fired the maneuvering jets, eyes jumping between his scopes and the viewport. A moment later, they heard a *clunk* as the gig connected with the *Comet*'s belly.

"You're locked," Carlo said. "Nice flying, old man."

"Not so bad yourself, kid," Mavry said.

On the quarterdeck, Tycho saw Yana glance curiously at the carryall and strongbox, and he grinned at his sister.

"We found the memory core, and the captain's—"

"Belay that and strap in," Diocletia said sharply. "We're not out of this yet. Mox's cruiser will be in range in two minutes."

Pausing only to remove his helmet and take a grateful gulp of the cooler, cleaner air aboard the *Comet*, Tycho sat down hurriedly. Huff emerged from the ladderwell a moment later, artificial eye gleaming.

"Arrr, whoever these bandits are, they're tricksy," Huff grumbled. "Best me and the lads could do was clip that frigate once or twice."

"Not now, Dad," Diocletia said. "Tycho—"

"Already calculating a route back to our tanks," Tycho said.

"That frigate's going to rake us pretty good on the way out," Carlo muttered, swinging the privateer around to race back the way she'd come.

"It can't be helped," Diocletia said. "We'll just have to hope the stern armor holds up."

"Arrr, fire on the comet, Dio," Huff growled.

Diocletia looked puzzled, then nodded and smiled.

"Mr. Grigsby? Have all missile crews fire on P/2. Doesn't matter where—just hit it."

"What good will that do?" Yana asked.

Huff grinned. "Plenty. 'Tis an ol' pirate trick."

"Wait—belay that last order, Mr. Grigsby," Diocletia said. "Sending you specific coordinates on the surface. Direct your fire at that spot. I want nothing left."

"The wreck?" Tycho asked. "But if the treasure's still down there, it'll be destroyed."

"Would you rather it wind up in the hold of Mox's cruiser?" Diocletia asked.

The *Comet* shook as Grigsby's crews launched a flight of missiles at the gray blob of P/2. Flashes marked the point of impact.

"Keep firing," Diocletia ordered.

A moment later, jets of silvery light erupted from P/2's surface, soaring kilometers into space—and shielding the *Comet* from the view of the enemy gunners.

"That's a pretty good trick," Yana said.

"See you around, Thoadbone!" Tycho called as cheers bounced up the ladderwell from belowdecks.

"Won't last but a few minutes, but 'twill be long enough," Huff said, grinning at the fans of ice now drifting in front of them. "An' besides, how many folks can say they've made their own comet tail?"

6

THE HUNTED

When the *Comet* was safely away from P/2093 K1 and on her way to Ceres, Diocletia removed her headset, shook her hair out of its ponytail, and exhaled deeply. Her black hair was streaked with silver, Tycho noticed. When had that happened?

"That could have been a lot worse," Diocletia said, swiveling in the captain's chair. "Because you all did your jobs, it wasn't. Tycho, hopefully what you brought back from P/2 will make the trip worth it. Carlo, your piloting was excellent, particularly that maneuver to protect the gig. And Yana, if you hadn't broken that jamming, we would have had to run for it and leave the crash site to Mox."

Yana dropped her eyes, then gave up being modest and grinned, enjoying the moment. Diocletia smiled back, but then her face turned stern again.

"But remember, success will teach you as much as failure," she said. "Analyze what you did, Yana, and make a note of it. Because something tells me we'll encounter that kind of jamming again."

"I hope not," Yana said. "I've never seen a signal that powerful that also affected every scanning frequency."

Diocletia and Mavry exchanged a quick look—one Yana didn't miss.

"But *you* have," she said, leaning forward. "Where?"

There was no sound but the *shush-shush* of the air scrubbers.

"At 624 Hektor," Mavry said quietly.

Yana looked surprised at the mention of that normally forbidden name.

"The Martian freighters on that day were carrying jammers, and the Securitat gave our pirates software to counteract them . . . ," she began carefully.

"Avast," Huff growled, the flesh-and-blood corner of his mouth turned down. "Bad luck to speak of it."

"But I need to know," Yana said. "The Securitat said the software was infected by Earth's agents—"

"'Twas an evil hour," Huff said. "Leave it at that."

"Grandpa, we *have* to talk about it. This isn't something from a long time ago—it just happened to us. I need to know how to stop it if it happens again."

"Next time, just do whatever yeh did this time," Huff said.

"Yana, Vesuvia should have a record of the jamming from back then," Carlo said hurriedly. "Maybe she could help you find what you need."

"But—" Yana objected.

"Good idea," Diocletia said. "We barely escaped back there. If I know Mox, he and his pals hoped to use P/2 as cover but didn't have enough time to set up a good ambush—the missile boat was the only thing fast enough to beat us there."

"What were a bunch of pirates doing out there, anyway?" Tycho asked.

"Waiting for us, which is what's really bothering me," Diocletia said. "We didn't set our course until we left Saturn's rings. Which means someone, somewhere, slapped a tracker on us. When we get to Ceres, we're going to have to search every meter of the ship."

"They put it on the gig," Yana said, eyes wide. "At Kraken Station."

"Maybe," Diocletia said. "Or they could have put it on the *Comet* at Enceladus."

"Shouldn't we stop and find the tracker now?" Tycho asked.

"And risk Mox catching us in deep space? No thanks. I don't care if he knows we're going to Ceres—not even

Thoadbone would be crazy enough to try anything in a well-patrolled port. But while we're there, be careful. Be aware of your surroundings, and watch what you say. Not one word about the *Iris* treasure, where we've been, or where we might be going. We're being hunted. We have to start behaving like it."

She looked at each of her children in turn.

"Now that that's settled, let's take a look at what we came all this way for," she said, nodding at Mavry.

"I'll get the memory core from the wreck hooked up and see what data we can pull off it," Mavry said. "But the really interesting thing is what Tycho found. Let me present you with the captain's strongbox."

Huff clanked over for a closer look.

"Now that there is a bona fide *antique*," Huff said. "Ain't seen one of them since I was a lad. An' it's still got power—will probably run for centuries. Back then folks made things to last."

"Makes me wish they hadn't," Tycho said. "How do we get it open without burning up whatever's inside?"

"Arrr, that's easy," Huff said. "You'll want to stand back, though, Mavry."

Mavry gave Huff some room, and the old pirate bent down awkwardly, his artificial eye fixed on the seam between the self-destruct unit and the strongbox.

Yana raised her eyebrows at Tycho, who shrugged. Maybe their grandfather was more familiar with such devices or had seen something they'd missed.

Apparently satisfied with his inspection, Huff

nodded, grunted, and raised his forearm blaster cannon, pressing it against the self-destruct unit.

"Grandpa, don't!" Tycho yelped amid the clamor.

"This course of action is strongly discouraged," Vesuvia said. "Desist at once."

"Be quiet, you bossy calculator," Huff growled. "See, the trick is takin' a clean shot. . . ."

"Dad, absolutely not," Diocletia said.

"Nothin' I ain't done before," Huff insisted. "Remember that time at the Hygiea roadstead? Avast, Mavry, I told yeh to stand back, not get closer. . . ."

"I *do* remember Hygiea, in fact," Diocletia said. "You incinerated half of what was in the box *and* blew a hole in a pressure dome."

"I did?" Huff asked, looking startled.

Diocletia just nodded.

Mavry, seeing his chance, put his arms around the strongbox.

"Before we do anything drastic, let's ask around belowdecks," he said. "Some of our retainers have talents that are . . . let's say, a little more *exotic* than what you'll find on the quarterdeck."

7

RETURN TO CERES

Mavry was right. When Tycho and Yana showed the strongbox to Dobbs, the *Comet*'s master-at-arms grinned and summoned Celly, a crewer with a shaved head and a mouthful of black ceramic teeth filed down to points. She looked the strongbox over with a practiced eye and asked the Hashoones to give her an hour.

As it turned out, she only needed half that time to drain the self-destruct unit of its power, detach it from the strongbox, and drill out the lock. Tycho and Yana hurried back to the quarterdeck with the box, only to find the rest of their family gathered around Mavry's console, where their father had just connected the wreck's memory core to his own computer.

"Doesn't look like there's much left," Mavry said as he typed. "Course data's mostly gibberish, but the registration information's intact, at least. I'm bringing it up now."

"The *Foundling*," Diocletia read over her husband's shoulder. "Registration last renewed by Josef Unger, 2808. That's eighty-seven years ago."

"She was registered on Europa," Mavry said. "You don't see that anymore. Huff, do you know the name Unger?"

Huff nodded.

"Sure. Ol' Josef was a Jupiter pirate back in my father's day. Associate of his, even. But the Ungers quit the life long ago—last I heard, they was in Port Town somewheres."

Diocletia looked back down at the screen.

"Anything else you can pull off it?"

"Vesuvia might be able to help, but looks like most of the data's trashed," Mavry said. "Besides, I really want to see what's in Tycho's strongbox."

Carlo and Huff stepped aside so Tycho could set the strongbox on his father's console. After Mavry nodded, Tycho bent down and opened it.

It was empty.

"Long way to come for nothing," Carlo grumbled.

Tycho peered into the strongbox unhappily.

"Wait a minute," he said. "I see something."

He reached into the box and removed a thin plastic card with a pattern of magnetic dots on it—the kind of card used every day in data readers across the solar system. Lettering on the card said *BoC* in ornate script.

"Bank of Ceres," Mavry said. "What you've got there is a key card for a safe-deposit box."

Ceres was an airless, barren minor planet in the asteroid belt, neutral in the conflict between Earth and the Jovian Union and patrolled by warships from both. The little yellow world had evolved into a shipping hub, and its chaotic sprawl of half-buried pressure domes offered everything a spacer might need. Inside the tunnels and domes, naval officers rubbed shoulders with shipping-company bureaucrats, while tourists gawked at tattooed men and women with the rolling gait of veteran spacers.

"We should hurry," Tycho said after a near collision with a burly spacer, followed by a hard-eyed stare.

"Stop being paranoid," Carlo said. "You're so busy thinking about treasures and key cards that you're not watching where you're going."

"Belay that," Huff growled. "You lot heard yer mother—best to keep the matter dark."

When finally given the chance to inspect the *Comet* in orbit above Ceres, Huff had located not one but two trackers—one on the gig and the other attached near the frigate's docking ring. Now he was muttering about sneaky Saturnians and gazing mournfully into the empty socket of his forearm cannon. Weapons were illegal on Ceres, but in Huff Hashoone's view, no sane pirate ever went anywhere without his persuader.

Tycho knew he shouldn't, but he couldn't resist patting the key card in his jumpsuit pocket to make sure it was still there. He didn't relax until they'd followed the twisting passages from the chandler's depot into the better-patrolled corridors that housed the admiralty courts and the consulates of the Jovian Union and Earth.

The consulates and courtrooms had impressive entrances with real wooden doors, but the Bank of Ceres put them all to shame: its double wooden doors led to a vestibule decorated with twin trees, each perhaps six feet high with a trunk as thick as Tycho's fist. Tycho wanted to stop and look through the thick glass that kept curious visitors from plucking off leaves as souvenirs, but Carlo insisted that there was no time for sightseeing.

They emerged from the vestibule to discover a broad screen displaying the Bank of Ceres seal. On either side of the screen was an open doorway and a Ceres guardsman standing at attention. As the Hashoones approached, with Huff trailing along behind them, the seal rippled and was replaced by a man's smiling face. The face was smooth and perfectly symmetrical—a giveaway that this was an AI like Vesuvia, not a real person.

"Welcome to the Bank of Ceres, serving customers

across the solar system since 2574. How may we assist you today?"

Carlo elbowed Tycho, who stepped forward, holding up the key card. The AI's eyes jumped to it, the artificial pupils widening. Tycho thought that was supposed to be reassuring, but it felt creepy instead.

"We have a key card for a safe-deposit box," Tycho said.

The face on the screen smiled but said nothing. Tycho wondered if something was wrong, but a moment later the handsome artificial face began to speak.

"Welcome back to the Bank of Ceres, Mr. Unger," it said. "It certainly has been a while!"

"I'm not—" Tycho began, only to get an elbow in the ribs from his sister.

"Solar system was a better place without all these blabbermouth machines," growled Huff.

"I'm sorry, Mr. Unger, I didn't understand what you said."

"I, uh, just want to look in my safe-deposit box," Tycho said.

"Very well, Mr. Unger," the face said. "Please proceed to the left and the line for special services, where one of our representatives will be happy to assist you."

The face faded away and was replaced by a schematic of the bank, with a green path. Then this too disappeared, and the screen displayed a large green arrow pointing to the left.

Beyond the screen, five lines of customers waited to

speak to tellers sitting behind a tall rampart of polished imitation wood and marble. The tellers wore navy-blue uniforms with gold braid and oversized black monocles, and their fingers were set in armatures of metal, trailing wires. A hologram over the farthest line said SPECIAL SERVICES in filigreed gold. A long line of people waited there, shifting impatiently from one foot to the other. The Hashoones took their places at the end of the line, behind a sour-faced woman wearing the uniform of a shipping lines pixel pusher.

"This is going to take *forever*," Yana grumbled, which caused the woman to turn and fix them with a pitying smile.

"Oh, honey, you have no idea," she said.

Tycho put the key card back in his pocket and folded his arms. Because of their elevated desks, the tellers' heads were a full meter above those of their customers. The teller presiding over the special services line was a bald man with a little bump of a nose and a wispy mustache. His hands moved languidly through the air above the desk, pointing here, then pinching there, his fingertips lighting up with each gesture.

After several minutes the spacer at the head of the line finished conducting his business, nodded to the teller, and strode away. The next person in line stepped forward, only to be halted by a glowing fingertip from the man behind the desk, which sent him scuttling back to his former place. The teller rose, shucked off his armatures, and descended a staircase behind the other tellers, vanishing from view.

A red shimmer appeared over the special services line, and music began to play softly—cheesy orchestral synth grunge that had already been out of fashion when Tycho and Yana were babies. The shoulders of the woman in front of the Hashoones dropped, like a marionette whose strings had been cut.

After a few bars the music stuttered briefly, then started again. Yana groaned. Carlo sighed. Tycho observed that the shoulders of the woman in front of them could, in fact, slump lower.

"Arrr," Huff said. "Think I'll fetch a nip of grog while yeh all cool yer heels."

"We all know that's not a good idea, Grandfather," Carlo said.

Huff's living eye bulged dangerously.

"Yer a mite young to tell me what is an' what ain't a good idea," he said, jabbing a metal finger at his grandson.

Carlo held up his hands apologetically as Huff stalked off, growling that he'd be back.

"Great," Carlo muttered. "Now he's off to the grog shop and who knows what trouble."

"Trouble that will be your fault," Yana said. "Why do you talk to him like he's an old man, like he's in the way?"

"Because he *is* in the way." Carlo sniffed.

"He's a Hashoone and a former captain," Yana said. "Which means he deserves your respect."

"He's a relic—a leftover from another time. Pretty soon the *Comet* will have a new captain. You think when that happens, Mom will hang around the quarterdeck with nothing to do, like Grandfather does? She won't—she'll retire to Callisto and let the new captain do his job."

"*His* job?" Yana asked. "Oh, because it's so obvious that you'll be the next captain. Right, Carlo?"

"Isn't it?" Carlo asked. "Why waste time being polite about it? I'm the best pilot in the Jovian Union, I've handled numerous boarding actions, and I can do every job aboard the ship. Neither of you can say that. Tycho can't fly, and whenever there's a boarding action, Mom makes you stay on the quarterdeck, where it's safe."

Tycho looked away, his face flushing with anger and shame. His brother was out of line, but it was true that his piloting left a lot to be desired, and everyone in their family knew it.

Yana didn't look away, though. Instead she shook her finger in Carlo's face.

"I'm on the quarterdeck because I run sensors," she said. "And I run them better than you."

"Cut it out, you two," Tycho said. "People are staring." Carlo ignored him.

"There's a lot more to being captain than running sensors," he told Yana.

"Yes, there is," Yana said. "There's respecting the crewers, and your fellow officers, and your family. None of which you understand."

They stood simmering for a minute while the synth grunge burbled mindlessly.

"I'm getting a jump-pop," Yana said disgustedly, turning and bumping into a burly cargo wrangler who'd joined the line behind them. Annoyed, the man fixed Yana with a warning stare.

"What are you looking at?" she demanded. The man shrank back, then stared at Yana in disbelief as she stomped off.

"Go ahead, Tyke," Carlo said. "I'm sure you've got something to say too. Want to lecture me about not respecting my elders?"

"Not really," Tycho said. "I was just remembering something, though. It was back when Yana and I were still kids on Callisto, and you'd just made bridge crew. You came back and told us how you'd just gotten to fly the *Comet* for the first time. Mom didn't think you were ready, but Grandpa insisted you could do it and told her how proud he was of your simulator work. That convinced Mom to let you try."

Carlo looked away.

"It was only for a few minutes, and in deep space, but you were so excited," Tycho said.

Tycho had lost track of how many times the snippet of music had played by the time the top of the teller's bald head reappeared. The teller settled back into his seat behind the desk, adjusted his monocle, then carefully put the fingers of each hand into its armature.

The red light above the special services line faded

away, the gold lettering reappeared, and the music cut off. Someone ahead of them in line clapped briefly, stopping at a sharp look from behind the desk.

Yana returned, followed a couple of minutes later by Huff, who betrayed no sign that he'd had too much grog. Tycho tried to make conversation, but his sister and his grandfather were both too angry. Yana extracted her mediapad from her bag and stared into it with a glower. Huff continued muttering to himself, while Carlo alternated humming and inspecting his fingers. Tycho just stared—at his boots, the ceiling, the hologram sign, the teller's fingers, or nothing in particular—as the line of customers ahead of them slowly shrank, and the woman in front of them finally stepped up to the desk.

"How long has it been?" Yana asked, putting her mediapad away.

"You don't want to know," Carlo grumbled.

"At least it won't be much longer now," Tycho said.

"Belay that, Tyke," Huff muttered.

"Seriously," Yana muttered. "Now you've jinxed us."

And indeed he had. The woman from the shipping lines reached into a carryall and pulled out a stack of currency chips, followed by a bundle of data disks and, worst of all, a folder of actual paper. Yana shut her eyes and sighed.

What followed was a deep discussion of several somethings, none of which Tycho could understand. The conversation required the teller to leave twice for consultation with a manager. While he was gone, Tycho estimated he heard the snippet of music more than fifty times.

The woman finally collected her belongings and marched away with an annoyed shake of her head. The teller adjusted his monocle, examined the joints of his left-hand armature, and then lifted his chin at Tycho.

The four Hashoones stepped forward.

"I understand you have a key card, Mr. . . . Unger?" the clerk asked, staring into the world of data only he could see.

Tycho retrieved the card from his jumpsuit pocket and held it up. The teller stared into his monocle, then extended a hand encased in metal and wire. Tycho handed over the key card and leaned against the desk.

"Customers are requested to maintain a courteous distance from the working area of bank representatives," the teller said.

"Sorry," Tycho said, hastily drawing his arms back.

"Bureaucrats," Huff rumbled.

"You are Mr. Unger?" the teller asked.

"Well—"

"Since you do not appear to be one hundred twenty-three years old, I shall conclude that you are not," the teller said.

"He never said he was," Carlo objected. "Your stupid AI said that."

The teller peered at Carlo. So did Tycho, simultaneously annoyed at his brother for stepping in and relieved that he'd done so.

"Not disagreeing with an incorrect statement is the same as agreeing with it," the teller said.

"No, it isn't," Carlo said. "If that were true, we'd spend our entire lives disagreeing with each other."

"Isn't disagreement a necessary part of a more complete understanding and thus cooperation?" the teller asked.

"Sometimes. But other times disagreement is a distraction. For instance, an unhappy customer might say, 'The service at the Bank of Ceres is horribly slow, and the tellers' behavior is shockingly rude.' Another party might disagree but seek to prove the customer wrong by helping him conclude his business in a speedy fashion."

Carlo smiled at the teller, and Tycho felt a flash of irritation that his brother's scar had only made his handsome features more distinctive.

"If it were not banking hours, I would be fascinated to discuss your example, which is no doubt hypothetical," the teller replied. "But as you can see, the Bank of Ceres is quite busy."

"On this we are in complete accord," Carlo said with a smile. "Let us therefore move on to cooperation and the matter of this key card."

"I am glad you have at last decided to use our facilities for a discussion of actual banking," the teller said. "But I suspect you are not Mr. Unger either, sir."

His eyes jumped briefly to Yana.

"At the risk of making a perilous leap of logic, I will rule you out as well."

As Huff growled something, Carlo drew himself up

to his full height, though that still left him a good way below the teller's eyes.

"I am not Josef Unger but Carlo Hashoone," he said. "This is my brother, Tycho, my sister, Yana, and our grandfather, Huff Hashoone. We are officers aboard the *Shadow Comet*, registered under a Jovian Union letter of marque, and the key card is our possession as legal salvage."

The teller sighed.

"It appears our discussions have moved backward," he said. "It sounds like you require the service of an admiralty court judge. Let me direct you—"

"We are more than familiar with the admiralty courts. Our business is with you—or with someone else at this bank, if you are unwilling or unable to help us conduct that business."

The teller waved his fingers in the air.

"Purely to give you an example of the power of cooperation, I shall review your case briefly with my superiors," he said.

"Wait—" Tycho began, but the music had already begun to play.

"I'm going to cry," Yana said. "No, I'm not. I'm going to get a projectile cannon and blast this bank off the face of Ceres."

"Now yer talkin'," Huff said.

"I bet the line to do that would be *really* long," Tycho muttered.

Carlo just raised his eyebrows and whistled along with the synth grunge.

The teller returned, looking faintly disappointed to see the Hashoones still there. He sat in his chair and spent a minute verifying that his armatures were working properly before returning his attention to them.

"This is a most irregular case," he said. "A long-standing agreement directs us to produce the item or items held in security here upon presentation of a valid key card."

"Excellent news," Carlo said. "Since we have given you a valid key card, let us—"

"A moment, please," the teller said. "The agreement stipulates that the item or items shall be produced if a valid key card is presented *and* a captain of the Collective or his or her heir is present. Is there a captain of the Collective or valid heir present?"

Tycho, Yana, and Carlo looked at one another, puzzled.

"The Collective," Huff muttered. "That's what the surviving pirates from the *Iris* raid called themselves."

"We can proceed, then," Carlo said to the teller. "Johannes Hashoone was a member of the Collective as captain of the *Shadow Comet*, and we are his heirs."

"I see," the teller said. "Our scanning services have verified your identities. As the merest formality, let me cross-index those against registration information for your vessel."

"Still say we should leave this be," Huff said. "Fool's business, diggin' up the past."

"But aren't you curious, Grandfather?" Tycho asked.

"Curiosity ends at the wrong end of a carbine," Huff grunted.

After a moment, the teller smiled.

"According to the records, none of you is captain of the *Shadow Comet*—and therefore none of you is a valid heir to the Collective," he said. "Would any of you care to disagree, as a point either of business or of philosophy?"

"I certainly would," Carlo said. "The agreement referenced the presence of a captain *or* a valid heir. If you examine the registration records of the *Shadow Comet*, you will see our grandfather's extensive history as captain. And as Johannes Hashoone's son, he counts as his valid heir. As do the three of us, I might add."

"One moment," the teller said, fingers tapping in midair. "Registration records verified. However, registration information indicates Huff Hashoone is no longer captain of the *Shadow Comet*."

"No longer captain . . ." stammered Huff, his forearm socket jerking back and forth.

"What does that matter?" Carlo said. "It's true that our grandfather is no longer captain. But that doesn't make him no longer a valid heir."

"There you are incorrect," the teller said with a smile. "The Collective agreement includes a number of relevant subclauses. A captaincy takes precedence over any claim to being an heir. Is there a Dee-o-cle-sha Hashoone present?"

"Take it easy, Grandpa," Tycho said, seeing the flesh-and-blood half of Huff's face turning an alarming shade of red.

"DIE-o-cle-sha," Carlo said. "That's our mother. She's in court."

"How unfortunate," the teller said, handing the key card back. "If you return here with the current Captain Hashoone, or proof that the captaincy has been dissolved, we will be happy to further explore your request. Have a nice day."

"But we just waited in that line for an hour and a half!" Carlo exclaimed.

The flesh-and-blood half of Huff's face was now purple.

"Without the current Captain Hashoone, I cannot proceed. Please stand aside."

"But this is ridiculous!" Carlo sputtered.

"We of course welcome customer feedback on our operating principles and business procedures. Please ask our lobby AI for a comment form."

Tycho was tucking the key card back in his pocket and so missed Huff's lunge for the teller's throat. He fell short by a centimeter or two, and his metal hand clanged on the imitation marble. The other tellers' heads snapped around to stare at the disturbance.

"Grandpa, don't!" Yana yelped.

"Bankers!" roared Huff, taking another swipe at the teller. "Biggest swindlers in the universe, the whole wretched lot of yeh! At least when pirates try to rob yeh, yeh gets to shoot 'em!"

Guardsmen rushed in from either side of the screen, black batons raised.

"Arrr, I've seen better service from a Martian royal executioner," Huff said. "Now c'mere, you dirty bilge rat! I'm gonna tear that fancy glass off yer eye an' jam it—"

Tycho jumped in front of the guardsmen, hands raised, but they shoved him aside and grabbed Huff from behind.

"Wait!" Tycho yelled. "Let me talk to him!"

Huff flailed in the guards' grip, the socket of his forearm cannon twitching madly. The Hashoones watched helplessly as he was dragged off, foul oaths echoing through the bank.

"Shouldn't we go with them?" Tycho asked. "Grandpa's power indicators were flashing yellow—what if his cybernetic systems run out of power?"

"They have recharge ports in the Ceres lockup," Carlo said. "He's been hooked up to them before. I'd better send a message to Mom."

The teller adjusted his monocle.

"Unless one of you also intends some ludicrous outburst, please step aside and allow other customers to attend to their affairs."

"Why don't you kids move it already?" someone growled behind them.

Defeated, the Hashoones stepped out of line.

"Have a nice day," the teller said.

Diocletia looked tired when she and Mavry arrived, and her children's competing explanations of what had happened only made her look more tired.

"Welcome back to the Bank of Ceres, Captain Hashoone and First Mate Malone," the AI said as they entered the vestibule. "We are—"

"Zip it," Diocletia said, striding past the screen.

To Tycho's relief, the customers had thinned out with the end of the business day approaching—only eight people were in line.

"Are you sure Grandpa will be okay?" Yana asked Mavry.

Their father smiled. "Oh, by now he's having a grand time telling his cellmates how he forced the entire bank to beg for mercy."

"Is he going to be in a lot of trouble?" Tycho asked.

"A moderate amount," Mavry said. "I doubt there's anyone on this dismal little planet who hasn't fantasized about strangling a Bank of Ceres teller."

"I've certainly considered it," Diocletia muttered.

After a few minutes, the teller who'd debated with Carlo earlier indicated they should step forward. Diocletia approached, boot heels ringing. The teller mutely extended a hand, and she placed the key card in his fingers.

"Identity scan complete, Captain Hashoone," the teller said. "And registration lookup verifies your status as current captain of the *Shadow Comet* with rights stipulated according to the Collective agreement. Do you wish to retrieve the contents of the safe-deposit box?"

"I would be delirious with pleasure," Diocletia said.

"One moment," the teller said, removing his finger

armatures. He handed back the key card, then vanished from view.

"He sure is moving a lot faster than last time," Yana grumbled.

"That's because he's afraid of Mom," Carlo said.

"He isn't," Diocletia said, then cocked an eyebrow. "Yet."

The teller emerged from an ornate doorway beside the desk and indicated that they should follow him into the bowels of the bank. Beyond watchful guardsmen and several electronic gates was a room with blank walls, a lone computer console, and a bare metal table. Two bank functionaries appeared from another door with a long box. At a nod from the teller, they drew gleaming keys from their belts and stood on either side of the box. Both pressed their keys into locks and turned them, then stepped back.

The teller removed the lid. There were five hollow spaces inside the box, each with a light, a nameplate, and a slot for a key card. Three of the spaces were empty, their lights dark. The names by the empty spaces read ORVILLE MOXLEY, MUGGS SAXTON, and JOSEF UNGER.

The other two slots contained gray cylindrical devices about a half meter long. The lights beside those slots were red. Tycho read an unfamiliar name—BLINK YAKATA—before he came to JOHANNES HASHOONE.

Yana peered into the box. The strange devices were identical—one end flared into a bell, while the other was topped with a box and some kind of readout.

"What are those things?" Tycho whispered to his sister.

"Some kind of scanner," Yana whispered back. "I've never seen a model like it."

"A scanner for finding the treasure?" Tycho asked.

Mavry elbowed Tycho and shook his head. The teller pulled white gloves from somewhere within the recesses of his uniform and put them on.

"The key card, if you please," he said, then stopped, peering into the case.

"What happened to Josef Unger's device?" Tycho asked. "When was it removed?"

"You seem confused about our business, young man," the teller said, beginning to strip off his gloves again. "We are caretakers, not archivists."

"But you must have some record of when the device was removed," Tycho insisted.

"Yes, you must," Diocletia said. "I'd like to know the answer to that question myself."

The teller said nothing, concentrating on carefully folding his gloves.

"Any such information would be a private matter between ourselves and Mr. Unger," he said finally. "And as we determined in rather exhaustive detail earlier, Mr. Unger is not present."

"But you're letting us use his key card," Carlo objected. "That doesn't make any sense."

"It is consistent with our operating principles and business procedures."

"That's not the same thing."

"At the Bank of Ceres we hold confidentiality in high regard. Just as we honor our agreements with customers, despite the fact that we no longer deal with businesses such as yours."

The Hashoones' eyes jumped to their mother's face. Diocletia's expression didn't change, which is how Tycho knew the teller was in real trouble.

"Businesses such as ours?" she asked. "I'm afraid I don't understand what you mean by that."

"I was referring to irregular professions." The teller sniffed. "No insult was meant."

"It most certainly was. And I've had quite enough of it. First you abuse longtime customers, and now you act as if we're too stupid to recognize an insult."

"A fascinating perspective, but since our business appears concluded, I'll leave further exploration of the question to you and your brood."

"I've got a better idea," Diocletia said. "Let's go discuss it with Sir Armistead-Kabila."

"Alfonso Armistead-Kabila? You know our bank's chairman?"

"Since I was a little girl. Does that surprise you, Mr. . . . ?"

"Hohenfauer," mumbled the teller.

"Surely you're aware, Mr. Hohenfauer, that the chairmen and chairwomen of this bank have known my family since my ancestor Ulrika Hashoone became a founding director some three centuries ago."

Hohenfauer blinked rapidly, and his fingers twitched, trying to summon the information that would have been instantly available if only he'd been at his desk, where things suddenly seemed much safer.

"I'll lead the way—I remember where Alfonso's office is," Diocletia said.

"That—that won't be necessary," the teller sputtered, rushing over to a terminal. "What was it you wanted to know?"

"Don't trouble yourself—Alfonso will be happy to help us."

"My dear Captain Hashoone, let's not be hasty," Hohenfauer said. "There's no need to bother the chairman, is there? Ah—it seems the records were incomplete earlier. I have the information right here. The device was removed in 2816, by Josef Unger himself."

"I see," Diocletia said. "We'll take the other device now—the one that my grandfather left in your safekeeping."

"I—I'll need his key card for that," Hohenfauer said.

"We don't have it. But surely you aren't questioning my identity or my rights under the Collective agreement?"

"No, but regulations—"

"Very well," Diocletia said. "We'll discuss it with Alfonso. Unlike his subordinates, he is capable of showing a little imagination."

"Just a moment, Captain Hashoone—let me see what I can do," Hohenfauer babbled, typing frantically. A moment later he extracted a blank key card from within his uniform, yanked his white gloves back on, and pressed the card into the slot below Johannes Hashoone's name. The light beside the slot turned green. The teller removed the strange device and handed it to Diocletia, who studied it for a moment, brow furrowed.

"Are there instructions?" she asked.

"No . . . there's nothing," Hohenfauer said, waving for his colleagues to come and take the box away. "But as per the Collective agreement, you are entitled to review the association's articles of incorporation. I can print them out or send them to your mediapad. Or both, of course."

"Mediapad will do," Diocletia said. "Now that your records have been magically repaired, what else is in them?"

Hohenfauer scanned his terminal's screen. A bead of sweat ran down his forehead.

"There's a conditional transmission. When a slot is activated, a prearranged message is sent to all other members of the Collective, using receiver codes specified at the time of the agreement."

"There's no need to send the transmission," Diocletia said. "We'll see to it that the others are informed."

"I can't stop it," Hohenfauer said. "I really can't. It's automatic—set up decades ago!"

Diocletia scowled.

"What does the message say?"

"I don't know that either. But there's something

else—it says 'The quantum signal will now activate for the next twenty-one days.'"

Tycho looked at his father, who shrugged.

"Right, the quantum signal," Diocletia said. "Now, is there anything else in there I need to know?"

"I—I don't know what that means," Hohenfauer stammered.

Diocletia handed the strange device to Mavry, then took a step toward Hohenfauer, her lips pressed together in a thin line. The teller took an involuntary step back and bumped into his computer console.

"It means, Mr. Hohenfauer, that you don't want me to come back here because there was something else in those records that you didn't tell me. Because that would be bad customer service. And bad customer service makes me angry."

"Th-there's nothing like that," Hohenfauer said.

"Good," Diocletia said. "Now let's go see Alfonso."

"But why? Captain Hashoone, please! I've done everything you asked!"

"What choice do I have? When Alfonso learns his old friend Huff Hashoone has been jailed at the Bank of Ceres's request, he'll of course want to know what happened. I'm afraid he'll be very upset."

"The earlier incident? Why, anyone can see that was a misunderstanding. I'll contact the authorities and have him released right away."

Diocletia considered that for a moment, then nodded. "In that case, I suppose I could visit Alfonso another day, when I'm not so tired from court. And now, Mr. Hohen-fauer, our business really does appear to be concluded."

The teller babbled pleasantries as he escorted them back to the vestibule, then bade them a good day with undisguised relief.

"You never told me you spent your childhood hanging around with bank chairmen," Mavry said as they pushed their way through the crowded corridors.

"Please. I looked up the chairman's name on my mediapad while we were waiting in line. Though Ulrika Hashoone really was a founding director—the Bank of Ceres was started to give us pirates a safe place to stash our loot."

"So you've never met Alfonso Armi-What's-His-Name?" Mavry said.

"Of course not," Diocletia said. "Hang around with bankers? Honestly, Mavry. As the daughter of a respectable pirate, I was raised better than that."

8

THE MYSTERIOUS MESSAGE

The *Shadow Comet* wasn't scheduled to depart Ceres until late the following day, when the minor planet came into ideal alignment for traveling to Jupiter without burning excess fuel. Despite Tycho's and Yana's frantic warnings that they only had three weeks to figure out how to find the mysterious signal that had been activated, Diocletia insisted that they weren't going anywhere until then.

The extra time, she said as the gig rose from the

landing field, would allow Huff and Mavry to ensure the *Comet* was fully repaired and to make another sweep for tracking devices. The children, meanwhile, could use the hours to do something more useful than arguing with her: Yana would study the scanner, while Tycho and Carlo investigated the pirates who had made up the Collective.

Aboard the *Comet*, Diocletia clambered up the ladder-well for a rest, leaving Yana poking and prodding at the scanner while Tycho and Carlo offered suggestions.

"This is one weird machine," Yana said. "It's only sensitive over a very narrow range of frequencies. It would be pretty much useless for detecting anything outside of that."

"That sounds like it was made to detect a specific signal," Carlo said.

"Exactly what I was thinking," Yana said.

"Hohenfauer called it a quantum signal," Tycho said. "What's that?"

"It works based on quantum physics, which Vesuvia hasn't made you guys study yet," Carlo said. "Basically, you have a pair of signals, and when one activates, so does the other—no matter how far apart they are. Engineers have never been able to use it for a message more sophisticated than yes-no, but it works."

"And any kind of signal can be a quantum signal?" Yana asked.

"I don't see why not," Carlo said.

"Interesting," Yana said. "Because look at the bell on

this thing. It's clearly made to detect sound. But you could make an acoustic scanner by just wiring together a few parts, and this baby was built like an attack cruiser. I'm not kidding—you could use this housing for hull armor."

"Or the other way around," Tycho said. "It did belong to pirates, after all."

"Well, Yana, you've got a couple of hours to play with it before we give Mom an update," Carlo said. "Tyke, I told Dad I'd run diagnostics on our propulsion systems, but after that we'll try to figure out the workings of the Collective."

Tycho nodded, then turned at a beep from his console.

"You guys get a message?" he asked, strolling over for a look. Their father probably wanted them to look at something in the *Comet*'s fire room. Or perhaps their aunt Carina had sent something to all of them—they'd already been warned that family meetings awaited them at home on Callisto.

"Not me," Yana said, settling into her chair with the scanner in her lap.

"Me neither," Carlo said, calling up the diagnostics for the *Comet*'s steering and rudders.

"Looks like you're the lucky one," Yana said. "Let us know what you did wrong."

Tycho tapped the message indicator on his screen. The sender's recognition code was a scramble of nonsense letters and numbers. But the words were clear enough.

*TYCHO HASHOONE, I'VE GOT SOME PROFITABLE
INFORMATION FOR YOU. INTERESTED?*

"Good news—somebody's gonna tell me I won the Martian lottery," he scoffed. "Amazing, since I never bought a ticket."

"What was that?" Yana asked distractedly.

"Nothing," Tycho said. "Just a junk message."

He went to delete it, but before he did, his console beeped again.

*YOU DID US A GOOD TURN CRACKING THE THREECE
SUUD CASE. SOME HERE WANT TO REWARD YOU FOR THE
EFFORT.*

"Very funny, Yana," Tycho said.

"What's funny?" Yana asked, looking up from the scanner.

"Okay, fine. Carlo, cut it out," Tycho said.

"Cut what out?" Carlo asked. "I'm a little busy for jokes, Tyke."

Tycho silenced his console's message indicator.

Who is this? he typed. He looked at the message for a moment, trying to figure out which of his siblings would be laughing at him in a minute, then sent it.

The reply came back almost immediately.

*IT DOESN'T WORK THAT WAY. I'M SOMEONE YOU WANT TO
KNOW, AND I CAN HELP YOU. LET'S LEAVE IT AT THAT.*

Tycho pulled up the origin code for the message and saw it had been run through one of the public broadcast servers on Ceres, hiding its origin. A message sent from within the ship would have moved over an internal channel. Still, there were ways around that. And both Carlo and Yana had the technical know-how to pull off such a prank.

Help me with what? he typed.

One second turned into five, then ten.

BECOMING CAPTAIN, OF COURSE. ISN'T THAT WHAT YOU WANT?

Tycho sighed.

NOT FUNNY, YANA. OR IS THIS CARLO? NEVER MIND—I DON'T REALLY CARE WHICH.

This time the response came back almost instantly.

GOOD FOR YOU FOR BEING SUSPICIOUS. I'LL PROVE MYSELF. AS PRIVATEERS OPERATING UNDER A LETTER OF MARQUE, YOUR FAMILY GETS THE SECURITAT'S DAILY INTEL BRIEFING, CORRECT?

Yes, he messaged back.

In truth, Tycho rarely bothered to scan the document when it arrived each morning. The briefing didn't contain truly sensitive information—that was reserved for the highest ranks of the Jovian military. Occasionally there was a roundup of pirate activity, but mostly it was boring political stuff that only adults cared about.

> READ IT TOMORROW. I'LL WAIT TO HEAR FROM YOU.

Tycho looked at the message for a moment. Suddenly the faintly glowing letters on the screen seemed filled with menace.

What am I looking for? he typed.

> IF YOU CAN'T FIGURE THAT OUT, WE HAVE NOTHING TO TALK ABOUT.

On any other night, Tycho would have savored dinner, which included hydroponic vegetables and actual lab-grown beef, both welcome changes from the usual shipboard burgoos. As they served themselves in the familiar confines of the cuddy, the Hashoones were more cheerful than they'd been for weeks, with Huff even managing to guffaw about his brief time back in the Ceres jail. But Tycho's smile felt pained and fake—his curiosity about the mysterious message had curdled into anxiety.

The others ate heartily enough to make up for his lack of enthusiasm. When the ruins of a flummery had been cleared away and the cook had gone back down the aft ladderwell to belowdecks, Diocletia poured herself a mug of flip and cleared her throat.

"Now then," she said, "let's hear what you've found out about our scanner and the Collective."

"Blasted unlucky affair from bow to stern," growled Huff. "Best to leave the whole mess wherever it lies. That's what Father believed, leastways."

"And maybe that's what I'll decide too, Dad," Diocletia said. "But first I'd like a better idea of what we're dealing with. Yana, go ahead."

Yana had brought the scanner up from the quarter-deck and now placed it on the table.

"This device was built to detect sound waves in water," she said. "It contains an acoustical receiver and a decryption module that will only pick up a very specific signal. And look here: whoever built this used high-quality gaskets and heat-sealed the seams. It's waterproof, and built to withstand high pressure."

"You say waterproof, but do you really mean liquid-proof?" Carlo asked.

"As in, made to detect a signal in a lake of methane? That was my first thought too. But no, it was made for water. In one of Titan's lakes, an acoustic signal would fade so quickly that you'd have to get really close to the signal."

"How close?" Carlo asked.

"Reach-out-and-poke-it-with-the-other-end close," Yana said.

Mavry laughed. "And how close would you have to be in water?"

"Ten or fifteen kilometers, maybe."

"Why does it have a decryption module?" Tycho asked. "If everyone can still *hear* the signal, what's the point of encrypting it?"

"Probably to make sure you're hearing the right signal," Yana said. "Which implies that you'd be hearing other noise while you were searching."

"Interesting," Diocletia said. "Unfortunately, an underwater signal doesn't limit the possibilities much."

"That's true," Yana said. "Subsurface oceans are pretty common in the solar system—the early settlers picked moons that had them. There's Europa, Ganymede, and Callisto in the Jupiter system, plus Titan and Enceladus in the Saturn system, Titania and Oberon at Uranus, and Neptune's moon Triton."

"Don't forget the Martian aquifers," Huff interjected. "Hopin' I go to my reward never seein' that horrible rust ball again."

"And then there's Earth," Mavry said.

His children looked at him quizzically.

"What? I've heard Earth has rather extensive oceans."

"Why would a band of Jupiter pirates hide a stolen treasure on Earth?" Carlo asked.

"The mind of a pirate is a curious place," Mavry said, perhaps a bit defensively.

"All right, Yana. Good work," Diocletia said. "Now let's hear what Carlo and Tycho have found out about the Collective."

Carlo and Tycho dug out their mediapads.

"So the *Iris* raid happened in 2809, and the Collective

was created a year later," Carlo said. "We started by comparing its articles of incorporation to documents drawn up by other pirates over the years. They're similar—lots of pirates stashed stolen goods until the heat from the authorities died down, and they made agreements to make sure nobody cheated and grabbed the loot for themselves."

Huff chuckled.

"I ever tell you 'bout the fortune Madame Chang and her Crimson Raiders stashed in a surplus science balloon? Set it adrift in Jupiter's upper atmosphere with a tracker on it. Which worked great till an electrical storm fried the tracker. Somehows they found the thing in all that soup, 'cept it was caught in the outer bands of a cyclone, an' so—"

Diocletia reached over and put her hand on her father's arm. Huff glanced at her, then scratched at his beard with his forearm cannon.

"Arrr, ain't got time to tell that yarn proper. You kids'll have to wait. Go ahead, Carlo."

"The bylaws of the Collective allowed members to transfer or sell their shares, but none of them ever did—they passed them down to their heirs instead," Carlo said. "Which means we can get our hands on them."

"Why not skip all this paperwork and just take the treasure?" Yana asked. "Isn't the old saying that possession is a hundred percent of the law?"

"Now that's proper pirate thinkin'," Huff rumbled.

"Thanks, Grandpa," Yana said.

"If there's a treasure left to take," Diocletia said.

"You think it's gone?" Tycho asked.

"I do," Diocletia said, then held up her hand as Yana began to protest. "But let's not get ahead of ourselves. Go ahead, Carlo."

"If the treasure's still out there, and we find it, there are reasons we can't just grab it," Carlo said. "For one thing, the articles of incorporation are still legally binding: any legal heirs to the Collective could sue us for their shares and expect to win. On the other hand, as far as we know, there have been no real leads on the *Iris* cache for decades. That means the people who own those shares may have forgotten about them, or see them as worthless paper. We might be able to get them cheap."

"Except that a message went out to the Collective members when the case was opened," Diocletia reminded him.

"A message sent over channels set up eighty-five years ago," Tycho said. "Carlo and I were curious, so we messaged Aunt Carina to ask whether she received it at Darklands. She didn't get anything on any channel she could think of."

"The pirates who formed the Collective must all be dead by now," Yana said. "So who has their rights under the agreement?"

"That's what we looked into," Carlo said. "We only had one afternoon, so we couldn't dive too deeply into the records, but we found them all. They're a mix of children and grandchildren. Some are still starship captains, some aren't. Johannes we know about, of course. After that—"

"Let's see if we can make this simpler," Diocletia said, arms folded. "Start with the members whose scanners were missing from the case—Moxley, Saxton, and Unger."

"Very well, Mother," Carlo said, tapping at his mediapad. "Orville Moxley was born on Io and became the captain of the *Emin Pasha*, which he passed down to his nephew Thaddeus. But then it gets weird. The ship registration lapses in the 2840s."

"Under that name, sure," Mavry said with a smile. "She was reregistered, probably on Cybele, where they're more casual about legal matters. By then her captain had renamed himself and wanted to rename his ship, too. So he called her the *Hydra*."

Tycho gasped. "Thaddeus Moxley is Thoadbone Mox?"

"One an' the same," Huff said. "Bad idea to call him Thaddeus, though. There's a long list of folks he's shot for that."

"So Thoadbone has a way to find the *Iris* cache?" Tycho asked.

Yana grinned, her eyes bright. "This is good news."

"How is that possibly good news?" Tycho asked. His sister's delight in dangerous situations never failed to surprise him—the last thing he wanted was to cross paths again with Mox.

Yana rolled her eyes.

"Because even if he got the message, we don't have to worry about giving him his share," she said. "What's he going to do, take us to court? He's wanted everywhere in the solar system."

"Never mind that for now," Diocletia said. "Moxley's scanner is gone. How do we know Orville or Thoadbone didn't use it to find the treasure decades ago?"

"Arrr, if ol' Thoadbone had come into that kind of money, the shindy woulda been gigantic," Huff said. "Every Jupiter pirate worth his carbine woulda known about it."

"And Orville?" Mavry asked.

"Cut from the same cloth as his nephew," Huff said. "Plus Father would have blown a hatch seal. He didn't like talkin' about the *Iris* cache, but he wouldn't have stood for bein' robbed by a Moxley."

"Maybe," Diocletia said, clearly unconvinced. "Tell me about the other missing scanners."

Carlo nodded at Tycho—they had carefully negotiated for equal presentation time, determined that neither would have an advantage when it came to credit in the Log.

"Josef Unger was born on Europa and emigrated to Callisto in the final years of the Resettling," Tycho said. "He last raised ship at Callisto in 2816—the same year he retrieved his scanner from the Bank of Ceres. Given the condition of the *Foundling*, I think we know what happened to him. His son, Pieter, was a freight hauler for a number of small-time shipping lines, working his way up from lumper to supercargo."

"Dull work, that," Huff said. "Particularly for a pirate's son."

Mavry nodded. "I think we can assume Pieter wasn't hiding the *Iris* cache under his bunk."

"Agreed," Diocletia said. "But then what happened to Josef's scanner?"

"I don't know," Tycho said. "It could have been destroyed in the crash. Or, um . . ."

"When I blasted what was left of the *Foundling*?" Diocletia asked with a smile.

Tycho shrugged.

"Well, not every mystery can be solved," she said, sipping from her mug. "Go on, Tycho."

"Anyway, Pieter Unger died thirty years ago, when a runaway ore loader breached the *Reliable*'s hull above Ariel. That left his eldest son, Loris, as the Unger heir. He's a miner in Port Town, with no current residence listed."

"Does that mean he's dead?" Yana asked.

"Not necessarily," Huff said. "Plenty of rock scratchers travel light, with naught but their gear. They get a bunk in mining camp an' victuals as part of their contract. Miserable existence, even by dirtsider standards."

"So we'll have to find him," Yana said. "Who's next?"

"Muggs Saxton," Carlo said. "He was a small-time pirate from Ganymede when he joined the raid on the *Iris*. He managed to stay ahead of the Securitat for seven years until they dug him out of a bolt-hole on Ganymede and sent him to 1172 Aeneas."

"Spent some time there meself," Huff interjected. "Father never understood why he got locked up as long as he did. Back then, long as you didn't kill nobody, piratin' meant a fine and a year in the brig—an' with good behavior, you were out in three or four months. The men what hit the *Iris* got four years, with no early release."

"Not Muggs," Carlo said. "He got released for good behavior after two. All the other *Iris* pirates served their full sentences. Then, ten years after he got out, Muggs quit pirating and started making investments and buying property on Ganymede. *A lot* of property and investments."

"Enough to make you wonder where he got the money?" Mavry asked.

Carlo nodded somberly. "Particularly since his scanner was gone."

"Arrr, you ain't got to worry on that score," Huff said. "I know where Muggs got his livres. He jumped a prospector in the Kuiper Belt and stole his claim. Muggs always preferred shootin' at folks what couldn't shoot back."

Carlo looked confused. "That's not in any of the records."

Huff grinned, his metal teeth gleaming alongside his normal ones.

"An' where would you look, lad? The Department of Dirty Deeds? Don't get too fond of records, Carlo—the truly important business never appears in 'em."

"Point taken," Carlo said. "Anyway, Muggs's eldest grandson would be his heir—Honorius Saxton-Koenig, Lord Sicyon. He owns a huge homestead on Ganymede and a stake in Gibraltar Artisans."

At the mention of that name, Diocletia scowled and Mavry's face went cold.

Tycho had expected some kind of reaction. Sims Gibraltar had been the first mate aboard the *Ghostlight*, the Gibraltar family's pirate ship. He'd also been Aunt Carina's fiancé. At 624 Hektor, an Earth destroyer had cracked the *Ghostlight*'s reactor, flooding her with deadly radiation. The Gibraltars cared for Sims and the other survivors as best they could but announced a few weeks later that all had died. A devastated Carina had sworn never to return to space, and the captaincy of the *Shadow Comet* had gone to her sister, Diocletia.

"We now have Johannes's scanner," Diocletia said. "So the last Collective member to discuss is Blink Yakata."

Carlo looked apologetic. "Yes. He had one child—a daughter."

"Oshima," Mavry said.

Like the Hashoones, Oshima Yakata had been one of the Jupiter pirates ambushed at 624 Hektor. But the computer virus that left the other pirates helpless hadn't affected her ship, and she'd fled as the Earth destroyers opened fire. The surviving pirates accused her of plotting against them with Mox, a charge she had answered with stony silence before selling her ship and retiring to Io.

"I remember Blink when I was jus' a middie," Huff

said. "He warn't a bad sort. Not his fault his daughter did what she did."

"Oshima will never sell us her shares in the Collective, though," Mavry said. "She lives in the Io outback, and the only way she sees visitors is down the barrel of a carbine."

"Well, when it's time for that conversation, we'll bring carbines too," Yana said.

The corners of Diocletia's mouth dipped.

"Let me make this extremely clear: no one is dying over a treasure hunt," she said. "If we agree to keep pursuing this, no one is going to die chasing miners around Port Town, or rushing off to shoot it out with Mox, or feuding with Ganymedean lords. And definitely not confronting Oshima Yakata. She and Mox have caused our family too much pain already to risk more—particularly over a treasure that somebody else may have found before any of us were born. Do you all understand that?"

Tycho nodded. So did Carlo.

"So you think the treasure might still be out there," Yana said eagerly.

Diocletia took a long drink of flip, her eyes closing momentarily.

"Maybe," Diocletia said. "*If* a member of the Collective didn't use one of the missing scanners to find it. And *if* the Securitat didn't find it first—or some spacer who got lucky, like we did with the *Lucia*. But it's possible. Now, does anybody have any other questions?"

"I do, Mom," Tycho said almost apologetically. "Carlo and I asked you to search the Log for anything regarding the *Iris.*"

Diocletia looked startled, then nodded.

"I forgot," she admitted. "I did search Johannes's entries in the Log, but there's nothing about the *Iris* cache. In fact, there's no mention of the ship at all."

Tycho hadn't expected the secret to be revealed so easily, but he was still surprised by the absence of *any* information.

"That's strange," Tycho said. "We know Johannes took part in the raid."

"It's not that strange," Diocletia said. "Captains can restrict access to portions of the Log—and every captain, including me, has done so. Vesuvia is programmed to honor those restrictions, even after a captain's death."

"But why would Johannes have done that?" Tycho asked, frustrated. "Why go to all that trouble for a treasure and then put it forever out of reach of his own family?"

"I don't know," Diocletia said. "But every captain has secrets—and every captain is entitled to them."

Tycho tossed and turned in his berth for half the night, waiting for the *Comet*'s bells to announce that another half hour of sleeplessness had gone by. Finally he gave up and fumbled for his mediapad, thinking he'd tap into Vesuvia's data banks and try to learn more about the members of the Collective.

But he found it impossible to focus on that task too. He put the mediapad back on the shelf by his bunk, then nested his fingers behind his head and exhaled in frustration.

The soft glow of the pad's screen illuminated the ceiling of his cabin, which was covered with initials left by generations of previous occupants. Tycho's eyes sought out his own TH, located where the ceiling slanted to meet the wall, then jumped to a spot he knew by heart, above his chest.

Huff had pointed out the HH to Tycho on his grandson's first day as a midshipman, then handed him a stylus and watched approvingly as he added his initials to the constellation of letters on the ceiling. Now, three years later, the letters struck Tycho as small and uncertain compared with the confident slashes left by the young Huff Hashoone.

Tycho let his eyes wander over the other initials. How many of those long-dead Hashoone middies had won the captain's chair? And how many had been passed over, ending their careers with a final voyage back to Callisto and a life spent dirtside, below the stars instead of among them?

And which fate would be his?

At some point Tycho must have succumbed to sleep, because four bells woke him at 0600. He rubbed his eyes groggily, blinking at the ceiling, then sat up with a start, remembering the Securitat briefing and the mysterious message he was expecting within it.

He pulled on his jumpsuit, threw a little water on his face, then grabbed a milk and a nutrient bar from the galley. His mother and father were already on the quarterdeck and turned in surprise at the sound of his feet on the ladder.

"What kind of teenaged pirate gets up early when he's at liberty?" Mavry asked with a grin.

"Privateer," Diocletia corrected her husband, but looked curiously at their son. "You *are* up awfully early, Tycho."

"Couldn't sleep," Tycho said as he settled into his chair, nibbling at the nutrient bar. He activated his terminal, called up the daily intel briefing from the Securitat, and read it quickly, his heart thudding.

There was nothing but the usual dull mix of politics and reports of fleet maneuvers.

He forced himself to read it again, looking for a reference to Threece Suud or anything else his mysterious contact might have mentioned yesterday. But nothing caught his eye. There were a few paragraphs about diplomatic contacts between Earth and the Jovian Union, followed by brief, boring items: *Hydraulics firm contracted with shipping line for . . . Earth's Parliament close to passing law addressing . . . Liability established in accident above . . . LaGrange point near Mars seen as site for . . . Ordnance limits seen unlikely for Hygiea roadstead . . . Titania ore find examined by . . . Yearly meteor shower to snarl Floras shipping until . . . Consulate of Earth renovations expected on . . . Hygiea shipping guild protests . . .* And finally, *Oberon taxation fight grinds on as* . . .

Tycho rubbed his eyes, baffled. He had assumed that since his contact had access to the intel briefing ahead of time, he or she must be a member of the Securitat. But maybe Tycho was thinking about it wrong. Maybe something in the briefing was supposed to make some other connection obvious.

He read it again, and again, and again.

Until finally he saw it.

Hydraulics . . . *Earth's* . . . *Liability* . . . *LaGrange* . . . *Ordnance* . . .

He scanned the first letter of each of the briefs, then did so again to be sure.

Titania . . . *Yearly* . . . *Consulate* . . . *Hygiea* . . . *Oberon* . . .

Read from top to bottom, they spelled out *Hello Tycho.*

Tycho reached for his keyboard, annoyed to see his hands were shaking, and called up yesterday's message.

And hello whoever you are, he typed. *Okay, I believe you. Now what?*

The answer came back immediately.

WELL DONE. AS A REWARD, I HAVE AN EARTH FREIGHTER FOR YOU. WON'T MAKE YOU RICH, BUT SHE'S AN EASY PRIZE. CAN INTERCEPT HER IN THE THEMISTIANS ON YOUR WAY HOME.

Tycho frowned. Many a pirate's career had ended with a tip about an easy prize that turned out to be an invitation to an ambush. But then tips like that didn't come from the Securitat, did they?

What's the course data? Tycho typed.

I'LL GIVE IT TO YOU WHEN WE MEET.

That, Tycho thought, was the *last* thing he wanted to do.

Why do we have to meet? he asked.

A MINUTE AGO YOU SEEMED LIKE A SMART KID. WHAT WILL YOU TELL YOUR MOTHER ABOUT THE COURSE DATA? THAT A MYSTERIOUS STRANGER MESSAGED IT TO YOU?

Tycho looked up from his console to where his parents sat at their stations. He should be able to make a short trip—Diocletia had promised them light duty before their departure for Jupiter, and there were plenty of gigs and taxis available to ferry him down to Ceres.

But taking the next step meant lying to his mother, who was also his captain. And that would do far more damage to his bid for the *Comet*'s helm than any flaws in his piloting.

Or it would *if* he got caught. Which he wouldn't.

And wasn't this deception in service of a good cause? The prize money would help his entire family—and right now the Hashoones needed all the help they could get.

"Say, Mom," Tycho said, yawning in a way he hoped

sounded casual, "you mind if I go dirtside for an hour or so? I was thinking I'd get some dried fruit. And I, uh, need another mediapad adapter."

Diocletia glanced back at him.

"Another one? I swear, Tycho—you and your sister have lost enough adapters to create an asteroid belt of them."

"I know," Tycho said. "I think I lost this one at lunch yesterday. I'm sorry."

Diocletia looked back down at her console.

"Fine—you can have a few hours' liberty. But both the adapter and the ride are coming out of your shore allowance. And I need you back here by 1430 to check the crew roster."

"I'll be here," Tycho said. "No problem."

I'm in, he typed.

The man who sat down across from Tycho was neither tall nor short, thin nor fat, old nor young. He was completely unremarkable, from his gray jumpsuit to his expressionless face and short brown hair. His eyes were the only exception—they were dark and alert.

"Call me DeWise," the man said. He had no accent Tycho could place.

"Is that your real name?" Tycho asked.

"Of course not. Here, you'll want to take this."

One of DeWise's hands advanced smoothly to the middle of the table, then retreated. Tycho pocketed the piece of scrap left behind, willing himself not to look at the numbers written on it.

"Thanks," Tycho said. "Though I still don't understand why you're doing this."

"Like I told you—we owed you one. Maybe someday you'll owe us one."

"What could you possibly want from me?" Tycho asked, but DeWise just shrugged, the movement no more than a brief lift of his shoulders.

"Who's to say? Solar system's a busy place. One day a smart kid like you might be in the right place at the right time, and that could be useful to us."

"You're doing me a favor because I might be useful to you?"

"Our business is figuring out who and what might be useful to us someday. That way, when things happen, we're prepared. And things *are* happening."

DeWise's eyes flicked around the café.

"The balance of power between us and Earth is growing unstable and threatening to tip," he said. "Your pal Threece Suud's little scheme was a symptom of that. So too, maybe, is what's happening around Saturn. You saw that for yourself on Titan."

"How do you know about that?" Tycho demanded.

"Relax, kid," DeWise said. His face hadn't changed. A spacer two tables away looked over briefly, then returned to his own conversation.

"Since you know so much, tell me what's happening around Saturn," Tycho said. "Who were the people we ran into on Titan? And who's behind them?"

DeWise's eyes flickered around the café again, then returned to Tycho.

"That question may have more than one answer," he said. "Mix dissatisfaction and money, and you get some interesting kinds of trouble. Just what kind of trouble is something we're still trying to understand."

DeWise leaned forward.

"Here's some free advice. Your little treasure hunt? You're too late. If you're looking to get rich, you're better off taking what I can give you."

Tycho started to speak, then shut his mouth and waited.

"But since I know that won't stop you, listen carefully," DeWise said. "We don't care about the money—just the other thing. Which you don't want anything to do with."

Tycho felt himself starting to smile and forced the expression off his face. Despite what DeWise had said, the Hashoones weren't too late—the *Iris* cache was still out there. Or at least the Securitat thought it was.

"I'll make up my own mind about that," Tycho said, trying to sound casual. "Starting when you tell me what this 'other thing' is."

"Information, of course."

"Awfully old information."

"That's right. It's useless to you—only an organization like ours would care about it. But we do. You need to remember that."

Suddenly the history of the *Iris* made a little more

sense. The ship must have been carrying some kind of sensitive information—something important enough that its loss had angered Earth, set the Securitat on the pirates' tails, and earned them longer-than-usual prison sentences. But what was it?

"You okay, kid?" DeWise asked.

"I'm fine. You know, you sure are full of advice about something you're going to find first."

A smile flickered across DeWise's face, vanishing almost before it could register.

"That's why I like you, kid. We *are* going to find it first. But in my line of work, you always have a Plan B. And that's you, Tycho. Now get going. You don't want to miss your ship."

9

WATER AND ORE

I t was a far happier crew that brought the *Shadow Comet* into her familiar docking cradle above Callisto nine days later. Tycho and Yana stood beside the port airlock belowdecks, mustering out the retainers and crewers as they boarded ferries for the journey down to Port Town, Callisto's largest settlement. Duffels and chests hoisted on their tattooed shoulders, the Comets boasted about what they'd do on shore leave, showed off treats and trinkets for sweethearts and children, and traded congratulations on a cruise that had shaken off murmurings of ill luck to prove profitable in the end.

Without exception, every one of the Comets offered Tycho a deep bow, a crunching handshake, or an exuberant whack on the shoulder, praising Master Tycho for capturing the prize that would let them swagger through Port Town like conquering heroes, full of currency chips and tall tales.

Tycho rubbed his shoulder and winced as the last ferry pulled away and silence settled over the *Comet*'s lower deck. The crewers' enthusiasm had left his shoulder bruised.

Yana closed her mediapad with a snap. "All hands accounted for, so I'm afraid there's no one left to drool over you and your good fortune, *Master* Tycho."

The ship had been right where DeWise had said it would be—a Tamias-class freighter called the *Portia*, bound for Earth's outpost on Hygiea with a month's worth of supplies in her hold. The *Portia*'s captain had meekly surrendered the moment the *Comet* displayed Jovian colors. He'd presented his papers without complaint and given the prize crew not a peep of trouble during the journey to Ganymede, where condemnation hearings had taken less than an hour. It wasn't the biggest payday the Comets had ever had, but it might have been the easiest.

Yana was apparently thinking the same thing, because she suddenly socked Tycho in his tender shoulder.

"Ow!" he gasped, giving his sister a wounded look as

he retreated. "What did you do that for?"

"Because it annoys me how lucky you are. Who loses an adapter and finds a ship?"

"I didn't find a ship—I found a mediapad. It just happened to belong to someone who worked for a shipping line."

"*And* it just happened to be unlocked *and* open to the freighter's flight plan," Yana moaned. "I'm surprised you didn't get a reward for returning the mediapad, too."

"Like I told Grigsby, serves them right for being cheapskates! If they'd given me a few livres for giving back their mediapad, maybe I wouldn't have taken their freighter!"

"Ugh, not that stupid line again. From now on, every time you say it I'm punching you."

Tycho had come up with the tale of the misplaced mediapad after his meeting with DeWise, practicing his story as the ferry carried him back to the *Comet*. He'd felt his knees shaking while Diocletia questioned him, but his mother had thought his nervousness was excitement, not fear—and, he suspected, she'd been too eager for a bit of good news to ask questions.

He was still embarrassed by the secret he was now forced to keep, but every time he repeated the story it felt a little easier, as if he was beginning to believe it himself. Besides, he'd told himself while staring at the ceiling in his cabin, he hadn't done anything Yana or Carlo wouldn't have done if DeWise had contacted one of them instead.

That was true, wasn't it?

* * *

Callisto was tidally locked to Jupiter, with one side of the moon always pointed at the gas giant. Because Jupiter's magnetosphere blasted Callisto's exposed surface with radiation, Callisto's colonists had settled on the far side, using the moon as a shield.

The Hashoones' home, Darklands, had been a mine shaft during the days of Gregorius Hashoone, who'd left Earth with his family more than four centuries earlier. Minerals and frozen gases had made him wealthy, saving his family from a life in the crowded mining camps that grew into settlements such as Port Town. But Darklands's ore had only lasted a century, leading Gregorius's great-grandson Lodovico to arm his ore boats with converted laser drills and convince the mine's employees to try new careers as space pirates.

A ramp corkscrewed down along the outer wall of Darklands's main shaft, connecting equipment lockers that had been converted into bedrooms. Iron and rock slabs sealed the ancient mine tunnels where, rumor had it, old robotic drills still sat abandoned in darkness. At the bottom of the thirty-meter shaft, a comfortable living room and simple kitchen surrounded humming filtration equipment and a giant steel water tank, linked by pipes to the deep ocean of water and ammonia that lay nearly two hundred kilometers below Callisto's icy crust.

Tycho could hear voices echoing up the shaft as he descended the ramp for the family meeting called by Aunt Carina. As he walked, he let the fingers of one hand trail absently along the bumps and ridges of the rock wall.

It was an old habit. As a boy, Tycho had been certain there were diamonds in the rock and had chipped stubbornly away at the wall with a little hammer he'd found in one of Darklands's many storerooms. And he and Yana had raced scooters down the ramp, pursued by horrified governesses and cheered on by convalescing pirates pressed into service as babysitters. The winner had claimed the captain's chair—or at least Gershom Hashoone's ancient armchair—while the loser had insisted that the winner had cheated.

Now Darklands's only inhabitants were Carina Hashoone and Parsons, the homestead's dignified major-domo. And Tycho found his feelings had changed, too. Darklands no longer represented normal life, but an interruption of it. Now, staying here meant nights of tossing and turning without ship's bells to clang every half hour, and days of missing the thrum of engines beneath his feet. Darklands meant family meetings and quarreling over simulator time and waiting to hear he could go back to space, which was where he now belonged.

Tycho nodded at Mavry, Carina, and Yana as he pulled a chair up to the dining area's big table. Made of actual wood from Earth, it had been a prized Hashoone possession for centuries, seized by an ancestor in some long-forgotten pirate raid.

Carina lifted her gaze from her mediapad. Like her younger sister, Diocletia, she had long limbs, dark eyes, and a glare that had backed down pirates twice her size. But Carina lacked Diocletia's deep tan, and her short hair was now mostly gray.

"Our shares from the condemnation of the *Portia* just came through," Carina said as Carlo approached the table, followed by Diocletia. "Congratulations, Tycho, on a fine piece of work."

Yana wrinkled her nose but added her voice to the chorus of praise.

"Arrr, hoped them Earthfolk would show a little backbone, meself," said Huff, emerging from the kitchen with a mug in his metal hand. "Nothin' settles a jumpy crew like the smell of blaster fire."

"A full wallet helps," Diocletia said. "I've smelled enough blaster fire for a lifetime, thank you. Any day that's peaceful and profitable is fine with me."

Huff waved that away with an irritable flip of his forearm cannon, nearly clipping Parsons, who had followed him out of the kitchen with a teapot and cups on a tray. The majordomo pivoted smoothly and noiselessly out of danger, one gray eyebrow arching momentarily, then began to serve the tea as Huff settled his bulk into his chair, unaware of the near-disaster he'd caused.

Carina smiled at Parsons and warmed her hands around the teacup.

"Now then, the day's agenda," she said. "The first item will be an update on our civilian businesses. Our cousins will be arriving in a few minutes to brief us."

Tycho suppressed a groan—such conversations made

a deep-space watch seem exciting.

Carina, unfortunately, heard his protest.

"Since Tycho can barely contain his enthusiasm, we'll let him lead the lunchtime question-and-answer session," she said.

This time, Tycho didn't bother hiding his groan.

"Next item. There's a Defense Force meeting at Ganymede tomorrow, so after lunch we'll discuss what the Securitat has told us about pirates at work in the asteroid corridors and around Saturn."

"Did you tell them what happened at Saturn *and* at P/2?" Yana asked.

Diocletia generally let Carina do most of the talking when the Hashoones were on Callisto—the sisters seemed to have an unspoken understanding that Darklands was Carina's domain, while the *Comet* was Diocletia's. But Diocletia spoke up now, dark eyes fixed on her daughter.

"Saturn yes, P/2 no," Diocletia said. "The fewer people you invite on a treasure hunt, the better."

Yana colored faintly but nodded.

"Finally, I'll want to hear what you've discovered about the *Iris* cache, and we'll discuss how to proceed," Carina said.

"Good," Yana said. "Because we're running out of time."

Parsons appeared from the kitchen and stood waiting by the head of the table. Carina motioned for him to speak.

"Ulric Hashoone and his party have arrived," he said.

Tycho heard the newcomers' voices as they made their way down the corkscrew ramp, while Huff got a few muttered comments about cursed civilian business out of his system.

There were six visitors in all. Ulric, Huff's younger brother, ran Callisto's Water Authority, which also employed his wife, Anja, and Josiah Hashoone, who Tycho seemed to recall was a son of Johannes Hashoone's brother. Angus Hashoone was another cousin—he was an executive at Callisto Minerals, as were his son, Philemon, and his daughter, Farris Swaim.

"I know you all have privateerin' business to attend to, so let's get right into the particulars," growled Ulric from above his mediapad. He had Huff's blazing eyes and thick build, and the olive skin of all the Hashoones, but his gray hair and beard were neat and trimmed.

Tycho, remembering he'd have to ask questions later, hurriedly reached for his own pad and began tapping out notes. But despite his best efforts, he found his mind wandering—and looking around the table, he saw he wasn't alone. Yana looked dazed and Carlo's eyelids were drooping, while Huff was asleep, mouth open and pointed at the ceiling of Darklands far over their heads. Mavry was examining his fingernails, while Diocletia was looking down at her mediapad—which Tycho would have bet his shore allowance wasn't displaying Water Authority earnings reports. Only Carina seemed to be following the discussion.

Huff woke with a snort when Parsons brought more

tea and pastries, and the discussion turned briefly to privateering, with Ulric congratulating Tycho for his role in taking the *Portia* as a prize. Tycho mumbled his thanks, looking away from Yana so he didn't have to see his sister's scowl—only to find Josiah Hashoone regarding him with hard eyes and a downturned mouth.

Josiah caught Tycho's look of surprise and hurriedly bent over his cup of tea. But after that, Tycho noticed little things he hadn't registered before. White-haired Angus was merry and at ease, methodically devouring a startling number of scones and petits fours, and both Anja and Farris smiled as they discussed their business and how it worked. But the other three cousins said little, and now Tycho saw that Ulric glared at Huff whenever he spoke; Philemon drummed his fingers irritably when questioned; and a look of distaste crept across Josiah's lean, dark features when any of the Hashoones serving aboard the *Comet* spoke.

Ulric and Josiah had been middies with Huff, and both they and Philemon had served briefly on the *Comet*'s quarterdeck after Huff became captain. But then, one by one, they had been shunted aside. Ulric and Josiah had been sent dirtside when Carina and Diocletia became middies, while Philemon had served until after 624 Hektor, leaving the ship when Diocletia took over the helm.

Clearly, life dirtside had been comfortable and profitable for them. But their resentment was equally plain. They had lived aboard the *Shadow Comet*, just like Tycho and his siblings did, and dreamed of issuing orders from the captain's chair. But those dreams had been dashed, and that life was gone. Now home was the ice and rock of Callisto, space travel meant a berth aboard a commercial liner, and every few months they had to take a grav-sled to Darklands and talk about water and minerals while their privateer cousins looked bored or fell asleep.

Tycho sneaked a look at Yana and Carlo. All three of them imagined succeeding their mother as captain, and none of them had thought about what would happen if they failed. But failure was what awaited two of them.

Over lunch Tycho managed to come up with questions that he thought were neither painfully stupid nor insulting, and the Hashoones exchanged farewells with their cousins while Parsons cleared away the dishes.

After lunch, Carina summoned them back to the table.

"Arrr, now that we know Callisto still has rocks and water, maybe we can get back to discussin' the real family business," Huff said.

"Interesting way to put it, Dad," Carina said. "But very well. At Saturn you saw firsthand that dangerous things are happening in the asteroid belt and the outer solar system."

Carina pushed her mediapad into the center of the table and activated its projector. A map of the solar system sprang into being above the table, shimmering in the space between the Hashoones. A flurry of red dots blinked in the outer asteroid belt, with a scattering around Jupiter and Saturn and several more around Uranus and Neptune.

"Diocletia and Mavry, you heard some of this on Ceres, but I've learned more since then. About four months ago the Securitat began monitoring reports of well-organized attacks on Jovian shipping. The first ones were reported by prospectors returning to Jupiter from Uranus—there were five in one month, which means there were more that were never reported. Suspicions initially fell on Earth's intelligence services, but all of the ships seized were taken to Saturn."

"And the local authorities did nothing?" Carlo asked.

"They tried. A week after the first alerts went out, a Perimeter Patrol cruiser engaged in a shoot-out with three bandits escorting a captured ore boat. The cruiser was jumped by a pair of frigates and forced to retreat."

Carlo looked incredulous. "And what was the response? Did the Defense Force flood the area?"

"Easier said than done," Mavry said. "Saturn is a long way from here, and most of our defenses are meant to stop an assault from Earth."

"Right," Carina said. "And those defenses are increasingly stretched. The incident with the Perimeter Patrol got the Securitat poking around, and they started picking up chatter that these pirates were following a chain of command. Within a couple of weeks, there was no need to speculate—pirates from Hygiea to Triton were openly declaring their allegiance to Saturn. They call themselves the Ice Wolves."

"Good name," Huff rumbled appreciatively.

"That's what the wolf patches we saw on Titan meant," Tycho said. "So is Mox working with them?"

"Unknown, but given the firepower he threw at you over P/2, I'd assume so," Carina said. "What's more, the ship you encountered—the *Geryon*—was impounded by Saturnian authorities a decade ago. As for the Ice Wolves, they seem to be a mix of pirates and spacers with a history of working both sides of the law. Most of them are from Saturn, but a handful are from elsewhere in the Jovian Union or are spacers based in the asteroids."

"No surprise there," Huff said. "Yeh always got yer adventurous types what flock to a banner."

"True, but this is different," Carina said. "There have been credible reports of Ice Wolves throwing around a lot of livres to recruit crews and buy equipment."

"Money from Earth?" Yana asked.

"Possibly," Carina said. "But some of it seems to be coming from individuals and entities based on Saturn's moons."

"There's certainly enough money out there," Tycho said, remembering the refineries and traffic above Titan.

"You're right," Carina said. "And in the last three weeks, there have been reports of Ice Wolves raiding Jovian and Earth ships alike, but letting ones registered at Saturn go unmolested. In response, some spacers have started flying Saturnian colors. A number of ports have lost interest in good recordkeeping, making it harder for the Securitat to track the bandits' movements."

"They're in league with the Ice Wolves, then," Carlo said.

"Or scared of them, maybe," said Mavry. "What does the governor at Enceladus say?"

"What you'd expect," Carina said. "In public, he's dismissed the Ice Wolves as a few troublemakers, while in private he's appealed frantically to Ganymede for ships. But that brings us back to Earth. A lot of His Majesty's intelligence operatives lost their careers after you discovered Threece Suud's labor camps. But now that the scandal's been largely forgotten, Earth's intelligence services are looking to get even—and this time they're working openly with their military to do so. Earth has built up its forces in the asteroids. They're sending merchant convoys out under guard, stopping Jovian merchants on suspicions of piracy, and displaying very itchy trigger fingers."

"Earth's engaged in that kind of saber rattling before," Diocletia said. "It tends to last until His Majesty's taxpayers get the bill."

"Yes, but Earth has agents at Saturn too, and they've heard the same stories about the Ice Wolves that our people have," Carina said. "They know the Union's attention is divided, and they see us as vulnerable."

Everyone was quiet for a moment, considering that.

"No one knows what any of it means just yet," Carina said. "But these are perilous times. The Union's never had a confrontation with Earth while having to worry about the loyalty of Saturn."

"Are we really at that point?" Carlo asked. "It seems hard to imagine."

"Lots of things do, right up to the moment when they become reality," Carina said.

The grim look on Carina's face made talk of the *Iris* cache seem frivolous—even Yana looked reluctant to speak up. But Carina retrieved her mediapad, extinguishing the map with its ominous red dots, and sat back with her fingers knitted together in her lap.

"Now then," she said, "I believe there's a lost treasure to discuss. Diocletia's told me about the *Lucia*, and the Collective, and the device from the Bank of Ceres. The question is how we're going to proceed—if we decide to do so."

That was too much for Yana to take.

"If?" she asked. "I read the old media reports about the *Iris* raid, and we're talking about a lot of money, Aunt Carina—years' worth. Maybe it's not polite to talk about it, but we could really use that money. Unless we want to count on Tyke getting *incredibly* lucky at the end of every cruise."

"Hey!" Tycho said.

"Belay that, Yana," Diocletia said. "Remember what a wise old pirate once said: luck is the residue of design."

Tycho tried to smile, but he knew the luck was a lie, and the design had been DeWise's. For what purpose, Tycho didn't know.

"It is a lot of money, I agree. Perhaps millions of livres

in high-end cargo," Carina told Yana. "But the question is whether our chances of finding the treasure are worth the time required to try—time we won't have for other things."

"You want to talk about time?" Yana asked. "How about the fact that it's running out? While we sit around yapping, that quantum signal is beeping down to nothing."

"Don't let a countdown force you into a bad decision," Carina said. "What I'd like to establish here is where we think the treasure is. Because that will affect what we decide to do. If we think the *Iris* cache is in the hands of the Securitat—or in orbit around, say, Neptune—we may as well move on to our next order of business."

"Agreed," Yana said. "But it's *not* in orbit around Neptune."

Carina looked over at Diocletia, and Tycho saw his aunt's eyes warm as some old memory or joke passed between the sisters. Then Carina leaned back in her seat and gestured to Yana.

"You may as well go first," she said. "Where's the treasure, and how did it get there?"

"Europa," Yana said instantly. "I thought it over all the way from Ceres, and it's the only answer. The signal is the clue."

"Why Europa?" Carina asked.

"Josef Unger was from there, for one. But more important, the scanners were designed to be able to pick out an underwater signal from a fair amount of noise. Those are conditions you'd only find on Europa."

"So you think Josef put it there?" Carina asked.

"Josef, or members of the Collective working together," Yana said. "It doesn't really matter. The treasure's on Europa. Everything points to it."

"But nobody lives on Europa," Carlo objected. "Unless you count tube worms and armored fish."

"We're not talking about *now*—we're talking about eight decades ago," Yana said. "The Resettling wasn't until 2817, remember? The *Iris* was seized eight years before that. And Josef Unger registered his ship there."

Carlo looked embarrassed. "But hadn't most of the residents left by 2809?"

"Not quite," Mavry said. "The dead-enders resisted until the very end, when they were forced to leave."

"Which means there would still have been subs, and underwater transmissions between homesteads, and other noise," Yana said.

Every child of Jupiter knew the story of the Resettling and what had led up to it. Europa's thick ice hid an ocean warmed by smokers, undersea vents surrounded by mountains of rich minerals that served as oases for aquatic life. After Earth's mining subs destroyed many of the smokers, the Jovian Union declared Europa a protectorate, banning further economic development and paying its colonists to relocate. That had infuriated Earth and led to the Third Trans-Jovian War. Now the only inhabitants of Europa were a few rangers in research stations.

"If the *Iris* cache is on Europa, why hasn't anybody found it?" Carina asked.

"Because it's a big ocean," Yana said. "Given the scanner's short range, you'd have to be looking in the exact right place or get very lucky. And until we opened the case, the signal wasn't transmitting. Just like it won't be in eleven days, when we'll still probably be sitting here flapping our lips while everyone else with a working scanner uses it to find the treasure that could be ours."

"That will do, Yana," Diocletia said. "Can I remind you this isn't the first time the signal's gone off? It must have done so three times before. That's three opportunities for the treasure to be found, and for this argument to be a waste of time."

Tycho scrubbed at his hair, agitated, then forced himself to tuck his fingers between his legs and his chair. It wasn't a waste of time, he knew. But he couldn't say *how* he knew that. He had proof from DeWise that would all but end the argument, but he couldn't use it.

"We've discussed this," Yana said. "The Moxleys didn't get the treasure or everyone would have known about it. The Ungers didn't get the treasure or they wouldn't have lived the way they did. That leaves—"

"So why was Josef Unger's scanner missing?" Diocletia asked. "Never mind where it is now. Why was it removed in the first place?"

"The pirates could have tested one of the scanners to make sure they could find the treasure again," Yana said. "Josef's would make the most sense."

"That doesn't sound too convincing," Carina said.

"I admit that part bothers me too," Yana said. "But everything else fits."

"No, it doesn't," Carlo said. "Why would the pirates hide the treasure on a moon that was going to be abandoned?"

"They thought they'd retrieve it before then," Yana said. "They didn't know that Earth would get so angry about the raid, or that the Securitat would hunt them down as well. They thought they had time, but they were wrong."

And all of that happened because they found something they hadn't meant to find, Tycho thought. *Something the Securitat still wants, all these years later.*

"'Tis a fair point," Huff said.

"Thank you, Grandpa," Yana said. "It's the simplest answer—which you've taught us is usually the right one. The treasure's still where it's always been. And we're running out of time to find it."

"You're wrong—we're already too late," Carlo said. "Yana's quantum signal is beeping in a Securitat warehouse somewhere—because their agents found our treasure a long time ago."

"And how do you know that?" Tycho demanded.

"The other missing scanner," Carlo said. "I'll tell you what happened to it. Muggs Saxton gave it to the Securitat in return for a reduced sentence and a cut of the treasure—"

"You've got no proof of that," Tycho objected.

"Maybe not, but it makes sense," Carlo said. "Why'd Muggs get released early, then? He gave them the scanner, they found the treasure, and he got a cut of it— enough livres to quit pirating and make his investment in Gibraltar Artisans."

At the mention of that name, Carina flinched—just for a moment, but they all saw it.

"I'm sorry, Aunt Carina," Carlo said.

Carina leaned back in her chair, and Tycho could see the pain in her eyes. Diocletia, meanwhile, was looking down at her hands where they sat in her lap.

Tycho hoped Carlo would catch the hint and move on. But to his surprise, it was Carina who spoke first.

"It's all right, Carlo," she said. "There's a lesson here for all of us. I know you didn't want to hear about the Water Authority, or negotiations with the Mining Union, or any of it. But those things are important to this family. They're important to *every* family in our business. The Gibraltars . . . they suffered a terrible loss, but today they make millions of livres a year supplying armaments and technology to the Jovian Defense Force. Because they had an alternative to piracy."

She gestured at the walls of Darklands. "It wasn't just taking prizes that built what you see around you—it was the kinds of businesses our cousins run, that you think are boring. In fact, it's more accurate to say we depend on them than the other way around."

The flesh-and-blood half of Huff's face twisted scornfully, but he remained silent. So did the rest of the Hashoones.

"Anyway," Carlo said tentatively after a moment. "The point is, the treasure's gone."

"No, it isn't," Tycho burst out, before he could stop himself.

His family turned to regard him, and he felt himself flush.

"And what makes you say that?" Carina asked.

"Um . . . just a feeling," Tycho muttered.

"A feeling?" his aunt asked, eyebrows raised.

"Already told yeh—Muggs made his fortune by jumpin' a prospector," Huff said.

"I know you did, Grandfather," Carlo said. "But I don't believe it. It sounds like a convenient story to me. Where did you hear it, anyway?"

"Oh, around," Huff said.

"Well then," Carlo said.

"Not a terribly flattering thing to have people to say about you," Mavry pointed out. "If he were lying, wouldn't Muggs have made up something that didn't make him look bad?"

"No—that's the whole reason why people believed it," Carlo said.

Diocletia nodded. But Huff was shaking his head.

"From what Father and everybody said 'bout Muggsie, he weren't nowhere near that smart," Huff said.

"Maybe not," Carlo said. "But the Securitat is."

Mavry paused, then nodded. "Point taken."

"And you, Tycho?" Carina asked. "Do you have a theory to go with your feeling?"

"No," Tycho said, then saw his mother frowning and rushed to fill the silence. "I'm not worried about Muggs Saxton's scanner, or what happened to Josef Unger's. But I am worried about what happened to Moxley's. If

Thoadbone knows the signal's transmitting and has his uncle's scanner, he's going to do something about it."

"And if so, what should we do?" Carina asked.

"I agree with Yana. Everything about the scanner suggests the treasure was hidden on Europa. If someone moved it, our scanner's useless and we'll never find it. But if it is still there, we need to find it before the signal stops transmitting or someone else beats us to it."

"Hear, hear," Yana said.

Carina tapped at her mediapad. "So that's two Hashoones who think the treasure's on Europa and one who thinks it's gone. What do the rest of you think?"

"Wherever it is, let it stay there," Huff said.

"I think it's gone," Diocletia said.

Carina nodded. "I think it's gone too. I think the Securitat leaned on the Collective members pretty hard at 1172 Aeneas, and one of them cracked. Probably Muggs—Carlo's scenario makes a lot of sense—but it could have been one of the others."

"If you've all made up your minds already, why even have this stupid meeting?" Yana spluttered, drawing hard stares from her mother and her aunt.

"Yana, control yourself," Diocletia said.

"You know, I might have an opinion on this subject," Mavry said.

"And that opinion is?" Diocletia asked.

"That the treasure's gone," Mavry said.

"Dad!" Yana yelped.

"But I wouldn't bet the *Comet* on that," he added. "Stranger things have happened. And I don't see any harm in letting these three investigate further—yes, you too, Carlo. They could start by calling on Loris Unger and Lord What's-His-Name and seeing if we can acquire their shares and obtain some more clues."

"That could be an interesting exercise," Carina said.

"Exercise?" asked Yana incredulously.

"Exercise," Mavry repeated. "Who knows? It might even teach some of our midshipmen how to be more diplomatic."

Yana made a face.

"And what about Oshima Yakata?" Tycho asked.

Mavry's smile disappeared.

"That's different," he said. "Leave her for last. If we get to the point where we think it's worth calling on her, we'll discuss it then."

Mavry exchanged looks with Diocletia and Carina. Something passed among the three of them, silently debated and settled in that strange fashion reserved for adults.

"Very well then," Carina said. "The three of you can continue the hunt—provided you take a few precautions. Don't do anything without clearing it with the rest of us, and don't do anything rash. Parsons will give you currency chips to acquire shares, within a reasonable budget."

"And work together," Diocletia said. "You might not succeed even if you do—but you're guaranteed to fail if you don't."

10

LORIS UNGER

The moment the Hashoones' family meeting was over, Yana marched up the curved ramp of Darklands. Tycho hurried to catch up with her.

"Where are you going?" he asked.

"To find Loris Unger, of course," she replied. "If you want to come, better hurry."

"I'm coming. But relax, Yana. Port Town's not going anywhere."

He called down to Carlo, who looked up and nodded.

"Get the grav-sled ready and I'll be there in a couple of minutes."

"'Get the grav-sled ready,'" muttered Yana, wrinkling her nose. "Who does he think I am, Parsons? I don't care how good a pilot he is—when I'm captain, he's off my quarterdeck. He can enjoy the Water Authority or however he wants to spend the rest of his life. I'm serious. I'll get someone from belowdecks before I let him try to order me around."

"Don't blow a regulator—I didn't do anything. What are you so mad about? We got what we wanted, didn't we?"

"Easy for you to say—*you* didn't spend the whole afternoon being criticized," Yana snapped, then sighed. "It's just so unfair, Tyke. We're supposed to show initiative, but if you do, it goes in the Log that you were out of line. Sometimes I wish Mom would just admit we're judged on how close what we say is to what she's already thinking."

"But if you're captain, isn't that a good way to pick your replacement?" Tycho asked.

"If you're making the right decisions. But Mom isn't doing that. More and more she's distracted, or changes her mind, or forgets things. You've noticed that, haven't you?"

"No," Tycho said, but the thought stuck in his head the rest of the way up the ramp. Yes, Yana was blind to family signals, particularly the ones that indicated it was time to stop arguing. But Tycho knew he had blind spots of his own. And maybe his view of their mother was one of them.

Like Darklands, Port Town had originally been a mine, one dug much deeper into Callisto's outer crust. Atop the settlement, landing fields ringed a dingy transportation hub where the Hashoones rented a grav-sled stall. From there, elevators carried visitors deeper into the old mineshafts and the tunnels connecting them.

The upper levels were well lit and clean, home to government offices, guild halls, and the complexes of Port Town's rich—most of whom were related to the Hashoones in one way or another. Below those levels lay caverns that were still patrolled, but here and there lights were dim, waste pipes leaked, and heat units were broken. And finally there was the lawless maze of the underlevels, where the families of starship crewers and contract miners lived in hovels, waiting for mothers and fathers to return from the stars or the mines.

Carlo, Tycho, and Yana started their search in the mining offices of the midlevels. Several of the companies had employed Loris Unger at one time or another, but he wasn't working for any of them now. After six visits, the siblings had been asked repeatedly to give people's regards to Carina, but they didn't have a single lead on the man they were looking for.

At the seventh company, a guild recruiter said Loris had worked on a dig in the Valhalla craters a month ago. The woman didn't know where he was but said that between jobs he depended on the lower levels' churches for food and shelter, moving between houses of worship as he wore out his welcome or refused offers of help.

"I don't understand—what's wrong with him?" Tycho asked.

"The bottle is what's wrong with him, Master Hashoone," the woman said. "It's the same thing that's wrong with too many miners and crewers here."

The Hashoones thanked her, made their way through the throngs to the elevator banks, and descended into the lower levels. There they stepped out into a corridor lit by flickering lights. Fog wreathed their faces, and Yana zipped up the thin jacket she'd worn for the short trip from Darklands.

"I wish I had my parka," she muttered as they skirted shallow, evil-smelling puddles and piles of trash.

"And I wish I had my carbine," Carlo said, snapping his coat out of the grip of a ragged figure with a whee- dling voice.

"Should we go back?" Tycho asked, peering through the gloom.

"No," Carlo said. "But let's get this over with and be on our way."

At least the churches were easy to find—their doorways were brightly lit and free of graffiti. At the Harmonious Home of the Bodhisattva Jizo, a monk directed them to the Port Town Temple and Tzedakah. There, the rabbi apologetically suggested they check with the imam at the Musallah of the Third Pillar. Finally, they were standing outside a boisterous saloon, arguing about whether they were lost, when the door burst open and a trio of wild-eyed, bearded men in spacers' outfits scrambled out, splattering the Hashoones with muck in their haste to be elsewhere.

"And don't stop till you hit Saturn!" bellowed a brawny brown-skinned man with white dreadlocks, shaking a meaty fist at the fleeing spacers' disappearing backs.

"Mr. Grigsby?" Tycho asked.

The *Comet*'s warrant officer looked at them in shock.

"What in the name of thunder are you three doing down here?" he asked as a knot of rough-looking men and women rushed out behind him, hands clutching mugs, pistols, truncheons, and razors. The Hashoones recognized Dobbs, Laney, Naisr the loblolly boy, and other familiar faces from belowdecks.

The scrum of Comets came to an abrupt halt, colliding and cursing but managing not to shoot or stab one another. They stared at Tycho, Carlo, and Yana in amazement for a moment, then hastily bowed and muttered greetings.

"Sorry to interrupt what looks like a fine shindy," Carlo said.

"Oh, we were just settling a point of disagreement," Grigsby said. "But this is no place for you, Masters—down here you'll be swindled, robbed, or worse."

Carlo waved that away. "Oh, we'll be fine, Mr. Grigsby. We're Hashoones, after all."

Grigsby cocked an eyebrow.

"That you are—but this ain't the quarterdeck."

He turned to Dobbs and grunted something that sent the master-at-arms back into the bar with the rest of their shipmates, after a last round of fingers touching foreheads and tugging at caps.

"'Sides the usual riffraff, there's foreign dogs like the ones we chased out, bent on stirring up trouble," Grigsby said. "Now then. What brings you to these parts?"

"Just looking for somebody," Carlo said.

Tycho knew his brother was going to refuse Grigsby's help—because he wanted to get back to Darklands, because he didn't trust the warrant officer with the secret, or both.

"We're looking for a man named Loris Unger," Tycho said quickly, ignoring Carlo's angry look. "He's a contract miner. We heard he might be at the Musallah of the Third Pillar, but we've gotten a bit turned around."

"Loris?" Grigsby asked. "You mean old Pieter's son?"

"You know him?" Yana asked.

"Know of him, more like. Most of Port Town's old spacers and their kin are familiar to me. Loris wouldn't be at Third Pillar—kindly folks, but they ain't much for hard cases that can't handle their grog. Most likely he's holed up at Bodhisattva Jizo."

"We were just there," Yana said, shaking her head.

"Saint Mary Star of the Spaceways, then," Grigsby said. "Three levels below us, by the elevators. I better go with you—I don't fancy explaining to the captain how I sent you down there to get killed."

"It's really not necessary, Mr. Grigsby," Carlo said.

"Best let me be the judge of what's necessary down here, Master Carlo," Grigsby said.

Saint Mary Star of the Spaceways was a long single room with pews assembled from old grav-sled benches and an altar that Tycho recognized as a landing skid from a bulk freighter. Holographic Bible scenes shimmered along the walls, dissolving into static at random intervals. But the cross adorning the far wall had been gilded and made with care, and the man coming down the aisle had a broad, kindly face.

"Welcome to Saint Mary's," he said. "I'm Father Amoss."

Carlo introduced himself, his siblings, and Grigsby. Father Amoss nodded at each of them, then bumped fists with Grigsby.

"Oh, Alcides and I are acquainted," he said when the Hashoones looked surprised. "I like to say he has his ministry and I have mine, though our methods are a bit different. And you must be Huff's grandchildren, of Darklands and the *Shadow Comet*."

"That's right," Carlo said. "Father, we're looking for a man named Loris Unger. We heard he might be staying here."

"Is Loris in trouble?" Amoss asked, brow creased with concern.

"No, nothing like that. We just need to talk with him."

"Yes, he's sleeping here . . . but I don't know if he's

around right now. Let me look. We put cots in the old sacristy years ago—with the congregation so much smaller now, we don't need the space."

He crossed the nave to a narrow door, which he shut behind him.

"If Loris is here, I'll do the talking," Carlo said.

"After you nearly got us killed on Titan?" Yana asked. "No way. I'll do it."

"What are you talking about?" Carlo asked. "I'm the one who *saved* us on Titan, remember?"

Yana snorted.

"Saved us from your own mess, maybe. Everything started going wrong when you were rude to Captain Lumbaba's widow. Or have you forgotten that?"

"I was not rude," Carlo said.

Grigsby watched the argument curiously.

"You were definitely rude," Tycho said. "Let Yana do it."

Carlo started to protest.

"Look, Carlo, we're all good at different things," Tycho said. "For instance, you're a great pilot—"

"Who should never talk to people," Yana said.

The door to the sacristy opened, and the Hashoones hastily suspended their argument. Father Amoss shook his head.

"I'm afraid Loris isn't here. Perhaps later—"

"Do you know where he might be, Father?" Yana asked. "It's important that we speak with him as soon as possible."

Amoss hesitated.

"One of the grog shops?" Yana asked.

Amoss nodded. "Probably the Devil's Den. It's on this level, past the —"

"Know the place," Grigsby said.

"Of course," Amoss said. "If not there, I'd try the Hidden Diamond, or perhaps the Last Airlock. I presume you know those too, Alcides?"

"Might've been round a time or two."

"Please be kind to Loris," Amoss said. "He's a good man who's had more than his share of misfortunes."

"We mean him no harm, Father," Tycho said.

"In fact, there might be some money in it for him," Yana said.

"Money," sighed Father Amoss. "There's so much of it on Callisto, dug out of the rock, and yet so little of it makes its way down here, to the people in the holes left behind."

The Devil's Den was literally a hole in the wall of a gloomy, deserted corridor, which a hologram had turned into the mouth of a red-faced, pop-eyed demon, bordered by heaps of trash. Unlike at Port Town's other saloons, no raucous laughter, throbbing music, or squeals from interactive games leaked out from the door. The corridor was silent, and Tycho felt a prickle of unease as he followed Grigsby, Carlo, and Yana into the bar.

Inside, a few figures huddled in the dim chill. Behind the bar, a squat man was passing a dirty rag over cloudy glasses to no obvious effect.

"No kids," he growled, looking up.

"They're with me," Grigsby said, putting his big hands on the bar and leaning over it. Tattoos flared into life on the backs of his hands, ribbons of light disappearing up his sleeves.

"Grigsby," the bartender squeaked, retreating until his back was against shelves of bottles. "What do you want?"

"I want Loris Unger," Grigsby said.

"Outside," the bartender said. "Passed out or dead, I don't care which."

The heaps weren't trash after all, Tycho saw—they were men in ragged clothes, curled up for warmth. Grigsby squatted in front of one of them, shaking him by the shoulders until his eyes snapped open.

"Loris Unger?" he asked.

"N-no," the man said, extending a shaky hand. "Over there."

Another heap got to his feet and tried to stumble off down the corridor, but Grigsby grabbed him and turned him around. He was tall and thin, with short hair faded from red to gray and a few days' worth of beard. His eyes were glassy and watering.

"Loris?" asked Carlo, stepping forward to peer at his face.

The man nodded with a jerk.

"No need for rough stuff," he gasped. "I'll be moving on now. J-just need to catch my breath."

He coughed convulsively, face reddening as he hacked

and strained. Carlo stepped back, looking disgusted.

"No rough stuff," Yana said. "Loris, my name is Yana Hashoone."

Loris looked at her in bafflement.

"Hashoone? Know that name."

"I know you do. You're not in any trouble. We just want to talk to you."

"A-about what?"

Yana looked at Carlo, who shook his head. "Not here, and not now," he said.

Loris's head slumped forward; scowling, Grigsby put a tattooed arm around him.

"Carlo, it's all right," Tycho said.

Grigsby looked from one brother to the other.

"I've served your family all my life," he growled. "I know when to keep a matter dark."

Yana looked around the corridor, then stepped closer to Loris, who struggled to lift his head. He blinked at her, wheezing.

"It's about your grandfather," she said. "And the *Iris*."

"O-ho," Grigsby said with a wolfish grin.

Loris shook his head, then staggered against Grigsby, who struggled to keep him upright.

"Is there a canteen or a café around here?" Yana asked. "Someplace quiet?"

Grigsby nodded. "About five minutes' walk."

He got Loris headed in the right direction, half leading him and half dragging him a few paces behind Carlo, Tycho, and Yana. At the canteen, it took three cups of coffee for Loris to be able to focus on Yana's questions.

"Oh, yes, my grandfather was a grand pirate—gallant and brave," he said. "He and ol' Johannes Hashoone were friends, you know. Had many a caper together, took many a prize. But the *Iris*—that's an evil name, Miss Yana. You don't want to be mixed up with that trouble."

"We're not mixed up with it, Loris," Yana said soothingly, sipping a warm jump-pop. "The treasure's gone forever. We're just collecting stories that spacers used to tell about the *Iris* cache. You must have heard some great old legends, right?"

Tycho and Carlo exchanged a wary glance. This was the critical moment, when Loris might become suspicious or hostile. In which case all could be lost.

"Grandfather died years before I was born," Loris said. "He was lost in space—along with our ship."

Yana nodded. "I know, Loris. But maybe your father told you something? We have some money for you, if you talk to us."

"Money?" Loris asked. "For stories?"

"For your time. We were talking about your father."

Loris's eyes unfocused, and Tycho feared he'd slump over again. But then, after a brief coughing fit, he began to talk in a low, wistful tone.

"Daddy used to dream of the lost treasure. First it was his hobby, but then it became his obsession. Every place he worked, he'd hunt through the old manifests and flight logs and listen to the spacers' tales. But he never found a thing. And then the accident happened."

Loris stared at the drab rock wall of the canteen, his lower lip quivering, and Tycho felt a surge of pity for the broken man.

"I'm sorry, Loris," Yana said. "But do you remember any of the stories he told you? Like where he thought the treasure might have been?"

"Gone," Loris said.

"I know it's gone. I mean before it disappeared."

"There were so many stories," Loris said. "All crazy. Fables and wild talk, Miss Yana. Starting with how the treasure had been stolen from us."

"Stolen? By whom?"

"Daddy never told me." Loris wheezed. "I don't even know if it was true. He couldn't accept what people kept telling him—that the treasure was gone forever, lost beneath Grandfather's home."

Tycho leaned forward, biting his lip, then forced himself to wait.

"Your grandfather was from Europa, right?" Yana asked.

Loris had been coughing again, and Yana had to repeat the question. He nodded, one shaky hand rubbing at his eyes.

"Where did Josef live on Europa?" she asked.

"Southern end of the Sidon Flexus," Loris said, bowing his head.

Yana grinned at Tycho and Carlo.

When Loris raised his head, his eyes were wild. "You let that treasure be, Miss Yana. You just let it be. It's cursed, they say, and I believe it. It ruined my father and my grandfather before him."

"The treasure's gone, Loris—lost just like they told your father. We just want the stories, and we can't thank you enough for sharing them with us." She dug in her carryall. "I've got a currency chip for you with one hundred livres on it. All I need is your signature on some papers."

"What papers?" Loris asked foggily.

"Just a bunch of boring stuff for lawyers. They won't let me pay anybody the money unless they sign it first."

Yana held out her mediapad to Loris, who stared uncomprehendingly at the blizzard of words on the screen.

"Here, Loris, let me just skip to the screen where you sign," Yana said, then handed the mediapad back to the old miner, along with a stylus. Loris stared at the screen for a moment, then scrawled his name and pressed his fingertip onto the surface.

"Thank you, Loris," Yana said, pressing the currency chip into his palm. Loris blinked at it for a moment, then stuffed it deep into the pocket of his soiled coverall and got to his feet.

"Do you want us to walk back to Saint Mary's with you, Mr. Unger?" Tycho asked.

Loris looked down at Tycho distractedly.

"No . . . no. Got some people to see."

And with that he shuffled out of the canteen.

"Well," said Yana, "one down, three to go."

"And one grog hound headed straight back to the Devil's Den," Carlo said.

That made Tycho stop smiling.

"Rarely seen a finer fleecing," Grigsby said. "Your grandfather would be proud."

"I'm not sure *I* am," Tycho replied. "Loris doesn't have any money."

"Sure he does," Carlo said with a grin. "He has a hundred livres."

"Which will last him what, a few days?" Tycho asked. "What happens to him after that?"

"I swear, Tyke, you are the worst pirate in history," Yana said. "If we find the *Iris* cache, we'll send him a finder's fee, okay?"

"And what would be the point of that?" Carlo asked. "You saw what he is, what he's done to himself. If you gave that man a fortune, do you think it would cure him? He'd just use it to kill himself more quickly. We can't save the solar system, Tyke—that's a job way above our pay grade."

"You're probably right," Tycho said.

But his conscience continued to gnaw at him as they passed the Devil's Den and headed back to the elevators that would lift them out of Port Town's lower levels. When they passed Saint Mary's, he hesitated, then came to a halt.

"You go ahead. I'll catch up," Tycho said. "I just want to tell Father Amoss we gave Loris his money. Maybe he can persuade him to make better use of it. I'll be fine—the elevator's just around the corner."

"Don't go nowhere else, Master Tycho," Grigsby said. "Particularly not back to the Devil's Den. Your brother's right—you can't fix what needs repairing in that man."

"I won't, promise. I'll meet you at the landing field, okay? You wanted to visit the fruit sellers anyway."

He found Father Amoss in his small office off the sacristy and told him about Loris and the money, though he left out what the man had told the Hashoones and the fact that Loris had signed his share of the Collective over to Yana.

Father Amoss sighed.

"It'll go where the rest of his money goes, unfortunately. He's sick, the poor soul."

"I know," Tycho said. He reached into his own coverall and found one of his own currency chips.

"Will you take this, Father?" he asked. "It's not much, maybe forty livres, but it's what I have. Will you use it to look after Loris?"

Father Amoss took the chip and patted Tycho's hand.

"I'd do that anyway," he said. "But there's many more in Port Town who could use looking after, and this will help. Bless you, Tycho—you're a good lad."

Tycho thanked him and left, and a minute later he was in the elevator, wondering if he was really the worst pirate in history or if he was really a good lad, and which was more important.

11

A PRINCELING OF GANYMEDE

Tycho's gloom began to lift as the grav-sled bumped
across the scarps and hills between Port Town and
Darklands. Yana's delight at their early success
proved hard to resist, and before they were halfway home, Carlo had joined them in discussing how to
outmaneuver Lord Sicyon and Oshima Yakata. Tycho
wasn't sure if their conversation with Loris had made
Carlo less certain the treasure was gone or if Carlo was
simply enjoying the hunt. Either way, it made for a

more pleasant journey.

Plus there was the sight of open space above them, dotted with starships in orbit and dominated by the gigantic sphere of Jupiter. Tycho peered at the familiar gas giant through the radiation shield, tracing its bands of gray and tan, white and rust, forever being churned into whorls and swirls by the tumbling storm known as the Great Red Spot.

The poverty and hopelessness of Port Town had gnawed at Tycho, but more than that he'd hated feeling trapped beneath hundreds of meters of rock and ice. Out here, under the vast vault of space, he felt free again. By the time the Hashoones descended the spiral stairs of Darklands, he and Yana were whooping and yelling like conquerors bearing the spoils of war, and even Carlo was smiling.

To their disappointment, this commotion went unnoticed—unless you counted Parsons, who stood waiting for them outside the simulation room, head cocked in polite expectation.

"Where are Mom and Dad?" Yana asked.

"Your mother and father are in dry dock, running diagnostics on the *Shadow Comet*," Parsons said in his slow baritone. "Your grandfather is in the crypt, and your aunt is in her office."

"Oh," Yana said. "Well, can we see Aunt Carina? We have news!"

Parsons rarely if ever asked about news, but they were still mildly disappointed that he betrayed no curiosity.

"Your aunt is preparing for tomorrow's meeting," he said. "I will tell her you are in the living area. But you may have to wait awhile."

He was correct—five minutes dragged into ten, and then ten dragged into fifteen, and still there was no sign of Carina.

"Calm down," Carlo said, annoyed by the *rat-a-tat-tat* of Yana's fingers drumming on the table. "You look like you're about to go into orbit."

"You heard what Loris said! We know where the treasure is, and we have the scanner we need to get it. He told us it's—"

"Under old Josef's home," Carlo said. "Which was at the southern end of the Sidon Flexus. I heard him, Yana. But Pieter knew where his father lived—so why didn't he dig the treasure up?"

"Because he never had a signal to receive," Yana said.

Carlo shook his head. "I've been thinking more about that. Pieter spent his whole life searching for that treasure, and *he* didn't think it was on Europa. And remember, he thought someone had stolen it."

Yana tossed her head in exasperation. "Loris said that was crazy talk. The signal's transmitting—don't you want to at least take a look? Let's tell Aunt Carina and then go get it."

"I don't think it's going to be quite that simple," Carlo said, getting to his feet and stretching. "I'm going to put in some time on the simulator—I feel like my flying's getting rusty already."

"Don't complain when we head for Europa without you," Yana said.

"I'll take my chances."

Carina finally appeared after another couple of minutes and sat quietly as Yana recounted what Loris had said.

"Yana, slow down and listen to me," she said. "Going to Europa isn't like hopping over to Port Town. We'd have to get through the ice into the ocean and then get out again. We don't have the equipment or training for that."

Yana brought her fists down on the table, rattling the plates and glasses. Parsons poked his head out of the kitchen, looking mildly concerned, then disappeared from view again.

"None of you are taking this seriously—it's just another stupid exercise for the stupid Log! You lectured us about precautions, and gave us currency chips, and let us go to Port Town, but you never thought we'd get anywhere, so you never bothered making a plan in case we did. That signal will stop transmitting in less than eleven days. If you won't let us actually look for the treasure, why don't you just lock us in the simulator room until then? That would at least be more honest!"

Carina ran her fingers through her gray hair but said nothing. Yana started to say something else, then stopped, her shoulders slumped.

"Yana—" Tycho began.

"Now you're going to tell me I'm being disrespectful,

and then that will go in the Log," Yana said in a small but still angry voice.

She was probably right. And Tycho's instincts told him to stand aside while his sister kept letting her turbulent emotions lead her into further mistakes. The only problem was that he agreed with Yana—and why should she be punished for being brave enough to say what they were both feeling?

But then his aunt surprised him.

"I'm not going to tell you that, and nothing's going in the Log," Carina said. "Because you're not entirely wrong. We didn't take this very seriously. And we did treat it like an exercise."

Yana looked up at her aunt, wary but hopeful.

"But you're not entirely *right*, either," Carina said.

"It's different now that we've learned . . . ," Yana said, but subsided at the sight of her aunt's upraised hand.

"I'll speak to our cousins at the Water Authority about borrowing an underwater suit and an impeller sled—they're used for well inspections here on Callisto. And I can set up simulator exercises for training with that equipment."

"Simulator exercises?" Yana asked unhappily.

"If you do get to Europa, you'll have to know how to maneuver underwater. In the meantime, tomorrow your parents are headed to Ganymede. Isn't that where Lord Sicyon lives?"

Yana nodded.

"Well, it wouldn't do to find the *Iris* cache and have

to give him his share, would it?"

"I think Lord Sicyon has enough money already," Tycho said with a smile.

"You two may not believe it, but I do remember what this is like—and so does your mother," Carina said. "She knows, just like I do, that it's hard enough being bridge crew without having to spend every hour thinking about what you did wrong and what that means for your future."

She smiled at them, but the smile didn't reach her eyes. Tycho saw the hurt there and thought of what their aunt might have added—that what was even harder, so much harder, was reaching that future and then having it ripped away from you forever by a few terrible minutes.

Renting a grav-sled on Ganymede cost nearly twice as much as it did on Callisto, but Tycho supposed he shouldn't be surprised—the pressure domes of Tros, the moon's largest settlement, were filled with luxury retail shops that made Port Town look like a refugee camp.

"To your average Ganymedan noble, a refugee camp is exactly what Port Town is," Carlo said after Tycho shared this observation from the grav-sled's backseat.

Gaining an audience with Honorius Saxton-Koenig, properly addressed as Lord Sicyon, had been surprisingly easy. The Hashoones had claimed to be students making an interactive documentary about notable families of the Jovian Union, which led Lord Sicyon's personal secretary to grant them a thirty-minute interview at his estate, located on the edge of the jumble of scarps and grooves known as Sicyon Sulcus.

"I'm doing the talking this time, right?" Carlo asked as the grav-sled bumped down the track into the shadowy hollow that contained Lord Sicyon's estate.

"Of course," said Yana, tugging irritably at the collar of her formal tunic. "Of the three of us, you're the obvious choice to make small talk with a snooty nobleman."

Carlo, busy activating the grav-sled's transponders, either missed the remark or chose to ignore it. Yana turned, stuck out her tongue at Tycho, and grinned.

The grav-sled garage at Sicyon Sulcus looked the same as the one at Darklands, but all comparisons between the two homesteads ceased when the Hashoones emerged from the garage airlock.

The pressure dome they found themselves in was small but paneled in wood and filled with greenery— small trees reached from thick pots toward warm yellow lights overhead, while planters were full of flowers, with ferns and ivy spilling over the sides.

Carlo ran his finger over the paneling and raised his eyebrows, impressed.

"Real wood," he said. "Must cost a fortune."

"The floor's wood too," Yana said, taking a nervous step back onto the concrete apron leading to the garage. "I don't think we're supposed to walk on it."

A door slid aside on the other side of a dome, and a

man entered, dressed in a formal suit of black velvet that seemed to ripple and shimmer in the light.

"Lord Sicyon?" Tycho asked.

The man's eyebrows shot skyward.

"His butler," he said, dipping his chin in a minuscule bow. "Calvert, at your service. If you'll follow me?"

They passed through two more domes, each more lavish than the last, walking on carpets and wood floors and gawking at paintings, mirrors in gilt frames, and shelves crammed with old books. Tycho spotted objects he'd never seen except on a screen—a piano, a jukebox, a grandfather clock, an easel, a chandelier. He felt like he was in some kind of trivia game or an interactive drama of old Earth, and he desperately wanted to stop and pick up everything and examine it for hours or days or until he got tired of it, which he suspected would be never.

Calvert led them through the main dome to a door of wood edged in gilt, which led to a small study with thick carpets, tall bookcases, and a long sofa made of sumptuous-looking scarlet material. An ancient desk stood against one wall, with a top-of-the-line mediapad set in a cradle atop it. Papers were scattered across the desk—crisp white paper, not scrap turned beige by endless recycling.

"Make yourselves comfortable," Calvert said. "May I fetch you something to drink?"

"Sparkling water, if you please," Carlo said.

Calvert dipped his chin, then turned to Yana.

"Jump-pop?"

"I shall have to see," the butler said. "And for you, Master Hashoone?"

"Um . . . do you have any juice?" Tycho asked.

"Orange, apple, cranberry, carrot, acai, mango, or pomegranate?" Calvert asked.

"Whatever you think is best," Tycho managed.

Calvert glided away as the Hashoones sank into the sofa. Tycho couldn't resist feeling the cushion, then poking at it. Embarrassed, he looked up to find Yana and Carlo doing the same thing.

Something began chirping, and Yana grabbed Tycho's arm. He followed her gaze to a cage on a stand near the desk. Inside it, several bright forms darted back and forth.

"*Birds,*" Yana said, getting to her feet and crossing the study to stare in fascination. "*Real* birds. Oh, they're *beautiful*. Come see!"

Tycho got to his feet to look at this latest wonder, but before he could join his sister, a man entered the study—though Tycho had to look twice to convince himself it really was a man. He was tall and wore a black uniform—vest, tight-fitting short-sleeved shirt and trousers, polished boots. His forearms were cradled in metal, with one hand wrapped around the chrome barrel of a carbine and the other forming a fist around wicked-looking spikes that crackled with brilliant light. A mirrored lens hid his right eye, and a halo of wires crowned his head.

The new arrival's eyes jumped from Carlo to Tycho

and then to Yana, indicator lights flaring to life on the harness around his head.

"No need for alarm," said a deep voice in a Ganymede accent. "Matthias is my bodyguard."

The voice belonged to another man, one with close-cropped gray hair and a mustache, wearing a bright blue jacket and a lemon-yellow waistcoat. On his shoulder sat a bird with bright red feathers and a hooked black beak, shifting uneasily back and forth.

"Is that a parrot?" asked a wide-eyed Yana.

"Indeed it is," said Lord Sicyon, crossing to the desk and settling the bird on a perch of dark wood. "And those lovelies in their cage are tanagers."

The parrot cocked its head at the visitors and squawked, provoking a flurry of chirps from the songbirds. Matthias came to stand beside Lord Sicyon, arms held loosely at his sides. Tycho noticed that he left enough room to bring his weapons up without clipping either the desk or the man he was guarding.

"Please sit," Lord Sicyon said as Calvert arrived with their drinks. Carlo introduced himself and his siblings while Tycho took a sip of the deep-red juice. The smell of it and the way it felt on his tongue were like nothing he'd ever experienced.

The parrot squawked again, while its master looked them over with mild curiosity.

Tycho eyed the bodyguard, then tried to cover a start of surprise. The man's forearms weren't cradled in metal, as he'd first thought. Rather, the metal was fused with the skin, just as the mirrored eyepiece was set in his face, and the sensors from the metal crown plugged into sockets near his ears and nose.

Lord Sicyon saw Tycho's gaze and nodded.

"Matthias is outfitted with military-grade hardware—a rapid-fire cannon and an energy prod," he said. "Plus his reflexes and senses have been enhanced dramatically. He has superior hearing, a remarkable sense of smell that references a state-of-the-art chemical-signature database, and eyes—quite literally—in the back of his head. I'd give you a demonstration of his capabilities, but it would be a shame to burn down my study. You've no doubt seen prosthetics used for those who have suffered injuries that can't be regenerated, but this is next-generation technology. And of course the augmentations were voluntary."

Tycho tried not to look horrified. Huff's body was more metal than flesh, but he needed his cybernetic parts to stay alive. This man had apparently changed himself of his own free will, agreeing to have parts of his own body carved away and replaced with machinery.

"If you'll forgive my asking, Lord Sicyon, why do you need a bodyguard amid such . . . peaceful surroundings?" Carlo asked.

"You're no doubt aware of my work with Gibraltar Artisans' research-and-development division?" Lord Sicyon asked.

When Carlo shook his head, Lord Sicyon's handsome features darkened.

"No? I would have thought you'd be more prepared, given the subject of your documentary."

"We like to have our subjects tell us what they do in their own words," Yana said quickly. "It makes for a more natural presentation."

"I suppose," Lord Sicyon said. "Well then. I control a substantial stake in Gibraltar Artisans, headquartered on this moon . . . say, shouldn't you be recording this?"

"Oh, of course," Yana said, blushing. She took her mediapad out of her bag under Matthias's watchful gaze, then held it up in front of her, aimed at Lord Sicyon.

"That's what you're using?" Lord Sicyon asked, looking bewildered.

"It's just a student project," Yana said.

Lord Sicyon shook his head.

"Anyway, Gibraltar Artisans supplies military technology to the Jovian Union and is one of our greatest assets in the struggle with Earth," he said. "Matthias here is the product of decades of research into mental and physical augmentation for personal security and defense."

Lord Sicyon smiled, revealing an expanse of white teeth. "So understand that I'm not just a shareholder—I'm also a product tester."

"We appreciate that, Your Lordship," Carlo said. "Though we are familiar with the Gibraltar family. I believe they once gained . . . notoriety as some of the more successful Jupiter pirates."

Lord Sicyon's back stiffened.

"Completely different side of the family," he said. "Gibraltar Artisans has nothing to do with that rabble."

"On that subject, Lord Sicyon, we wanted to ask about your own family," Yana said.

"'On that subject?' What subject do you mean?" Lord Sicyon asked. Beside him, the parrot made a disagreeable noise.

"Are you familiar with the *Iris* cache?"

"Never heard of it," Lord Sicyon said as Carlo shot his sister an annoyed look.

"It was the cargo of a mailboat, seized some eighty years ago by a group of Jupiter pirates—" Carlo began.

"And what could such a thing possibly have to do with me?" Lord Sicyon said, hands clasped in his lap. His knuckles had turned white, Tycho noticed. "My family has no connection to pirates—none whatsoever."

"Begging your pardon, Your Lordship, but you *do*," Tycho said. "The pirate Muggs Saxton's eldest son was Carolus Saxton, who married Honoria Koenig. Carolus and Honoria were your parents. That's correct, isn't it?"

Lord Sicyon had turned an alarming shade of red. Matthias regarded the Hashoones impassively, sensors whirring.

"Stop recording," Lord Sicyon said.

Yana lowered her mediapad.

"Let me be perfectly clear about this," Lord Sicyon said through gritted teeth. "I have not the slightest interest in the ancestor you speak of, nor in any criminal schemes he might have pursued during his misguided life. I am a loyal son of Jupiter, as my mother and father were before me. And our deeds speak much more loudly than any gossip about the past."

"I assure you, Lord Sicyon, that we don't doubt your patriotism in the slightest," Carlo said. "What interests us is the story of the *Iris* treasure. Over the years, all sorts of crazy legends have grown up around it."

"If this is a joke, it's in very poor taste. What do I care for some ancient connection to a shameful dirty matter? If you want to succeed making documentaries, young man, perhaps you should start by not spreading rumors and tittle-tattle."

"Oh, but they aren't rumors," said Yana. "Here, take a look at my mediapad, Your Lordship. We have proof that Muggs Saxton was a member of the Collective, the pirate band that made off with the *Iris* treasure. Which means you are heir to his share of that treasure, should it ever be found."

"Look around you, young lady," Lord Sicyon said. "Do I look in need of money?"

Yana sat back and sipped her jump-pop. "We wanted to talk with you, Your Lordship, because you're an heir to the Collective. A lot of Jovians will be fascinated to learn what's become of the Collective families since the days of Muggs Saxton."

Lord Sicyon seemed to flinch at that name.

"I told you I've never heard of this Collective," he said. "There's nothing whatsoever that I could add to your little project."

"Oh, you have a great deal to add, Your Lordship!" Yana said. "Having found an actual heir to the Collective, we can't very well leave you out of the project, now can we?"

"You can and you will," Lord Sicyon said. The parrot squawked again.

"We've found such amazing images of your grandfather to use too—there's even video of him in prison. The contrast between the two of you is amazing—there's his clothes, and his up-country accent. People will be so surprised to learn you're related."

The noises Lord Sicyon and the parrot were making struck Tycho as oddly similar.

Yana bit her lip, then leaned forward. "Though I suppose if you were no longer an heir, there would be no need to include you in our project. Or to discuss your grandfather Muggs or his connection to the Saxton-Koenigs."

"I wouldn't have the slightest idea how to stop being heir to some deplorable business arrangement I've never heard of," Lord Sicyon said.

Yana peered at her mediapad, as if wrestling with a difficult problem. Carlo took a sudden interest in his sparkling water. Tycho forced himself to breathe.

"There might be a way," Yana said. "As part of our research, we acquired some shares of the Collective—easy enough, since they're worthless except as historical curiosities. If you're really opposed to being discussed in our project, you could sign yours over to us as well."

Yana offered Lord Sicyon her mediapad. The man took it and glowered down at the screen, muttering under his breath, then scrawled his signature and pressed his fingertip against it.

"There," Lord Sicyon said, thrusting the mediapad back at Yana as if it were dirty. "Now let that be the end of this ridiculous episode—and our disagreeable interview."

He got to his feet with such haste that the parrot fluttered its wings and emitted an alarmed bray. "Calvert will show you out."

12

JUPITER INVASION

When the Hashoones returned to Darklands, two large crates awaited them in the living area at the bottom of the ramp.

"From our cousins at the Water Authority," Carina explained.

"You actually contacted them," Yana said.

"I do keep my promises, Yana Hashoone," Carina said sharply. "Now get this stuff set up—none of you is going near Europa until you've trained on it."

With Parsons's help, the siblings opened the crates and extracted their contents. The first crate contained an impeller—basically a long sled, folded into meter-long sections, with a navigation unit and handles attached to an engine. The second crate held segmented pieces of ceramic armor, a waterproof suit made of reinforced fabric, air tanks, a jet pack, and a helmet whose clear faceplate was as thick as Tycho's little finger.

"Underwater's different from deep space," Carlo said, seeing his brother tap on the faceplate in wonder. "The pressure's immense."

"Right," Tycho said. He'd never been immersed in water, unless the shower counted, and found it strange to think about a suit designed to protect you from an excess of matter, rather than its absence.

They carried the equipment up the ramp to the simulator room, a narrow chamber that had once been a break room for miners, with rectangles of blank iron marking long-sealed tunnels leading deeper into the rock of Callisto. There, a quartet of stations waited, similar to the ones aboard the *Shadow Comet*. Tycho and Yana had spent countless hours here as children—just as Carlo had before them, and their parents before him, and so on back through generations of Hashoone pirates.

"Two Collective members down, one to go," Yana declared as Carlo programmed the simulator. "When I get my share of the treasure, I'm buying myself a cage full of those pretty tangerines."

Carlo and Tycho exchanged a baffled glance.

"Oh—you mean *tanagers*," Carlo said with a laugh. "Tangerines are something else."

"Fine. I'm buying myself a cage full of tanagers *and* a cage full of tangerines. What are you going to buy, Tyke?"

Tycho looked up from separating armor pieces into left and right.

"A statue of Muggs Saxton, to stand in the entry hall at Tros. Don't you think Lord Sicyon would appreciate the gesture?"

All three started to laugh, and they were still smiling when they got Carlo's armor strapped on.

"Speaking of Muggs Saxton, Carlo . . . ," Yana said, handing her older brother the simulation goggles. "Do you still think he gave the scanner to the Securitat?"

Carlo pushed the audio inputs into his ears.

"I was wondering when you would ask," he said. "I still want to know how he got out of prison early, but no, I don't think he did. I believed Lord Sicyon when he said he'd never heard of the *Iris*. Unlike, say, when he tried to claim his family had no connection to piracy."

"Yeah, that was rich," Yana said. "Good thing Grandpa wasn't there to hear his opinion of pirates."

"Oh, it's not like he hasn't heard it before," Tycho said. "It's not like we all haven't heard it before."

"True," Carlo said, taking the helmet from Tycho. "It's ridiculous. Every family in the Jovian Union has a pirate ancestor or two. Makes you wonder what our grandchildren will say about us, doesn't it?"

"That's obvious," Yana said. "They'll say, 'Yana Hashoone was the best captain ever.'"

"Hah," Carlo said. "You know what? Sometimes I wonder if they'll be privateers at all. You heard Aunt Carina yesterday. And look at how the Saxtons changed in just two generations. Or the Gibraltars. Or half a dozen other families. Muggs was nothing but a small-time pirate, but his grandson's a financier and a respected nobleman."

"And a stuffed-shirt blowhard twiddling his thumbs dirtside," Yana said. "No thanks—I'd rather be a privateer. Wouldn't you?"

Carlo just grunted, twisting the helmet clockwise until it latched into the collar.

"You're green," Yana said, checking the suit indicators.

"Good," Carlo said, his voice muffled. "Fire up the simulator."

For the next half hour Tycho and Yana watched their brother perform an odd pantomime, seeing and hearing imaginary things fed to him by the computer and reacting to them. With the exercise complete, he shed the suit and checked his scores while Tycho helped Yana into the equipment. Then, a half hour later, it was Tycho's turn.

The simulator showed him how to operate the suit's systems, from the helmet work light to the cutting torch, then taught him maneuvers. He discovered you had to work a lot harder than you did in the vacuum of space, where the slightest push against something would set you drifting in the opposite direction. But Tycho adapted quickly and found himself quite comfortable. He was smiling when the simulation ended and Yana snatched the goggles off his face.

"Ow!" Tycho complained. "What was that for?"

"Look at your scores," she said. "You beat both of us."

"By a pretty decent margin too," Carlo said, not sounding nearly as unhappy about it.

"Huh," Tycho said, trying not to grin.

"No fair," Yana said. "You had an advantage because you went last."

"Don't be a sore loser," Carlo said. "Tycho can play fish all he wants; just the idea of being underwater creeps me out. Anyway, don't get too excited, Tyke—remember, we're not competing to be captain of a submarine."

The door to the simulation room opened, revealing their father.

"Dad," Yana said, "we've been training with the equipment. Believe it or not, Tycho scored the best."

Tycho was too happy to object to that but stopped smiling when he saw Mavry's face.

"You three better come with me," Mavry said. "Something's happening."

Tycho, Yana, and Carlo hurried down the ramp to find the rest of their family standing around the dining table. Shimmering in the air above Carina's mediapad was an image of High Port, the space station orbiting Ganymede that housed key ministries of the Jovian Union.

"You need to see this," Carina said. "They're live images from a passenger liner above Ganymede."

Bright dots were racing toward the station.

"That's a tactical formation," Carlo said. "Looks like a perimeter of frigates around a trio of cruisers. What's going on?"

"No one knows yet," Carina said. "The ships just arrived—and they're not ours."

"Earth's, then," Huff said. "The scurvy bilge rats 'ave finally declared war."

"They never would have gotten through Perimeter Patrol," Tycho said. "We have warships covering the approach vectors from the inner solar system."

"Which means they came from somewhere else," Diocletia said as Parsons glided out of the kitchen to stand behind Carina.

"To get that close to High Port, they must have dropped long-range tanks up above and come in hot," Carlo said. "Impressive flying."

As the Hashoones watched, the mysterious ships slowed and hung glittering against the blackness of space.

"They're not attacking—they've realigned into a defensive formation," Mavry said. "Looks like they're just short of firing range."

"Wait," Carina said. "There's a transmission coming through. I'll put it on speaker."

She pushed a basket of fruit aside and poked at the mediapad.

"—the people of the Jovian Union," said a calm, unhurried voice with a Saturnian accent. "My name is Hodge Lazander. I am the speaker of the group you call the Ice Wolves, but I represent many more people than that. We are not here to bring war. Rather, I hope we are here to make peace."

"Arrr, some peaceful gesture that is," Huff muttered.

"Shh, Dad—let's listen," Carina said.

"Many stories claim we are the creation of someone else," the voice said. "These are untrue. The government of Earth did not create us. Nor did Earth's corporations. No, *you* created us. You created us by taking our raw materials but doing nothing to help us develop our infrastructure. You created us by taxing us, but not representing our interests. You created us by defending your own interests, but ignoring our concerns."

A flight of Jovian pinnaces streaked past the passenger liner recording the scene, then raced around High Port toward the intruders.

"Little late, fellas," Carlo said.

Lazander continued. "If our tale sounds familiar, if our grievances echo in your ears, it is because once this was Jupiter's tale, and once these were Jupiter's grievances. Just as your settlers once demanded their freedom from Earth, so now our settlers seek our freedom from you. We are here to declare a new birth of freedom for the people of Saturn, Uranus, and Neptune—as well as the settlers, prospectors, and freed corporate serfs of the outer solar system."

The pinnaces formed a defensive line between High Port and the bandits.

"Jupiter Defense Force frigates are scrambling," Carina said.

Tycho heard a small, wet sound next to him and

turned to see his sister calmly eating a plum while listening.

"We seek peace," Lazander said. "Peace with the Jovian Union, and peace with Earth. We want free movement between the nations of the solar system, and free trade, and equal treatment under the law. Those cherished values were the foundation of your revolution, and they have inspired our quest for freedom. Deny us that freedom, and you will force us to fight for it. Grant it to us, and we shall form new bonds of friendship."

"Good speech," Yana said with her mouth full.

And then, moving as one, the frigates and cruisers pivoted smoothly and accelerated into deep space, leaving the warships of the Perimeter Patrol to confront a danger that had already passed.

The Hashoones were arguing, over the remnants of dinner, about how the Jovian Union should respond, when Parsons came and stood at the end of the table.

"It's the communicator for Master Carlo, Master Tycho, or Miss Yana," he said. "It's a Father Amoss from Port Town. He's quite insistent that he speak with you."

In the communications suite, the priest's face filled the wide viewscreen. He looked frightened.

"What is it, Father?" Tycho asked.

"Strange men," Father Amoss said, leaning close to the microphone. "They were here a few hours ago. They found Loris."

"What kind of men?" Carlo asked.

"Spacers," Father Amoss said. "Hard men with—"

"That's enough," Mavry said. "Nobody say anything else."

Tycho turned to see their father had followed them. His face was grim.

"This isn't a conversation for an unsecured line," Mavry said. "Father, stay where you are. We'll come to you."

Father Amoss nodded, and a moment later the viewscreen went blank.

"Get the grav-sled ready," Mavry said, then hesitated. "Load up the underwater equipment."

"What?" Yana asked. "Where are we going?"

"I don't know that we're going anywhere," Mavry said. "But events are moving fast, and I'd like to try to stay ahead of them."

The doors to Saint Mary Star of the Spaceways were locked. When he opened them, Father Amoss glanced fearfully in each direction, then ushered them inside and barred the doors behind them.

"Is Loris safe, Father?" Tycho asked.

"The men looking for him—who were they?" asked Yana.

Father Amoss looked from Tycho to Yana.

"They had beards," he said. "Saturnian accents. They walked like spacers and smelled like fuel."

"Ice Wolves," Mavry said.

Father Amoss nodded. "They came while Loris was out. I tried to find him before they did, but they got there first. Loris said he thought they were going to kill him. So I hid him away, in case they came back."

"And did he tell them anything?" Yana asked.

"That's what concerns you, then," Father Amoss said, voice hard.

"You said you hid Loris," Tycho said. "Are you sure he's safe?"

"Yes," Father Amoss said, and his face softened at the relief on Tycho's face. "There's not much else to tell. I don't know what Loris told them—he was too frightened to make much sense. But they didn't look like the kind of men you'd say no to."

"Where is Loris now?" Tycho asked.

"Safe, like I said," Father Amoss said, then raised his hand before Tycho could ask his next question. "I think it's better to leave it at that. The fewer people who know, the less harm there is to be done. You've done enough of that already."

"We didn't tell anyone about Loris," Yana objected.

"That's not what I'm talking about," Father Amoss said, leading them to the door. "You know, one of the truest measures of a person is how they treat those over whom they have the advantage."

"What does that mean?" Yana asked.

"I didn't think you'd understand," Father Amoss said. "Now, if you'll excuse me, I have to get back to my work."

The doors shut behind them, and they picked their way down the chilly corridor.

"Father Amoss doesn't seem to approve of your methods," Mavry said as they waited for the elevator that would take them back to the surface.

"Oh, not you too, Dad," Carlo said with an exasperated sigh. "We're privateers, not a charity ward."

"For once I agree with Carlo," Yana said.

"And what do you think, Dad?" Tycho asked.

Mavry considered that for a moment as the elevator rose and they swallowed to keep their ears from popping.

"Our livelihood is a dishonest one," he said. "We take things that aren't ours—by deception if we can, by violence if we can't."

"Exactly," Yana said—but Mavry held up his hand.

"So how do we make our peace with that?" he asked. "I think it's by being honest within that livelihood. We place a high value on being honest with our crewers, with our adversaries, and with each other."

"We should be honest about being dishonest?" Yana asked.

"The life of a pirate is complex," Mavry said with a smile.

"Should we have told Lord Sicyon the truth about his shares, then?" Carlo asked.

"He doesn't need the money," Tycho said.

"And you think Loris does," Carlo said. "But why does that make it different?"

"I don't know," Tycho said. "I just know it does."

"When we get topside, Carlo, prep the gig for immediate departure," Mavry said. "We'll bring the equipment from the grav-sled."

"Wait, where are we going?" Tycho asked.

"Old Josef's home on Europa, of course," Mavry said. "It seems the Ice Wolves are on the trail of the *Iris* cache. I'd like to beat them to it."

"Shouldn't we talk this over with Mom and Aunt Carina?" Tycho asked.

"No time," Mavry said. "I'll explain it to them later."

"The Ice Wolves must have found about the cache from Mox," Tycho said. "And gotten his scanner."

"Which means that money could go to finance their insurrection," Carlo said grimly.

Or maybe it's not the money at all, Tycho thought. *Maybe Mox knows about what else is in the cache—the thing that Earth wanted all those years ago and that the Securitat wants now.*

"So what's our story, Dad?" Yana asked.

Mavry smiled.

"Why, we're engineers and apprentice engineers on a maintenance mission to whatever research station is nearest to the Sidon Flexus. Yana, you'll figure out what that is."

"Engineers have fourteen-year-old apprentices?" Carlo asked.

"They might," Mavry said, then shrugged. "Look, if you don't think it's worth a try, we can wait around at Darklands until we hear someone else has our treasure."

"No way I'm letting that happen," Yana said.

"That's the spirit," Mavry said.

13

EUROPA AND IO

The journey to Europa took a little over an hour. As the moon grew in the gig's viewports from a dot of light to a white ball crisscrossed by dirty brown streaks, Mavry ran through a rapid-fire checklist.

The gig's transponders were broadcasting an affiliation with Callisto Space Engineering—a firm that did no real work but had existed for centuries as a cover story for such situations. The impeller and underwater suit were stowed in the rear of the gig, along with Johannes

Hashoone's scanner. Mavry had loaded a mediapad with engineering diagrams and maps of Europa's oceans. All of the Hashoones had practiced answering likely questions about who they were and what they were doing.

"Incoming vessel," Carlo warned from the copilot's seat. "Heading 93.8, and coming hot. Transponder profile indicates she's a Jovian Defense Force cruiser."

Mavry whistled. "That's a lot of firepower for Europa. Show's about to start, kids."

A moment later the gig's communicator crackled.

"Unknown ship, we have you on our scopes," said a man's voice. "You are trespassing in the Europa Protectorate exclusion zone. Reduce speed and identify yourself."

"We see you, cruiser—no need to run us down," Mavry said, sounding peevish. "Our destination is Abelard Research Station. Didn't they tell you we were coming?"

"That's a negative," the cruiser replied. "Reduce speed at once."

"Look, son, we've got three inspections today. You ever try cleaning algae out of a shunt vent? Get on the comm to Callisto Space Engineering, and Harvey will give you the work order number and flight plan ID—like he was supposed to this morning. We'll file the paperwork when we return. That way we can both get on with our day."

"Negative. Heave to immediately. That's an order."

"Son, I don't have time for—"

"Our next communication will be a warning shot," the cruiser said. "Be a shame if we missed."

"We're shutting down the engines, cruiser," Mavry said, flicking switches. "Can we make this quick? Like I said, we've got three inspections—"

"I heard you the first time. Turn to oh eight six and prepare for boarding. Maneuvering jets only."

Mavry sighed and tapped the gig's retro rockets, inching the little ship into alignment with the cruiser. A moment later, a shadow fell over the gig as the two-hundred-meter warship passed overhead, blocking the sunlight reflected by Jupiter. Tycho looked up at the cruiser's cannons, which swiveled to keep the gig in their sights. If one of those gunners got nervous, the gig would be torn apart before any of them could so much as flinch.

"Beginning docking procedure," the man on the cruiser said.

A moment later they felt the gig shudder and heard a scraping noise from above, followed by the whine of a docking tube engaging with the gig's topside airlock. Mavry shut down the gig's systems and switched on the cabin lighting.

"They're jumpy today," he said, unbuckling his harness and getting to his feet. "Keep your hands where they can see them, and let me do the talking."

There was a hiss and a flutter of wind as the air in the gig and the cruiser mixed. A Jovian Defense Force marine in combat gear clattered down the ladder one-handed, black carbine pointed at the Hashoones. He eyed them for a moment, then gestured to someone above him. Another marine entered the craft, followed by a JDF lieutenant.

"Boys, this is all an unfortunate misunderstanding—" Mavry began.

"Save it, pal," the lieutenant said. "This is a restricted zone, and all facilities are in lockdown due to the current emergency. Which means there's no algae cleaning going on at Abelard Research Station or anywhere else on Europa."

Mavry looked outraged.

"Wait till I get back to Callisto and get my hands on Harvey! No one ever tells me anything! When I think of how much of my time he's wasted—"

"Who's Harvey?" the lieutenant growled as another pair of boots appeared at the top of the ladderwell. "Never mind—we'll find out on Aeneas. Because that's the only place the four of you are going."

"That won't be necessary, Lieutenant Csonka," another voice said.

The newcomer was average sized and plain faced, in a military uniform that lacked insignia. Tycho looked at him, then tried to hide his shock.

It was DeWise, the Securitat agent from Ceres.

DeWise's gaze skittered over Tycho with no obvious sign of recognition, alighted briefly on his sister and brother, then settled on Mavry.

"Mavry Malone, I presume," he said.

"I don't know who that is. I work for—"

"You work for yourself, like all privateers," DeWise said. "And this would be Carlo, Yana, and Tycho Hashoone. Your exploits are quite well known, of course."

Mavry opened his mouth to protest further, then thought better of it and just waited.

"You can go now, Lieutenant," DeWise said. "There's no need to detain these people. I'll deal with them."

"But our orders are to defend the security perimeter—"

"And you have, most admirably," DeWise said. "I will take it from here, Lieutenant."

"Yes, sir," Lieutenant Csonka said sullenly. He nodded to the two marines, then followed them back up the ladder.

"I didn't catch your name," Mavry said.

"That's because I didn't say it," DeWise replied.

"I'm going to take a wild guess that you work for the Securitat," Mavry said.

"Correct—fortunately for you. Given the current hubbub, it might have taken some time to sort things out in detention. And the JDF might wonder whether letters of marque should be given to people who try to con their way past their own military officers."

"We've done no such thing," Yana said.

"Of course not. Just like that's not underwater equipment behind you, and you're not heading for the Sidon Flexus, once the home of a pirate named Josef Unger."

Yana gasped, then tried to turn that into a cough. Tycho refused to look at DeWise.

"Lieutenant Csonka doesn't know it, but we're

conducting an operation beneath the Sidon Flexus as we speak," DeWise said. "Nice try, but this little expedition of yours is over."

"You've no right to that treasure!" Yana sputtered. "It's ours!"

"Yana, quiet," Carlo said.

"Perhaps it shouldn't have been left in an ocean to be salvaged, then," DeWise said.

"It's *not* salvage!" Tycho said.

"Tycho—" Mavry began, then gave up trying to contain his rebellious children.

"You don't understand," Tycho said. "The Ice Wolves know where it is too. They'll be coming."

"I hope so," DeWise said, inclining his head up the ladderwell. "I've got a cruiser full of Jovians spoiling for a fight. And now, if you'll excuse me, I have a treasure to recover."

DeWise vanished up the ladder, and the hatch shut behind him. Mavry sank into the pilot's seat as the cruiser disengaged its docking port. When the warship was clear, Mavry powered up the gig's engines and slowly turned back toward Callisto.

"So that went well," he said.

"I was right about the salvage rules, though. Wasn't I, Dad?" Tycho asked.

"Tyke, honestly," Carlo protested. "It doesn't matter now. We're beaten. We did our best, but the Securitat got there first."

"At least it was them and not the Ice Wolves," Yana said.

"We're *not* beaten," Tycho said. "And we're not going to let them get away with this."

"You're right, we're not," Mavry said. "Hang on—I'm inputting a new course."

Carlo looked at his father in astonishment. "Where are we going now?"

"Io. Let the Securitat dig up the treasure—that's the hard part anyway. It'll make it more satisfying when they have to hand it over to us in court."

"We're going after Oshima Yakata's share of the Collective," Tycho said with a grin.

"Right," Mavry said. "When you've had a bad run at the card table, what do you do?"

"Walk away before you lose it all," Carlo said.

"That's one strategy," Mavry said. "Myself, I double down."

Mavry had been born on Io, but none of his children had ever been there, and as the gig neared the moon, they fell silent, awed by what they saw through the viewports.

The innermost of Jupiter's large moons, Io was a dark sphere against the bright bulk of the massive gas giant beyond, with volcanoes blooming red and orange on the face kept eternally turned away from Jupiter. It was a perilous but profitable place to live, rich in minerals and gases belched up from the molten interior.

The gig descended through a nimbus of crackling light that stretched out into space around the moon.

Flashes of green and blue followed pulses of yellow and white, and now and then a fork of brilliant purple energy crackled for kilometers across space.

"Jupiter's magnetic field is so strong that it strips the atmosphere of dust and gas particles, which then pick up a charge in orbit," Mavry explained. "Makes for an impressive light show, but it also plays havoc with your instruments. We'll have to have everything recalibrated when we get back to Callisto."

As they passed through Io's thin outer atmosphere, ball lightning skittered eerily across the viewports and particles of dust rattled against the hull. The landscape below was a yellow waste, pockmarked by canyons and mountains that heaved themselves up from the plains.

"Oshima lives on the edge of the Colchis Regio," Yana said, poking at her mediapad. "Looks like about an hour from Galileo Station by grav-sled."

"Yeah, a bunch of mineral hounds and gas extractors live out that way," Mavry said. "Crazy coots, every one of them. Now listen. When I knew her, Oshima was a difficult woman—suspicious of everybody, quick to take offense, and able to hold a grudge for decades. And that was on a good day. I doubt a dozen years in the Io outback has made her better company."

They could see the lights of Galileo Station below—a cluster of habitation domes built on stilts above Io's surface. Mavry brought the gig down in a graceful arc, firing the retro rockets so they barely felt the bump of the landing skids.

"Smooth landing, Dad," Carlo said, sounding impressed and a little jealous.

Mavry just waggled his fingers and smiled.

"Now then, environment suits," he said. "And bring emergency flares and a communicator—your mother's going to be mad enough about this little excursion as it is. If I get us marooned in a grav-sled with a bad case of sulfur burn . . . well, it won't be pretty."

Carlo removed a box of flares from the gig's equipment locker and passed them to Tycho.

"Should we bring carbines, Dad?" he asked.

Mavry hesitated. "Yeah, we'd better. But only as a last resort."

They suited up and crossed the landing platform, grit pinging off their visors, then descended in a rickety elevator that sounded like it might plummet down its shaft and embed itself in the frost-covered plains below.

Inside, Mavry signaled that they could remove their helmets. Yana wrinkled her nose: Galileo Station's air was a foul brew of sulfur mixed with an acrid whiff of burned electronics.

The station wasn't much easier on the eyes. Everything was rusty and looked ill kept. The people were hunched and sallow, with darting, suspicious eyes—though at least there was no sign of burly spacers with thick beards and Saturnian accents. They descended to the lower levels, rented a battered grav-sled from a surly clerk, and were soon driving across the Colchis Regio toward the anvil-topped mountain known as Prometheus.

Filaments of color danced in the skies: streamers of gold and silver, purple and green, that swelled and then melted away.

"I can't decide—is that pretty or scary?" Tycho asked.

"A little of both," Yana said after a moment. "I think I'll be glad I saw it once I'm far away from here."

"Shh, you two," Mavry said. "We're getting close."

Carlo checked the navigation unit and guided his father to a ridge on the lowermost slopes of Prometheus, where their headlights revealed shallow ruts left by wheels. They came to an old metal sign that had been rammed into the ground at a cockeyed angle. It was pitted and corroded but still readable.

NO VISITORS
INTRUDERS WILL BE SHOT

"Well, we know we've got the right house," Mavry said.

A flash of lightning revealed a small homestead on the next rise—a low building that looked like it had begun life as a bulk freighter's shipping container.

The grav-sled was halfway to the little house when something pinged off the windshield, leaving a crescent-shaped nick in the thick glass. Mavry hit the brakes as their suit radios crackled to life.

"Turn around and get lost," said a croaking voice over the speaker. "Do it right now. Or I'll shoot you all."

"Take it easy, Oshima," Mavry said. "We just need to

talk to you for a minute. Hold your fire—we're getting out of the sled."

Mavry shut down the filtration system and popped the grav-sled's doors, releasing a puff of air that instantly froze into a coating of rime on the seats and the Hashoones' enviro suits. Then he got slowly out of the vehicle, keeping his hands raised, and inclined his head to indicate that his children should do the same.

Another flash of lightning revealed a figure about twenty meters ahead, wearing an enviro suit and staring down the barrel of an antique rifle. The figure picked its way across the frozen plain, rifle still raised, and stopped about three meters away. The Hashoones' ears were filled with the sound of labored breathing.

Oshima Yakata was small and bent—Tycho was pretty sure her environment suit was a child's model. But her black eyes were hard behind her helmet's faceplate, and her gloved hands were steady on the rifle.

"Who are you?" Oshima demanded.

"It's Mavry Malone, Oshima. It's been a long time."

The dark eyes widened.

"And these are my children," Mavry said. "Carlo, Tycho, and Yana."

"Your children? That means they're Hashoones."

"Yes. Diocletia is their mother. You're not going to shoot us, are you? Because you're making me nervous."

"Shame to have Hashoones in my sights after all these years and not pull the trigger," Oshima said, but lowered the rifle.

"Thank you. Now, can we go inside and discuss things like reasonable people?"

"No Hashoone sets foot in my house. Whatever you've got to say, you can say it out here."

"All right. Go ahead, Carlo."

Carlo stepped tentatively forward.

"Ma'am, have you heard of the Collective?" he asked. "It was a group of Jupiter pirates formed in your father's day, after the raid on the *Isis*."

"Of course I know what the Collective is," Oshima snapped. "Think I'm old, eh? That I don't remember? My father, Blink, was one of them, along with Johannes and Josef Unger and Orville Moxley and Muggs Saxton. Oh, I remember just fine. Now let me guess—you want my share of it."

"Well, purely for the historical novelty," Carlo stammered. "The treasure's gone forever, of course—just a fairy tale told belowdecks. We're interested because—"

Oshima's laugh was a humorless grating bark.

"You're a liar, boy—and a bad one, too. The treasure's gone, eh? Is that why my father's old communicator lit up with a message saying Johannes's scanner had been removed from the Bank of Ceres? And is that why the Securitat has spooks drilling through the ice on Europa? Oh, yes, I know about that, too. Go home, Hashoones. Go home and watch the Securitat bring up the treasure. Go home and wish Josef and that old swindler Johannes had found a better place to hide it."

"Swindler?" Tycho said. "It's the government that's

doing the swindling! They're stealing that treasure from all of us, you included."

Oshima brayed laughter.

"Such a shame—I could really spruce up the place. It's only what you Hashoones deserve. My father hated Johannes, did you know that? He hated him because he cheated everyone he ever met out of whatever he could. Just like you're trying to cheat me. Your family's never had a trace of honor—not since Gregorius's day."

"Who are you to talk of honor, you old witch?" demanded Yana as forks of lightning painted the plains a sickly purple. "Where was your honor at 624 Hektor? Do you remember that day, old woman? The day you betrayed your countrymen?"

Snarling with fury, Oshima raised the rifle and pointed it at Yana's face. Tycho's ears filled with static as Oshima screamed at Yana, Mavry tried to say something soothing, Carlo yelled, "Stop!" and Tycho himself made some desperate noise of protest. But Yana held her ground, gloves balled into fists, staring back at Oshima.

"Go ahead, if you've got the guts. Wait, let me make it easier for you."

She turned around.

"Now you can shoot me in the back. That's what you're used to, isn't it?"

Oshima's hands began to tremble. She lowered the rifle, letting the butt rest on the icy ground.

"You stupid girl," she said, in a voice that sounded more tired than angry.

Tycho looked at Carlo and saw his brother's fright and disbelief—an expression he knew mirrored his own.

"All lies," Oshima said. "Yes, I survived the battle. Yes, my ship was undamaged. It was undamaged because I saw what was happening and fled for my life. Do you know why I was able to run, while everyone else's engines misfired?"

"Because you're a traitor," Yana said. "Just like Thoadbone Mox."

"No. I was able to run because I never installed the software program we were given—the one that was going to protect us against the jammers we'd been warned about, but shut down our systems instead. The program that was given to us by Thoadbone Mox and Huff Hashoone."

"You're lying!" Tycho exclaimed. "Our grandfather had nothing to do with that! Our ship was damaged, and he was nearly killed!"

Oshima just smiled.

"Ask your father if I'm lying."

The Hashoones' eyes turned to Mavry.

"Yes, Huff helped distribute the program and told the others to install it," he said, the words emerging slowly and unwillingly.

"What?" Tycho gasped.

"But that's because he was tricked—tricked by your pal Mox," Mavry said to Oshima. "The two of you knew what Huff didn't—that Earth saboteurs had hidden a virus in the program. But Mox was smart enough to install it on his own ship, so he'd look innocent if something went wrong. You didn't even have the guts to do that. When Earth's destroyers failed to kill the rest of us on the first pass, like they were supposed to, you got scared and ran."

Oshima scoffed.

"Don't you get tired of being a fool, Mavry? Earth had nothing to do with it, and neither did I. It was the Securitat. They wanted to bring the Jupiter pirates to heel, and Thoadbone and Huff helped them do it. 624 Hektor was a trap for greedy pirates—with the promise of a big score for bait."

"If that's what you thought, why were you there?" Carlo demanded. "Why weren't you safe here on Io?"

"Because I was greedy too," Oshima said quietly. "Greedy, and stupid, and not willing to trust myself that I was right."

"You're no victim," Yana said. "You survived. A lot of Jupiter pirates didn't."

Oshima nodded, then waved her arm at the wasteland surrounding them.

"Yes—and behold my glorious reward. Exile, and disgrace, and a lifetime of lies spread about me by your grandfather and others."

"That's enough, Oshima," said a disgusted Mavry. "Huff's not a liar, and you know it."

The old woman shook her head.

"You're a little late for loyalty, Mavry," she said. "I expected you and Diocletia to unplug that old buzzard

218

years ago. What made you lose your nerve?"

"I don't know what you're talking about," Mavry said, staring out across the plains.

"Oh, yes you do. Before 624 Hektor, you and Diocletia were plotting with Cassius Gibraltar to get free of Huff—even though it meant breaking up the Hashoone clan. Funny how you wound up stuck with him instead."

Tycho's eyes turned to Mavry, as did those of his siblings. Their father's mouth was a thin line in a face gone pale.

"Ohh, I guess that was a secret," Oshima said, baring her yellowed teeth at Tycho in a predatory smile. "Let that be a lesson for you, boy. Secrets don't stay secret. Just like treasures don't stay buried."

In the grav-sled, Mavry saw his communicator's message light was blinking. He listened, then shook his head in dismay and tapped out a brief message in reply.

"It's your mother," he said, putting the grav-sled in drive. "Sounds important."

"Aren't you going to speak to her?" Carlo asked.

"Not from here. Best to get back as quick as we can."

"Dad, what did Oshima mean—" asked Yana.

"Not now," Mavry said sharply.

Tycho caught his sister's eye and shook his head. She scowled at him.

"When, then?" she asked.

"I don't know," Mavry said. "Just not now."

They rode back to Galileo Station in strained silence.

Tycho stared out the window at the grim landscape. Beside him, he knew, Yana was gnawing at the same disturbing questions he was. So too, he imagined, was Carlo. But perhaps not. And he was sad, suddenly, to think that he'd never know. Tycho could usually guess what his twin sister was thinking, but he and Carlo had never had a conversation like that and probably never would.

They finally reached Galileo Station and returned the grav-sled, haggling briefly over the nick in the glass, then took the elevator back up to the landing platform. Mavry looked around at the bleak landscape and shook his head.

"Well, it's been a lovely visit," he said. "Reminds me of why I wanted to get off this godforsaken moon in the first place."

"Where did your family live?" Yana asked tentatively.

"Nowhere near here—our homestead was out by the Amirami flows," Mavry said. "I couldn't wait to get into space, but my father actually liked it here. Or at least he liked it better than Europa."

"Grandfather Malone was from Europa?" Yana asked.

"Yes and no," Mavry said. "Came here in the Resettling, with his father, and was happy to do so. He'd get mad if you brought up Europa. He said it didn't matter where he'd been born—he was from Io."

Tycho came to an abrupt halt, and Yana smacked into him, dropping a case of emergency flares.

"What are you doing?" she demanded.

"We have to get back to Callisto," Tycho said.

"Great idea. It would help if you'd get out of my . . . wait a sec. What is it you think you've figured out?"

Tycho shook himself and met the curious gazes of his siblings and father.

"Not till we're on the gig," he said, looking around suspiciously.

Yana managed to restrain herself until the gig emerged from Io's envelope of plasma into the emptiness of space.

"Now what's this great revelation of yours?" she asked.

"The treasure," Tycho said. "There's somewhere else it could be—somewhere we didn't think about."

"Tyke, enough," Carlo said. "Let's just go home."

"Good idea—because the treasure's in the ocean beneath Callisto."

"What? That doesn't make any sense," Yana said.

"Listen to me. Our cousins have run the Water Authority for a long time—what if Johannes and Josef borrowed equipment from them, just like we did, and hid the treasure where they could get at it a lot easier than they could on Europa?"

"But Loris said it was beneath Josef's home," Carlo objected.

"He didn't say *which* home. Grandfather Malone was from Europa, but he was also from Io. Just like Josef Unger was from Europa, but he was also from Callisto. They both emigrated during the Resettling. Remember?"

"Tyke, this is crazy," Yana said. "I asked about Josef's home, and Loris said it was at the southern end of the Sidon Flexus. He talked about Europa, not Callisto."

"No, that's not what you asked him. You asked him where Josef lived on Europa. And he told you."

"Why is the Securitat drilling there, then?" Mavry asked.

"Because they're making the same assumptions we have, Dad. They've got someone's scanner, they know it works best in water, and they know where Josef lived. But what if we're all overlooking something?"

"Even if you're right, Loris said the treasure was lost or stolen," Carlo said. "Callisto's ocean goes down hundreds of kilometers—if it fell in there, the pressure crushed it into a pancake."

"Maybe," Tycho said. "But don't you want to find out? Before we decide we're beaten, isn't it worth taking a look at home, right beneath our own feet?"

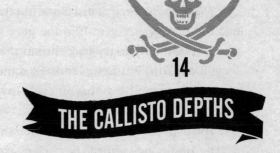

14

THE CALLISTO DEPTHS

When they returned to Darklands, Diocletia was waiting at the bottom of the ramp with her arms folded.

"Uh-oh," Mavry muttered under his breath.

"And how was Europa?" she demanded as Huff clanked up behind her, his artificial eye gleaming up at them. Tycho tried not to stare at his grandfather and betray the thoughts chasing themselves through his head.

"Europa was better than Io," Mavry said.

"Io?" Diocletia asked, looking stunned.

"Arrr, Mavry," Huff rumbled. "What've you gone and done now, lad?"

"Things," Mavry said. "There wasn't time to discuss it."

"There wasn't time to discuss it, but there was time to load the underwater gear into the grav-sled?" Diocletia asked. "You'll have to try harder than that."

"I'll explain. But first, I can tell something else has happened—something that doesn't involve us. What is it?"

"You'd all better sit down," Diocletia said.

The Hashoones settled themselves around the table. Parsons materialized with tea.

"Where's Aunt Carina?" Carlo asked.

"Trying to clean up your mess," Diocletia said. "Three hours after you rushed off to Europa without consulting anybody, the Ice Wolves raided it with a pocket cruiser and three frigates."

"Mox," Yana said.

"Yes . . . the cruiser was confirmed as the *Geryon*. JDF units in orbit drove Mox off after a brief skirmish."

"That's bold, even for Thoadbone," Mavry said. "But why is this our mess?"

"Well, Mavry, perhaps because they'd just intercepted *you*. Imagine you're a Securitat agent and connect the dots: the Ice Wolves have been recruiting Jovian spacers and pirates to their cause. Four Jovian privateers make a harebrained attempt to con their way down to the surface of Europa. Then, hours later, the Ice Wolves try to run the blockade."

"They think we were running interference for Mox?" Mavry asked, looking offended. "That's insane."

"Maybe so, but that don't mean there ain't folks what believe it," Huff rumbled as Parsons poured the tea.

"Carina's trying to talk sense into them, but it's a near thing," Diocletia said, taking a gulp of tea and closing her eyes. "So if you also shot up a Perimeter Patrol frigate above Io, you'd better tell me now."

"Nothing like that," Mavry said. "Just an unpleasant conversation with an old colleague. I'll tell you about it later."

Diocletia's teacup rattled in its saucer.

"You didn't," she said. "You're lucky she didn't shoot you."

"Oshima?" Huff roared. "You should've taken me, lad. Oh, what I wouldn't do to look through crosshairs and see that treasonous she-worm."

"Grandpa—" Yana began, but Mavry held up a finger in warning.

"Don't," he said.

"You're lucky the four of you weren't clapped in irons for trespassing and attempted piracy at Europa," said Diocletia. "You're lucky that . . ."

She subsided, shaking her head but still smoldering.

"So what happens now?" Carlo asked after a moment.

Diocletia exhaled slowly.

"The Union leadership is determined to hit the Ice

Wolves and hit them hard. There's a council of war set for the day after tomorrow at High Port. We'll be attending—provided we haven't been stripped of our letter of marque or locked up for treason before then."

She glared at Mavry over the rim of her teacup.

"Day after tomorrow?" Tycho asked.

His mother's eyes stopped trying to drill a hole in her husband and snapped to him.

"Yes, Tycho. Why? Do you have other plans?"

"It's the *Iris* cache. I know where it is. Where it *really* is."

Diocletia sighed.

"Let me guess," she said. "The *Iris* cache is beneath the presidential mansion on Ganymede. And you four geniuses want to wear fake mustaches and fly over there with shovels."

Tycho started to explain, but Diocletia, hand upraised, looked away before he was done with his first sentence.

"That's enough, Tycho. Chasing that treasure has been nothing but trouble. What's happening right now is deadly serious, and we need to focus on it, not rainbows and pots of gold. Wherever the *Iris* cache is, it can rot for all I care."

She got up from the table and strode away, heading for the ramp. Tycho pushed back his chair as well, determined to follow her and make her hear him out.

"No, Tycho," Mavry said. "I'll try later, but now's not the time for that discussion—or any others. Go over the underwater simulation again. Yana and Carlo will help you."

"Forget it. I've had enough of this nonsense," Carlo said.

"Belay that," Mavry said. "I promise you we'll sort things out later. For now, you three are crewmates and I need you to act like it."

Parsons, unperturbed as always, appeared to take away the tea.

Every Hashoone child learned that sound traveled through Darklands in ways that could be hard to predict—for example, from the simulation room to the bedrooms a level above and below. Over the years, many ambitious young Hashoones had failed to shut the door during an early-morning or late-night simulation, then looked up from the virtual world to discover angry relatives roused from sleep.

Tycho, Yana, and Carlo had just finished carrying the impeller and the underwater suit down from the garage when they heard the argument carrying up the ramp from their parents' bedroom a level below. From the sounds, Tycho guessed Mavry had walked up the ramp and encountered Diocletia leaving their quarters, and their disagreement had begun across the doorway.

They couldn't hear every word, but the bits and pieces told them enough.

". . . beyond foolish to do such a thing without discussing it . . ."

". . . no time to debate it . . ."

". . . lucky you're not all in jail . . ."

". . . wouldn't be saying that if we'd succeeded . . ."

"... endangered our letter of marque ..."

"... but they've worked so hard, and together too ..."

"... your insubordination put them and us in danger ..."

Until, mercifully, one of their parents shut the door.

"I really wish I hadn't heard that," Tycho said.

"I could say that about a lot of things today," Yana replied.

Carlo just looked impatient. "Come on, let's get this equipment hooked up so we can get this over with."

"That doesn't bother you, hearing something like that?" Yana asked.

"No," Carlo said, looking away. "Why should it?"

"Because they're our parents?" Yana said, incredulous.

"They are, but we're a starship crew. You heard what Dad said earlier—we have a job to do. So let's do it."

"Oh, cut it out, Carlo. It's *us*—you can get upset about something without its going in the Log."

"I'm not upset," Carlo said, crouching down to hook up the armor's diagnostic ports.

"Right. I forgot, you're above all this. None of it means anything to you—not Mom and Dad fighting, not what Oshima said about Grandpa and the software program, not the idea that our parents were going to break up the clan. . . ."

Carlo got abruptly to his feet, the armor's ceramic chest plate clattering on the floor.

"What about it?" he demanded, his scar white against a face gone red. "It's all ancient history! Haven't you had

228

enough living in the past, trying to measure up to the glory of the great Jupiter pirates? I'm tired of Grandfather's story, of Aunt Carina's story, of Mom and Dad's story. It's time for us to write *our* story. Why don't you see that?"

"Because there is no *their* story and *our* story!" Tycho burst out. "It's the same story!"

Carlo shook his head. "You just keep telling yourself that, Tyke. You keep telling yourself that and see how far it gets you."

If there were more arguments during the night, they took place behind closed doors. When Tycho sat down for breakfast, Diocletia and Mavry were in their usual places, not chatting like they usually did, but no longer projecting a prickly hostility.

Carina, however, looked up from her mediapad and nodded at Tycho pleasantly enough.

"So are you ready to go down the pipe and see if you're right about the location of our treasure?" she asked.

"Sure," Tycho managed to say. His eyes jumped instinctively to his father, but Mavry was studiously focused on chosing his next scone, while Diocletia stared fixedly into her teacup. Whatever drama had happened to change her mind, he'd missed it.

Tycho was briefly elated but wished his aunt had waited until after breakfast—his hunger had vanished, replaced by anxiety as pieces of simulator exercises unspooled in his head.

After breakfast, Carina called up the rarely consulted manual for Darklands' filtration system, a humming assemblage of machinery built around the homestead's hulking steel water tank.

"All right, let's review," she told the assembled Hashoones. "This hatch leads to a short maintenance shaft that enters the main pipe here. The main pipe runs nearly two hundred kilometers down to the ocean, beneath the crust. When I shut down the pump and filters, it will take about twenty minutes for the water to drain."

Carina pulled a key from a pouch on her belt and opened a panel on the side of the filtration machinery. She checked her mediapad, then tapped a combination of buttons. A red light began to blink, and a moment later the hum of the equipment rose in pitch, then abruptly ceased.

"It's so quiet," Yana said. "Feels creepy."

"Let's hope it's not for long. Now listen. The main pipe is a little over a meter wide. There's a detachable platform at the top that's used to ferry equipment up and down—such as the impeller sled and, in this case, one brave midshipman."

She smiled at Tycho, who smiled back.

"Once the pipe's drained, Tycho will ride the platform down with the sled and the scanner. Tycho, you and Yana work well together, so she'll be your point person for communications—but all of us will be here to help with anything you need."

Yana fitted her headset over her dark hair and nodded at her brother.

"We'll be fine. I've got plenty of experience telling Tyke what to do."

"Yeah, right," Tycho said.

"You've gone over how to use your equipment in the simulator, correct?" Carina asked.

"Tyke got perfect marks last time," Carlo said.

"Good to hear," Carina said. "The ocean is salty and mixed with a small amount of ammonia—that keeps it from freezing. Your suit was designed for these conditions. It's rated for three hundred meters of water pressure, but you won't need to worry about that—if the treasure's down there, it's almost certainly floating or anchored to something. Anyway, if you need it, you know how to use your suit's jet pack."

"Arrr," Huff said. "Terrible being down there under all that rock. Like a tomb—"

"Why don't we leave the briefing to Carina?" Mavry suggested.

"It's all right," Tycho said. "I'll be fine."

"I know you will be," Carina said. "The biggest uncertainty is signal range. We don't know how close the scanner has to be to the signal to detect it. We've loaded the coordinates of the old Unger homestead into the sled's nav unit. Once you're in the water, it should be about ten kilometers away."

Tycho nodded.

"Now listen carefully, Tycho. You have three days'

worth of air. That's for safety, not exploration. You know everything that's happening with the Jovian Union these days and with this family. The last thing we need is to launch a rescue mission on top of everything else. Do not be reckless."

"I understand," Tycho said. He blew his breath out in a long exhalation. "And I'm ready. Let's do this."

Once Tycho put on the bulky underwater suit, the hatchway looked a lot narrower. And the maintenance shaft smelled terrible—an acrid mix of ammonia and other chemicals.

"Ugh," he said. "How long is the trip down?"

"Oh, only about five hours," Mavry said with a smile.

Tycho gave the pipe another unhappy sniff. "I'll use my suit's air. Besides, if something's wrong, better to know at the top than at the bottom."

Carlo and Yana helped Tycho fit the helmet onto its collar and lock it. He adjusted the controls on the suit's wrist pad, his breath loud in the confines of the helmet, and air began to flow.

"You read me, Tyke?" Yana asked, the words coming a beat behind the sight of his sister's lips moving.

"Loud and clear. Do you read me?"

"All green," Yana said, giving him a thumbs-up. "First thing is to make sure the maintenance platform works."

Tycho stepped into the hatch and sank to his knees, ducking his head to crawl forward. After a meter, the maintenance shaft intersected the main pipe at a right angle. Tycho crept to the end of the shaft and activated his work light. Below him, an O of metal plunged straight down into darkness.

It was some two hundred kilometers to the ocean below. Tycho wondered how long it would take him to fall if he should slip.

"You okay in there, Tyke?" Yana's voice asked over his radio. He knew she was close enough to grab his foot. But it already felt like she was perilously far away.

"Just getting my bearings. The main pipe's clear—all the filtration equipment retracted successfully. Ask Aunt Carina to deploy the platform."

"Copy that."

Something hummed, and a broad metal disk emerged from the side of the pipe about half a meter below, filling all but a few centimeters of the shaft. It rotated and locked into a narrow track.

"Looks good," Tycho said. He reached down and shoved at the disk. It didn't move.

It was too narrow to turn around in the maintenance shaft. Tycho wormed backward and popped up in the familiar surroundings of Darklands, with his family gathered around him. Behind them, Parsons was clearing the breakfast dishes.

"You okay?" Diocletia asked. "You're sweating."

"I'm fine. I'll have plenty of time to rest in a minute. Who's got the scanner?"

Carlo handed it over. Tycho turned it on, verified that

the readout was working, then turned it off and secured it to his chest with a loop of hook-pile tape.

"All right," he said. "Let's do this."

Yana reached out and put her hand on her brother's faceplate, followed by Mavry, Carlo, Diocletia, and Carina. Tycho smiled up at their assembled hands, though he was mildly alarmed when Huff tapped his forearm blaster cannon against the helmet.

"Be safe, Tycho," Diocletia said. "Wait. Honestly . . . now there are handprints all over his faceplate."

She cradled his helmet against her side and swiped her sleeve repeatedly across the faceplate, which allowed her a chance to give him a private smile.

When his mother let go, Tycho lowered himself into the maintenance shaft again, scooched backward, and dropped down onto the platform.

"I'm in the pipe," he said. "Push the impeller sled over to me."

He guided the sled into position, the platform momentarily bobbing beneath him. It was a tight fit—he could barely extend his arms without touching the walls on both sides.

"Ready to go," he said, hoping he sounded more confident than he felt. "Send the platform down."

"Starting sequence," Yana said. "Talk to you in a couple of hours."

The maintenance shaft vanished into darkness, replaced by a featureless circle of metal as the platform accelerated and the walls became a blur.

Tycho had heard of spacers' children who panicked in tight spaces, rendered helpless by some ancient instinct left over from the time when humans roamed the vast plains of Earth under endless skies. He wondered how they'd react if they found himself where he was now.

Fortunately, he was a Hashoone and a born spacer—from her berths to her ladderwells and gunnery bays, the tight confines of the *Comet* had always felt comforting, not confining. He looked around once more, verified that everything was as it should be, then shut off his helmet's work light to save power. There was no sound but his own breathing as the platform hurtled through the darkness toward the hidden ocean far below.

"Tycho, do you read me? Tyke?"

Startled, Tycho looked around before he remembered there was nothing to see. His sister said his name again, concern creeping into her voice.

"I'm here. What's going on?"

"Did you fall asleep?"

"No," he lied.

"Unbelievable. You should be nearing the bottom of the pipe."

"Got it," Tycho said, his brain still a little foggy.

A few moments later, something beeped in the darkness, the noise surprisingly loud. Tycho turned on his work light, blinking at the glare. The platform came to a stop, then began to creep downward again. Water appeared around Tycho's feet, followed by a circle of darkness. The platform was descending into Callisto's hidden ocean, moving along a guide that extended below the pipe's terminus.

Tycho forced himself to relax. *Your suit's buoyant,* he reminded himself. *And you have a jet pack. You'll be fine.*

The water rose to his chest, then his neck, then his chin. Then he was completely submerged.

The platform stopped. His feet were trying to float. He grabbed hold of the guide connecting the platform to the pipe, then looked up. The end of the main pipe was above his head, a bright circle in the beam from his work light.

"I'm in the water," he said. "I'm all right. I'm going to set up the sled."

The sled demagnetized from the platform with a clank and unfolded itself, deploying floats with a puff of bubbles. Tycho unspooled a cable from its front housing and clipped it to the platform guide.

"I'm going to have a quick look around before I activate the nav unit," he told Yana.

Still gripping the platform guide, he looked up and let his work light play over his surroundings. Half a meter above his head, the main pipe emerged from the hard-packed rock and ice of Callisto's crust, which formed the ceiling of an immense underwater cavern. Off to one side and extending below him was the dim shape of the pipe's siphon, which had been rotated out of the way by great geared wheels. On the other side of the pipe, a cluster of antennae and probes and sensors had been rammed into the crust above and trailed down into the water.

Tycho let his feet rise until he was floating, activated his maneuvering jets, then tentatively let go of the guide and drifted in the water. A tap on the jets sent him gently away from the pipe, past the impeller and the siphon, until there was nothing but rock and ice above his head.

He tapped the jets again, a bit too hard, and found himself shooting upward. Instinctively he flung up his arm to protect his head. His arm and shoulder mashed into the cavern's ceiling, which gave slightly under the impact. He squeezed his fingers, and gray mud squished out between them. He dug tentatively, and bits of rock and muck came free, clouding the water around his helmet.

A chunk of bright white rock slipped from his grasp and he looked down, following its descent as it fell. The water was crystal clear—he could see every detail of his boots where they hung below him. The falling rock slowly shrank to a dot, then a bright pinpoint, caught now and again by the fading illumination of his work light until it was finally swallowed up by the vast darkness below him.

Tycho heard his breath quickening and realized he'd shut his eyes. Directly above him lay the unimaginable weight of two hundred kilometers of ice and rock; directly below him lay the unfathomable abyss of two hundred fifty kilometers of water. He was in the heart of a moon, suspended between two enormities his mind could barely grasp.

"Tyke? You okay?"

His sister must have heard him gasping.

"I'll be all right," Tycho said, eyes still shut, arm still braced against the cavern roof.

"Have you turned on the scanner?"

"No. Uh, I was about to."

He forced himself to open his eyes, then to push himself down, away from the ceiling. He let some air bleed out of his tanks, sinking a couple of meters. Being away from the cavern roof made him feel a little better—this was almost like the familiar, floating feeling of a space walk. He reached down and unfastened the scanner, reminding himself to focus on it and not on his feet or the yawning dark below them.

"Okay," he said, hefting the device. "Turning it on. It's working."

"And?" Yana asked, excitement leaking into her voice.

"I'm not receiving anything," Tycho said, peering at the readout to make sure the scanner was functioning properly.

"Let me sweep it around," he said, firing his maneuvering jets to turn himself in a slow circle.

There was nothing. The scanner was silent.

"No signal anywhere," he said, frustrated.

"You're probably just out of range," Yana said. "Activate the sled's nav unit so you know you're pointing the scanner in the direction of the Unger homestead."

"Right," Tycho said. "I can do that."

The impeller and the equipment platform were on the other side of the siphon. He tapped his maneuvering jets and craned his head, looking for the outline of the sled or the bright circle of the pipe.

Among the sensors and antennae he saw four rectangles, one on top of the other. Tycho fired his jets and moved closer, trying to make sense of what he was seeing. The rectangles were greenish gray, each separated by a short length of cable. He looked up and saw that the cable was shackled to a clump of instruments, secured by its own weight.

"Strongboxes!" he yelled.

He heard Yana gasp, then her muffled voice telling the others.

"And the signal?" she asked.

"No signal," Tycho said, pointing the scanner at the boxes until it nearly touched them. "That's strange."

"Are you sure it's the treasure, then? I mean, why leave it right under Darklands and not tell anybody?"

"I don't know. But there's nothing else it could be. Four strongboxes—I can see where the chain holding them was welded to the machinery."

"Amazing. You were right, Tyke."

Grinning, Tycho tapped the jets and drifted around the boxes, examining them from every angle.

"The boxes are corroded—so's the cable—but they're intact," he said. "They look too heavy to move to the platform all at once. I'll work from the bottom and cut them free one at a time."

He reattached the scanner to his suit, then tugged the

cutting torch free of a pouch on his leg and thumbed the igniter. The torch blazed like a star in the water, which began to boil around the superheated arc of plasma.

Remembering his simulation exercises, Tycho bled some air from his tanks, sinking to the level of the last strongbox. A loop of cable hung below it, hanging free in the water. Above it, another cable attached the box to the next one in the chain. Tycho grabbed the loop of cable at the bottom, clambered awkwardly onto the lowermost box, and looked for the best place to cut the cable.

Then he was tumbling head over heels, moving very fast, with his breath hammering in his ears. The torch pinwheeled away from him, a spark of brilliant light in the darkness.

"Tycho!" Yana yelled.

Somehow the cable had snapped above him. The boxes were plummeting into the abyss on a one-way trip to the moon's distant core—and they were dragging him along like an anchor.

His body thrashed back and forth as he plunged deeper into the ocean. The suit was rated for three hundred meters—below that, his faceplate would crack and he would die.

"Tyke! What's happening?"

He managed to get his head pointed up, still clutching the loop of cable that was now at the top of the chain of strongboxes. It felt like his arm was going to rip free of its socket. He fumbled with his other hand for the jet-pack controls, missed them, then found them on the second try. The maneuvering jets roared to life on full blast, trying to push him back up.

He was still plummeting downward. He had no idea how deep he was.

"Come on come on come on come on come on . . . ," he gasped.

He was still falling, though he thought he was slowing down. Or perhaps that was his imagination.

"TYKE!" Yana was screaming.

"COME ON!" he yelled.

No, he was definitely slowing. The pain in his shoulder was excruciating. He got his other hand on the loop of cable, trying to distribute some of its weight.

"Tyke! Talk to me!"

"Cable . . . broke," he managed to say. "Still got . . . boxes."

His descent had slowed to a crawl. But he was still going down.

"Let go!" Yana yelled.

"No."

Tycho hung in the water, the jet pack's force having finally counterbalanced Callisto's gravity and arrested the strongboxes' plunge. The jet pack was hot against his back. Tycho prayed it wouldn't burn out or run out of fuel.

As he slowly began to rise, he heard a tiny sound inside his helmet, above his eyes.

A small crack appeared at the upper left corner of his faceplate, where it joined the helmet. A faint whiff of ammonia reached his nose.

He was rising more quickly now, the pain in his shoulders running down his arms into his hands. Sweat was pouring down his back. His sister was screaming at him.

The small crack suddenly zigzagged halfway across his faceplate. He tried to will the jet pack to propel him faster. A tiny drop of water formed at the center of the crack, on the inside of his faceplate. The droplet hung suspended for a moment, trembled, then hit him in the nose.

Something gleamed above him. It was the siphon. There was the sled, floating in the water next to it. And there was the platform.

He shut off the maneuvering jets and almost smashed into the platform as he shot past it, crying out as he let go of the cable with one hand. His hand was numb and spasming. He started to sink again, but the third strongbox hit the edge of the platform and stuck there, the top two boxes settling atop it with a clank. The fourth strongbox hung just below the platform. Exhausted, Tycho wrapped his arm around the platform and shut off the jet pack. His back was burning.

"Remind me never to do that again," he told Yana between gasps.

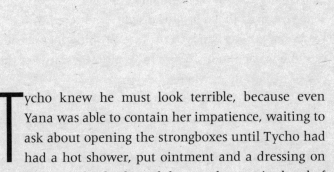

15

THE *IRIS* CACHE

Tycho knew he must look terrible, because even Yana was able to contain her impatience, waiting to ask about opening the strongboxes until Tycho had had a hot shower, put ointment and a dressing on the blisters on his back, and devoured an entire bowl of hominy and a plate of soft tack.

It was like Christmas morning, he thought, enjoying his sister's exasperation as he accepted Parsons's offer of a second cup of tea.

Finally feeling somewhat restored, he pushed his chair back from the table and turned to look at the corroded strongboxes, now sitting side by side in the living area of Darklands, next to the sled and his muddy suit and damaged helmet.

"We broke the locks but didn't open them," Carina said. "Tycho, you do the honors."

Tycho crouched down in front of the first strongbox, amazed at how tired he was. He looked up at the Hashoones surrounding him, smiled, and threw back the lid.

The first thing he saw was the jewelry—there were necklaces, and brooches, and things he didn't know the names of. Diamonds and rubies and tigereyes gleamed amid loops and curls of gold and silver.

"Oh my goodness," Yana said.

"Arrr, ain't that a beautiful sight," muttered Huff.

Tycho put his hands in the box, pushing them inside until he was up to his wrists in wealth. He stared at the rest of his family in wonder.

They opened the rest of the boxes, exclaiming in amazement at a bag of uncut emeralds, a diadem that glittered and flashed like a comet, old-style watches and pendants and a hundred other astonishing objects.

"It's a pirate hoard of old," Mavry said. "There's five or six million in livres here at least. Sometimes the legends are true."

"Hate the thought of givin' part of it to that blasted Oshima," Huff growled.

"We can spare it," said Diocletia, sounding giddy.

"And Mox's share?" asked Carlo, grinning as he showed off two hands festooned with rings.

"Arrr, I vote we jes' shoot that one this time," Huff said. "Even my generosity has its limits."

Tycho laughed along with the rest of his family, but all the while he was looking for something out of place—something that would quicken the pulse of a Securitat agent with an interest in old secrets.

He spotted it in the third box—the black square of a data disk, almost invisible beneath a spill of golden coins. He palmed the disk quietly and pointed at a necklace of lapis lazuli Yana had just held up triumphantly, and when heads turned toward his sister, he slipped the disk into the pocket of his jumpsuit.

And then he realized how desperately he needed to sleep.

This time all Yana had to do to wake him was poke her head into his darkened room.

"Dinner's almost ready. We would have let you sleep, but Aunt Carina wants to discuss tomorrow's meeting at Ganymede."

Tycho forced himself upright in his bunk, groaning at the ache in his shoulders and back.

"Okay, I'm up," he said. "What else have I missed?"

"Not much. Mr. Knackert's going over the valuables downstairs, figuring out what they're worth."

"And is it good news?" Tycho asked anxiously. His

last thought before vanishing into sleep had been a flash of paranoia that the jewels would somehow turn out to be fake.

"Very good news. Knackert's about ready to drown in a puddle of his own drool. He's thinking eight million. Maybe more."

Tycho relaxed and grinned at his sister.

"We found it—we really found it! Everyone thought the *Iris* cache was gone, or an old legend, or cursed, but we found it."

"*You* found it," Yana said.

"We all helped. Without you we wouldn't have gotten Lord Sicyon's and Loris's shares."

Yana snorted. "I'm sure you'll insist that Mom note that in the Log alongside all the details of your triumph."

"Of course I will," Tycho said, suddenly serious.

Yana shook her head, but she was smiling.

"You know what? I believe you," she said, turning to go—but then she turned back.

"Something's bothering me, though," she said, looking at him gravely.

"What's that?"

"It's about what was missing from the treasure."

Tycho froze. He had been sure no one had seen him pocket the disk.

"We never found the quantum signal," Yana said, and Tycho was suddenly able to breathe again.

"Maybe it fell off when the chain broke," he said, flexing his abused shoulders.

"Then the scanner would have picked it up before that. No, I don't think the signal was there in the first place. That's strange, isn't it?"

"It is. But everything to do with the treasure has been strange."

"That's true. Anyway, you'd better hurry if you want any candied yams," Yana said, and the door shut behind her.

Tycho waited a moment, then dug his mediapad out of his duffel bag and entered the password for the hidden file where he'd transferred DeWise's messages. Soon he would be rid of the Securitat agent, his schemes, and the sleepless nights that had come with them.

I have something you want, he typed, then looked down at the glowing letters on the screen. He imagined the Securitat agent reading the message on his cruiser above Europa, or in some nest of bureaucrats on Ganymede, and allowed himself a satisfied smile.

Tycho found the other Hashoones standing behind a hunched, bald little man in a dirty jumpsuit who was rummaging through the last of the strongboxes, humming happily to himself. Knackert was one of the more discreet members of Carina's network of Port Town dealers who specialized in goods of uncertain pedigree.

Knackert looked up from his work, calipers and sensors jangling from bandoliers and straps on every limb. He smiled hugely at Tycho, then dissolved into red-faced mirth. Tycho, used to the old dealer's fits of laughter, knew enough to wait.

"Master Tycho!" Knackert said at last, giggling as he turned a diamond-encrusted case for a personal communicator so it caught the light. "So good to see you again, ho ho! Oh, yes! And congratulations on such a remarkable prize! You'll see these beauties again, come high season on Ganymede—and on Earth and Mars, too. Oh, yes, Master Tycho—hee hee!—your discoveries will adorn lucky wives, husbands, mistresses, consorts, and concubines for years to come. Ha! Such a pleasure to bring such marvelous objects back into circulation!"

"An' to pocket yer biggest commission in years, right, Knackey?" Huff rumbled amiably.

Knackert waved that off with a chuckle and punched numbers into his mediapad. Then, with Parsons's help, he bundled the strongboxes onto a floater cart and waddled up the ramp.

"I'm kind of sad to see it all go," Yana said, judging Knackert's progress by the chortling and cackling that bounced down the well to the dinner table. "Some of that stuff was really pretty."

"When have you ever cared about that?" asked Carlo.

"I'm allowed to think things are pretty," Yana said, looking annoyed.

Diocletia raised an eyebrow.

"You know what I find pretty?" she asked her daughter. "Retuned engine baffles. Longer-range bow chasers.

And not thinking an unsuccessful cruise will send us to the poorhouse."

"Longer-range bow chasers?" Yana asked, all thoughts of jewelry apparently forgotten. "Can we really get those?"

"We can discuss it, at least," Carina said, smiling. "There are a number of things we can discuss now. But after dinner. And after we talk about tomorrow."

After Parsons cleared away the dishes, Huff pulled the black stump of a cheroot out of a pouch on his bandolier and leaned back in his chair with a look of quiet satisfaction on the living half of his face. The cheroot smelled vile even before Huff lit it, but the other Hashoones didn't bother to argue, instead scooting their chairs back to what they'd learned was more or less a safe distance.

"Now then," Carina said. "The Jovian Defense Force was badly embarrassed by the Ice Wolves' grand speech at Ganymede and further rattled by the attempted raid on Europa. There will be a considerable military response, one involving JDF warships as well as privateers."

"What does that mean?" asked Tycho.

"It means we're going back to Saturn," Mavry said.

"Yes," Diocletia said. "We're getting our orders tomorrow at High Port and leaving immediately after that."

"The Union wants to send us off to war again?" Yana asked. "They didn't exactly keep their promises to us after the hunt for the *Hydra*."

"Our letter of marque is a military document—we're members of the Jovian Defense Force," Carlo pointed out.

"Come off it, Carlo. We're members of the military when it's convenient for politicians," Yana said. "When it's not, we're pirates that nobody wants to talk about— and who can have our rights taken away until the next time we're needed."

"You sound like an Ice Wolf all of a sudden," Carlo said.

"So what if I do? Maybe the Ice Wolves are right. We're not really that different from them, if you think about it—we're raw materials the Jovian Union makes use of but doesn't really care about."

That silenced everyone for a moment. Huff puffed on his cheroot in contemplation.

"I'm not saying I disagree with what the Jovian Union stands for, or anything like that," Yana said. "But if our government isn't working for the people of Saturn, why shouldn't they be allowed to go their own way? Isn't that what we did when we wanted our freedom from Earth?"

"But look at how they're doing it," Tycho said. "Show-ing up with warships at High Port? Raiding Europa? That's not the way to convince people you deserve freedom."

"Why does anyone have to convince someone else that they deserve freedom?" Yana asked.

"Arrr, politics," Huff rumbled.

Carina held up her hands for peace.

"The Jovian Union can't afford to have its attention divided between threats from Earth and trouble at Saturn. So the Defense Force plans to hit the Ice Wolves fast and hard—to head off whatever they're planning next and to show Earth that we won't take such threats lightly."

"Good," Carlo said. "We can't appear weak at a moment like this."

Yana rolled her eyes.

"So now what?" Tycho asked. "Do we vote on it?"

"Not this time," Diocletia said, turning to Mavry. "Your little expedition to Europa has caused our loyalty to be questioned—and it will be questioned further if we don't join this mission. I've already ordered our crewers at Port Town to be ready to fly."

Tycho nodded. Carlo was beaming, obviously excited by the chance to fly with Jovian warships. Yana scowled, but then she nodded too.

"Can I take you into Port Town tomorrow?" Tycho asked his mother. "I, uh, want to work on my grav-sled piloting."

Yana was looking at him quizzically—and so, he realized, was everybody else.

"Now what are you up to?" Yana asked, peering at her brother. "Ah. I know what's going on."

"And what's that?" Tycho asked, hoping he didn't look as nervous as he felt.

"You're still fretting about Loris Unger, aren't you?"

Tycho tried to look embarrassed, rather than grateful

that his sister had accidentally given him the excuse he hadn't thought of himself.

"Fine with me," Diocletia said. "Just be ready to go when we get back. And watch your step in Port Town."

"I will."

Yana shook her head sadly. "Tycho Hashoone, patron saint of sad old grog hounds and other lost causes."

DeWise agreed to meet Tycho in Port Town, naming a nondescript café near the guild hall of the Most Honorable Union of Surveyors and Metallurgists. Tycho spotted the Securitat agent at a table near the back, hands around a chipped coffee mug, and couldn't resist grinning at the sour expression on the man's face.

He made DeWise wait while he got a jump-pop and a nutrient square, then sat down across from him at the dented metal table.

"So how was Europa?" Tycho asked with his mouth full.

"Cold."

"Find what you were looking for?"

The Securitat agent sighed.

"I think you already know what we found—nothing. We spent two weeks below the ice with one of those scanners and our own equipment for nothing. So are you going to tell me how you found it?"

"Maybe," Tycho said. "You first. Whose scanner did you have?"

"Muggs Saxton's."

Tycho nodded. "Which he gave you in exchange for a reduced prison sentence."

"That, plus access to his personal communications and everything he knew about the *Iris* raid and the Collective."

"I'm listening."

DeWise frowned, then shrugged. "I suppose it doesn't matter anymore. The Collective members all trusted Josef Unger because he was that rarest of things—an honest pirate. He and your great-grandfather were the ones who hid the *Iris* cache when the members of the Collective were forced to scatter. Moxley got his scanner and tried to dig up the cache, but we caught him and sent him to 1172 Aeneas—where we already had Josef, Johannes, and Blink Yakata in custody."

"But you didn't get Moxley's scanner," Tycho said.

"No—and none of the pirates we'd already caught would cooperate," DeWise said. "We had agents follow Johannes and Josef when they were released in 2815, but they slipped our grasp. We tried to keep an eye on the Collective members, but never got a hint that the treasure had been found—by them or anybody else. And no message came from the Bank of Ceres for eight decades."

"So there was no signal to follow," Tycho said.

"Right," DeWise said. "We tried looking anyway, and pursued every kind of crazy theory—that the treasure was encased in the ice beneath the Unger homestead, or buried in the side of a smoker, or moving around in a robot sub. Eventually we had other priorities, and all we could do was wait. We're good at that, when we have to be."

Tycho smiled. "Too bad you were looking in the wrong ocean."

"Don't be a brat, Tycho. It was Callisto, wasn't it?"

Tycho nodded. "Right beneath Darklands."

DeWise considered that for a long moment, and Tycho could almost see his mind calculating. Then he cocked his head, and the corners of his lips twitched.

"That's very interesting," he said in a way Tycho didn't like at all.

"Why is that interesting?" he asked.

"It just is," DeWise said. "Now, we have other matters to discuss. Do you have it?"

"Yes."

"And does anybody know?"

"No," Tycho. "What would happen if they did?"

"Things would be more complicated. I'll take it now, if you please."

"It's not that simple."

"What you have is dangerous, Tycho. We're all better off if it's in the right hands."

"I'm not sure I believe you. What do I have, exactly?"

"Like I said before, information. Information that could help the Union in the current crisis."

"And if I don't give it to you? What happens then?"

"It would go badly for your family," DeWise said, face expressionless.

Tycho considered that.

"I want something in return," he said.

DeWise smiled.

"In addition to everything I just told you? And the fact that you weren't jailed for piracy after your little stunt at Europa?"

"The information was a trade," Tycho said. "As for the rest, spare me. If we were in the brig on 1172 Aeneas, you'd have one less ship to take to Saturn."

DeWise's eyes leaped around the café.

"Be quiet," he said. "But point taken. What is it you want?"

"The *Hydra*—free and clear. No more of this nonsense in the courts."

"That's not my department, Tycho. It's out of my hands."

Tycho nodded. "I had a feeling you might say that."

He reached below the table into his jumpsuit's hip pocket and brought out the black data disk, holding it in his hand. DeWise's eyes leaped to it, then shifted to the carbine in Tycho's other hand.

"Oh, so now it's an old-time pirate drama. What are you going to do, kid? Blow a hole in me?"

"In you? No."

Tycho cocked the carbine, careful to keep it pointed away from the Securitat agent, then held the muzzle against the disk.

"The *Hydra*," he said.

DeWise took a sip of coffee. It spilled down his chin

and he wiped irritably at his face with a dirty napkin.

"All right, Tycho. I'll do everything I can. In recognition of your family's services to their country during the current emergency and all that."

"And will that be enough?"

DeWise sipped his coffee.

"I can't promise you it will be, but I would think so. Plus I won't forget that you were helpful to us. Don't give me a look like that's nothing, kid. Didn't I already bring you a prize when both you and your family needed one? Couldn't help like that be useful to you in the future?"

Tycho bit his lip. He had been certain that his tangled relationship with DeWise was ending, and with it the need to keep secrets from his family. Now DeWise himself was suggesting otherwise.

But DeWise's tip about the *Portia* had been a good one, and its capture had been a big help to the Hashoones. And his account of the *Iris* cache fitted with what Tycho and his siblings had discovered. What if he was telling the truth about the disk too? Could Tycho really deny his country an advantage now, when it was caught between enemies?

"All right," he said reluctantly, and handed over the disk.

"You've done your country a considerable service," DeWise said, getting to his feet.

"I hope so," Tycho said. "But I want to know what was interesting about the cache's being right under Darklands."

"You're out of information to trade," DeWise said over his shoulder—but then he paused and turned back.

"I like you, Tycho—so here's one more freebie. It's impressive that you found the *Iris* cache—we didn't, after all. But have you asked yourself how it got there?"

"What's that supposed to mean?"

"To tell you the truth, I'm not completely sure," DeWise said. "But I've got a pretty good guess."

Before Tycho could ask, DeWise shook his head. "You've figured out harder puzzles than this one, kid. But this time you might not like the solution."

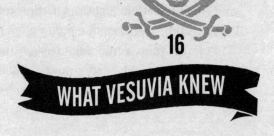

16

WHAT VESUVIA KNEW

N ow that is an impressive sight," Carlo said.

Ahead of the *Shadow Comet*, the rust-colored, oblong moon Amalthea hung in space against the seething mass of Jupiter. Arrayed around the moon was a quintet of Jovian warships and their long-range tanks. The crescent-shaped destroyers *Godfrid*, *Ingvar*, and *Ingolfur* were in the lead, ahead of a pair of angular, hammerheaded cruisers: the sister ships *Hippolyta* and *Antiope*.

Off the port wing of the formation, Tycho spied a pair of privateers—Spotted Jack Almedy's *Steadfast*, garishly painted with red-and-orange flames, and the graceful *Izabella*, captained by Garibalda Marta Andrade. Carlo maneuvered the *Comet* into place on the starboard wing, beside Absalom Garrett's needle-nosed *Ironhawk*—the same privateer that had joined the *Comet* in pursuing Mox two years earlier.

"Two cruisers, a trio of destroyers, and four privateer frigates," Tycho said. "Can't say we lack firepower."

"Arrrr," Huff said from his usual place near the ladderwell, metal hand clamped to a rung and feet magnetized to the deck. "Ain't the weapons what counts, but knowin' what to do with 'em. Seen plenty of fancy flotillas come to ruin, on account of bein' led by a fool."

"What makes you think Admiral Badawi is a fool?" Carlo asked.

"Ain't sayin' he is. But someone will see this here big parade an' shout the news clear to Saturn. Better to slip off from Jupiter separately and join up away from pryin' eyes."

Tycho and Yana exchanged a concerned glance, but Carlo waved dismissively.

"I'm not worried about that," Carlo said. "I'm looking forward to showing Admiral Badawi what I can do."

"What *we* can do, you mean," Yana said, rolling her eyes at Tycho.

Carlo, delighted by the chance to fly alongside pilots from the Jovian military, had spent their last night at

Darklands holed up in the simulation room, practicing fleet maneuvers until he wound up slumped over his console, asleep while unguided virtual *Shadow Comet*s smashed into virtual obstacles.

A light blinked on Tycho's console.

"Ship-to-ship communication from the *Ironhawk*," he said.

"Thank you, Tycho," Diocletia said. "Put it onscreen."

The handsome, red-haired Captain Garrett appeared.

"Diocletia," he said, smiling broadly. "It's been a while, but what a pleasure to fly alongside you again."

"Absalom," Diocletia said politely. "Nice to fly with you again as well."

Mavry, out of range of Vesuvia's camera, squashed his nose up against his face and began waggling his fingers at Garrett, tongue lolling out of one side of his mouth. Yana began to giggle. Diocletia gave her husband a venomous look.

"This is quite the task force they've assembled," Garrett said. "We'll make Mox and his new Ice Wolf friends wish they'd never come calling."

Mavry put his feet up on his console and pantomimed sticking his finger down his throat. By now Yana was red-faced with half-smothered laughter.

"Shh!" Tycho hissed at his sister.

Mavry turned and grinned at his children, which sent Yana diving under her console, sides heaving.

"We, um, have to check preflight, Captain Garrett," Diocletia said. "We'll talk to you soon. *Comet* out."

Garrett disappeared from the screen. Mavry was now pretending to be dead.

"Honestly," Diocletia said, pink spots on her cheeks. "Is this the quarterdeck of a privateer or a traveling circus?"

"I think that nice young man wants to take you to the Midshipmen's Ball," Mavry said.

"Maybe I'll let him. At least he conducts himself like an officer."

"Mom's right," Carlo said, frowning. "What if a member of Admiral Badawi's staff had seen that, Dad?"

Mavry raised an eyebrow. "And this would happen how? Is there an ensign hiding in the larder?"

"You know, I think I saw a guy in uniform behind the potatoes," Tycho said, which set his sister off again.

Carlo just shook his head and muttered something.

"Another message," Tycho said. "This one's from the flagship, to all ships in the task force."

"Arrr, maybe they've hired a brass band," Huff said.

"Onscreen, please, Tycho," Diocletia said. "And for the next minute, let's see if we can impersonate an actual starship crew."

Admiral Badawi himself stared down at them, the camera on the *Hippolyta*'s bridge capturing him from a low, dramatic angle. He was a beefy, chestnut-skinned man with an impressive white mustache, dark eyes that seemed to bore through the viewscreen, and a crisp black uniform heavy with gold braid. Behind him, harried-looking officers were rushing back and forth.

"Captains, it is my honor to command this mission," he said, hands clasped behind his back. "The right and proper authority of the Jovian Union has been challenged by a rabble—a mob bent on fomenting rebellion and disorder. When we arrive at Saturn, that rebellion will be at an end."

Badawi smoothed his luxuriant mustache with one well-manicured hand, then jabbed a finger at the screen.

"We have assembled this task force to teach these so-called Ice Wolves a lesson they will never forget. Our target is Refueling Station Gamma, which the Securitat has identified as a rebel hotbed. I intend to drive off its defenders and destroy it. When this demonstration is complete, no one from Saturn or Earth will doubt the resolve of the Jovian Defense Force or our ability to mete out justice."

The admiral nodded to someone out of camera range.

"My navigator is transmitting course data now. Lock in your courses and accelerate to cruising speed on her mark. It's two weeks to Saturn, ladies and gentlemen—and it's not going to be a pleasure cruise. When we arrive, it will be as an instrument of the Jovian Union's will. Whether you are hearing this on the bridge of a warship or aboard one of our . . . auxiliary units, I expect you to carry out my orders with discipline and resolve, and to make our Union proud."

Badawi's heels clicked together, and he lifted his chin.

"That is all. *Hippolyta* out."

The screen went blank.

"Auxiliary units?" demanded Yana. "Is that what that pompous old walrus just called us?"

"Belay that," Diocletia said. "For now, Admiral Badawi is our commanding officer."

"An' more's the pity," Huff said. "Now I'll say it—that man's a fool. An' a dangerous one too."

In addition to good grooming, Admiral Badawi believed in drills—within the hour, he had a list of simulations prepared and special channels reserved for communications among all nine crews. The Hashoones spent a full shift advancing on defensive lines of imaginary Ice Wolves alongside avatars of the other Jovian warships, virtual cannons spitting brilliant energy, then chasing down the stragglers with the rings of Saturn as a backdrop.

The fourth drill ended with Carlo heading off an Ice Wolf frigate before it could make a suicide run on the *Antiope*, then driving her back into the sights of the *Ingolfur*, whose volleys reduced the frigate to glowing fragments.

"Excellent flying, *Comet*," Badawi said. "Good thing the rebels couldn't see this latest drill unfold—they'd have laid down their arms and made our little expedition unnecessary. And where's the glory in that, eh?"

Carlo grinned at his family as Badawi announced a fifteen-minute break and signed off the shared channel.

"Did you see the way we broke that enemy formation?"

he asked, leaning back in his seat with his hands behind his head.

"I did," Diocletia said. "You did well, Carlo."

"Then why are you looking like that?" Carlo asked.

Diocletia and Mavry exchanged a glance, but it was Huff who spoke up.

"Because these puppet shows ain't got no connexion with reality," he growled. "Them Ice Wolves is experienced spacers, but in that old fool's sims, they line up to take their licks like malingerin' apprentices."

Diocletia started to say something, then folded her arms over her chest, looking unhappy.

"I'm right an' you know it," Huff muttered.

"Perhaps the admiral's working on basic tactics before introducing some more realistic scenarios."

"An' perhaps if I flap my arms, I'll fly to the Oort cloud. Badawi's brain ain't equipped for realistic scenarios, Dio. He's spoilin' for a fight and fixin' to get his people killed—and us, too, if we ain't careful."

The next two days of drills were much the same—in Admiral Badawi's relentless simulations, the Ice Wolves assembled to protect Refueling Station Gamma, forming a neat line outside the perimeter of Saturn's rings, then concentrated their fire on the *Hippolyta*. Each time, Badawi countered this attack by sending the privateers—or "auxiliary units," as he invariably termed them—to execute pincer movements, driving the Ice Wolves into the warships' overlapping zones of fire to be destroyed.

The drills were impressive displays of coordinated fire and precision tactics—but only Carlo still believed they would bear any resemblance to the actual fight awaiting them.

When Yana questioned what Badawi was doing, Carlo had an answer.

"The admiral thinks *how* we fight is as important as the results of that fight," he said. "Saturn fell to insurgents because the Jovian Union failed to enforce the rule of law. The way to restore order is to show Saturnians a demonstration of coordinated military action—not to fight insurgents with their own tactics."

"I don't know what's scarier—that you just said that or that you might actually believe it," Yana said.

"If we maintain formation and fire support, the Ice Wolves can't stand against us, Yana. This is a military operation, not a slugging match between pirates."

"Arrr, but there's the rub," Huff said. "Both fighters have a say in how things turn out. If I were this Lazander, I'd duck into the rings an' launch hit-and-fades against our forces from there, evenin' up the odds. Or jes' turn tail an' run."

"Then we win," Carlo said. "We destroy Refueling Station Gamma, making the Saturnians rethink the consequences of letting the Ice Wolves take over. Mission accomplished, and we go home."

"That's not winning," Diocletia said.

"Why not?"

"If the Ice Wolves don't fight, destroying one of our

265

own facilities will just turn more Saturnians against the Union. Dad's right. If Lazander's smart, he won't give this task force anything to fight. He'll disperse his forces and wait for us to go home—or to do something stupid."

Carlo looked doubtful.

"We haven't simmed that scenario," he said.

"That's 'cause there ain't no glory in it," Huff said. "The only sims Badawi runs are the ones he can win."

Everyone sat silently for a minute.

"There's another problem," Yana said.

"Oh, good," Tycho said.

"The jamming. We haven't run a single simulation in which the Ice Wolves use Mox's jammer—which we know they still have. The Defense Force knows what happened to us at P/2, right?"

Diocletia nodded.

"They do—I had Carina give them the data. You're right—I don't know why Badawi hasn't accounted for that."

"So what do we do?" Tycho asked.

"Is there anything we *can* do?" Yana asked.

"Arr, of course there is," Huff said. "We can go home, leavin' this fool mission 'fore it becomes our epitaph. We've plenty of livres, thanks to young Tyke here."

"And forfeit our honor?" Carlo demanded.

"Honor's cold comfort in the shroud, boy."

"I'm less concerned about our honor than I am about our letter of marque," Diocletia said. "It's still more than

266

a week to Saturn. All we can do is wait and see what happens."

Before the next day's final drill, Badawi warned his captains that he'd prepared a simulation that was a little different. Which was true, sort of: this time, the Jovian warships were swarmed by pinnaces determined to bloody the *Hippolyta*'s nose.

"Very good," Badawi said as the virtual wreckage disappeared from their computer screens. "You handled that well. Now, any questions about what we just faced?"

Diocletia thumbed her headset controls. "Admiral, this is Captain Hashoone. A related question for you?"

"Go ahead, Captain Hashoone."

"We've tangled with Thoadbone Mox multiple times, Admiral," Diocletia said. "The last time, he was in command of three ships and deployed a powerful jammer that overwhelmed our systems until my sensors officer was able to disrupt the interference."

"She means me," Yana pointed out to Tycho while covering her microphone. In return, he offered his sister pretend applause.

"How is that question related to the scenario we just explored, Captain Hashoone?" Badawi asked.

"It concerns unorthodox tactics typically used by, um, insurgents—like the ones we've now started simulating, Admiral. I can resend the data from our most recent encounter with Mox in case it's been overlooked."

"It has not been overlooked, Captain," Badawi growled. "Mox didn't use jammers in his raid at Europa, remember."

"But he might in a defensive situation against a superior force, Admiral. Particularly when the ships of that force are trying to coordinate offensive operations, as you've been teaching us to do."

"I wouldn't put anything past a known traitor and renegade. But let me assure you, Captain Hashoone, that our countermeasures teams are more than prepared for your scenario. If Mox uses his little toy, we'll have it analyzed and neutralized within seconds. Unless we just blast Mox and his ship to atoms—I've found that the simplest defenses are often the most effective. Does that address your concerns, Captain?"

"It clarifies things admirably, Admiral," Diocletia said, then plunked her headset down on her console in disgust.

"Yana, when we reach Saturn, have details of the procedure you used to break the jamming at P/2 ready to send to the other ships," she said. "Admiral Badawi may not think it's important, but I do."

"For the record, Captain Hashoone, you were very diplomatic," Mavry said.

"Great. These days, that and a letter of a marque will buy you a one-way trip to Saturn."

Tycho slept fitfully and started awake at five bells. He stared at the darkened ceiling above him, listening to the reassuring *shush-shush* of the *Comet*'s air scrubbers and the thrum of her engines. Normally the combination of those familiar sounds would nudge him back to sleep within a few minutes, but not tonight. With a groan, he abandoned his bunk and descended the ladderwell to the quarterdeck.

Diocletia was sitting in the captain's chair, staring at her monitor while absently twisting her ponytail behind her head with one finger. She turned at the sound of his feet on the ladder's rungs, and the alarm on her face was replaced by a smile and a nod.

"You're a bit young for the Hashoone curse," she said.

"What's the Hashoone curse?"

Diocletia indicated the empty quarterdeck. "Sitting at your console in the middle of the night with no watches scheduled. Or staring at your mediapad in your bunk."

"Oh, that. Doesn't seem to affect Yana, though."

"Your sister could sleep through an emergency reentry. But then the two of you have been as different as could be since the day you were born."

Tycho settled into his chair, closing his eyes at the familiar way the imitation leather creaked and then seemed to fit around him.

"So why are you on the quarterdeck in the middle of the night?" Diocletia asked.

Tycho hesitated. It was just him and his mother, and for a moment what he wanted most was to tell her what had happened with DeWise, how he had done something for what he swore was an admirable reason—or *mostly* an admirable reason—but one thing had led to another, and now he was stuck, unable to go back but not wanting to go forward.

"Oh, you know . . . everything," Tycho said, shrugging helplessly.

"I know," Diocletia said, then smiled. "It's not as bleak as it may seem, though. This mission is a bad idea, to say the least. But we'll be okay if we keep our heads. And in the meantime, here's something that should cheer you up."

Tycho got up and stood by the captain's chair. His mother typed on her console.

"Carina's people have sold off the *Iris* cache. That's the amount per share—four of the five shares are ours, since we're not giving Thoadbone his. We'll have to give the crewers their cut, of course, but I'd call it a pretty good payday."

Tycho whistled appreciatively. Two or three years' worth of cruises might not yield that much money.

"We barely got to celebrate your find—the solar system had other plans, as it so often does," Diocletia said. "But we will. And we'll get to do so because you saw what nobody else saw, and insisted we look where nobody else thought to look—including me."

This, Tycho thought, was a moment he should want to go on forever: his mother talking about how his success had helped their family, an accomplishment that would certainly be remembered when the time came to choose a new captain.

But he remembered DeWise's words, and his smile faltered.

"What is it, Tycho?"

"I'm glad I was right about where the *Iris* cache was, but something's still bothering me. *Why* was it there? Johannes must have hidden it under Darklands. But it's pretty clear he didn't tell anybody else."

"You don't know that. It was a long time ago, and the Collective members were being hunted by the Securitat. Maybe it was a temporary arrangement, and everybody forgot."

"That's a lot of money to forget. And the treasure got there without Johannes ever taking his scanner from the Bank of Ceres."

Diocletia bit her lip. "True."

Tycho was quiet for a moment.

"I wanted to think Orville Moxley was the one who ambushed Josef Unger at P/2," he said, going over the thoughts that had plagued his restless nights. "I tried to convince myself Thoadbone had the coordinates for P/2 from his uncle's logs, figured out we were going there and tried to head us off. But it was much simpler than that—Mox got our course heading from the trackers and found P/2 the same way we did, by searching against known orbits."

"Most likely," Diocletia acknowledged. "But what about Muggs Saxton? His scanner was gone too. Maybe he ambushed Josef. Or maybe it was the Securitat. Or some pirate we don't know about."

"Then how did the treasure wind up under our own home?" Tycho said. "Muggs didn't have the guts for a deep-space ambush. And the Securitat wouldn't have killed Josef unless they were sure they didn't need him anymore."

Diocletia looked surprised.

"That's a pretty ruthless thing for a fourteen-year-old midshipman to say. How did you get so knowledgeable about the Securitat?"

Tycho looked away, his stomach churning.

"But I think you're right," his mother said. "So what you don't want to say, Tycho, is that you think Johannes killed Josef Unger."

"Yes," Tycho said. *And ruined many lives that came after him,* he thought of adding, but decided not to.

"I wish I could tell you there are a million reasons why you're wrong, and Johannes would never have betrayed a fellow pirate. But I can't. Your theory makes a lot of sense."

"I know. I wish it didn't."

"Still, I can't tell you you're right, either—as I told you on Callisto, I looked in the Log. There's no mention of the *Iris*, unless Johannes restricted access to it. In which case we'll never know."

"I guess I have to learn to accept stuff like that and not let it drive me crazy."

His mother smiled. "When you figure out how to do that, tell me the secret."

Tycho smiled back.

"Still . . . ," Diocletia said.

"Still what, Mom?"

"Vesuvia, I need a course plot based on orbital coordinates."

"Acknowledged," Vesuvia said. "Awaiting input."

"Call up the orbital data for P/2093 K1," Diocletia said. "But this time I want the coordinates beginning in . . . what year should we start with, Tycho?"

"The raid on the *Iris* was in 2809."

"Vesuvia, can you calculate orbital positions for P/2093 K1 since 2809?"

"The calculations are straightforward," Vesuvia said, and Tycho thought the ship's AI sounded slightly offended. "Shall I display them on the main screen?"

"That won't be necessary. Do you have a record of any course intercepting those coordinates?"

"Yes," Vesuvia said.

Diocletia and Tycho looked at each other.

"When?" Diocletia asked.

"April 17, 2895. Twenty-three days, nineteen hours, twenty-one minutes, and nine seconds ago."

Tycho laughed. Diocletia shook her head, exasperated.

"I seem to remember that trip, Vesuvia," she said. "Do you have a record of any *other* course intercepting those coordinates? Set a confidence interval of 85 percent."

"Coordinates match no record."

"Does your definition of 'record' include data to which a captain has restricted access?"

"No. Records are limited to accessible data."

Diocletia drummed her fingers on her console,

eyebrows lowered, teeth working at her lower lip.

"Let's try it another way," she said. "Were coordinates intersecting the orbit of P/2093 K1 already in your memory before we plotted them last month?"

Vesuvia was silent for a second, then two. Then three.

"Yes," Vesuvia said.

"When were those coordinates entered into memory?" Diocletia asked quietly.

"On July 3, 2816."

"Seventy-nine years ago," Tycho said.

Diocletia nodded.

Tycho tried to think of another explanation, but there wasn't one. Seventy-nine years ago, when Johannes Hashoone was captain, someone aboard the *Comet* had used the ship's computer systems to plot the coordinates of a lonely ball of ice and tar, one of millions hurtling through the wilds of the solar system.

The *Foundling* had been there too. But unlike the *Comet*, Josef Unger's ship had never returned.

17

SHOWDOWN AT SATURN

Remembering the Ice Wolves' precision flying at Ganymede, Admiral Badawi had insisted his task force arrive at Saturn with similar flair. So the Hashoones weren't particularly surprised when the admiral ordered them to use their long-range tanks until they were barely outside Saturn's outermost F ring—close enough that the pale-yellow world's bulk filled the *Comet*'s viewports.

"At this speed, you'll need to vector nearly straight

away from the tanks, not down," Mavry warned Carlo.

"I've been simming this for two weeks, Dad."

"All ships detach," Badawi declared.

"Detaching tanks," Tycho said over the frigate's internal speakers. Belowdecks, he knew, the Hashoone retainers and crewers had formed into teams at the gunports, prepared for action.

"Sensors are up and green," Yana said coolly. "Refueling Station Gamma is dead ahead. We're still out of range for detecting other targets."

The *Comet* shook as clamps released, stabilizers disengaged, and fuel ports retracted, separating her from the massive fuel tanks she used for travel between planets.

"Disengaged from fuel tanks," Vesuvia said.

"My boards are green," Carlo said. He shoved his control yokes forward, accelerating down and away from *Comet*'s tanks.

"Gunnery crews, hold your fire," Diocletia said into her headset.

"Aye, Captain," Mr. Grigsby growled from his station belowdecks. "Easy on the triggers, you lot."

Checking over his boards, Tycho realized he was smiling. Despite his anxiety about the mission, his family was working together like the disciplined starship crew they were—and he was a part of it, as he'd always dreamed. Whatever lay ahead, there was no place in the solar system he'd rather be.

"Vesuvia, put the tactical view onscreen," Diocletia said.

"Acknowledged."

The view from the *Comet*'s forward cameras flickered and was replaced by an approximation of what an observer looking down from high above Saturn would see. Green triangles marked the cruisers *Hippolyta* and *Antiope*, sitting at the center of the Jovian formation. Ahead of the capital ships was a trio of green squares—the destroyer *Godfrid* at point, flanked by the *Ingvar* and *Ingolfur*. On the right flank, two green circles indicated the positions of the *Ironhawk* and the *Shadow Comet*; on the left, two more circles represented the *Steadfast* and the *Izabella*. Ahead of the Jovian task force, at the top of the viewscreen, the perimeter of Saturn's rings formed a wide arc, with Refueling Station Gamma a red cross just outside the A ring.

"*Ingolfur*, tighten it up," Badawi grunted, and Tycho pictured the admiral on the *Hippolyta*'s bridge, fuming that one of destroyers ahead of him wasn't maneuvering exactly as in his endless sims.

"That's better, *Ingo*," the admiral said. "Now maintain formation."

"Helmsman probably goosed the throttle before stabilizers were clear," Carlo said disapprovingly. "You'd expect better from a warship pilot."

"Military pilots, arrr," Huff said. "He's probably only got five weeks behind the sticks of a real starship. On t'other hand, I bet his uniform looks *perfect*."

"Quiet, Dad," Diocletia said, studying the display.

"Refueling Station Gamma's within sensor range,"

Yana said. "Updating with new target information."

On the display, red shapes began winking into existence on either side of the red cross of the refueling station.

"Six bogeys—looks like three destroyers, two frigates, and a pocket cruiser," Yana said.

"That'll be the *Geryon*," growled Huff, his forearm cannon jerking reflexively. As always before a battle, the old pirate was dripping with weapons. He had twin pistols in his shoulder holsters, bandoliers filled with ammunition forming an X across his chest, and a wicked-looking cutlass slung at his left hip.

"They'll have more than six ships," Mavry warned.

"Let's hope Badawi knows that too," Diocletia said. "Vesuvia, tag the bogeys as hostiles. And switch back to visuals."

"Acknowledged," Vesuvia said, and a moment later Saturn was in front of them again, surrounded by its hypnotizing gyre of rings. The *Comet* accelerated smoothly through the thin F ring, dodging chunks of ice and rock and leaving ripples in the drifting dust behind her.

"Preparing to hail the station," Badawi said. "All craft display colors and hold here."

Carlo eased up on the yokes, and the *Comet* drifted to a halt.

"So far so good," he said.

"So far," Mavry said.

"Vesuvia, display colors," Diocletia said.

"Transponders active, Jovian flag."

"This is Admiral Badawi of the Jovian Defense Force. I am addressing those insurgents who call themselves the Ice Wolves. Your illegal insurrection against the Jovian Union is at an end. Heave to and prepare for boarding. Any vessel not complying with these orders shall be treated as a hostile combatant."

"Hostile craft are activating transponders and displaying Saturnian flag," Vesuvia said.

"Here we go," Tycho said under his breath.

"All ships engage," Badawi said. "Eliminate the enemy craft but leave the station alone—let's see if we can bring them to their senses first. Just like we simmed it, people. Do your country proud."

"Engaging," Diocletia said over the shared channel, the acknowledgment echoed by captains up and down the line. Carlo pulled back on the control yokes, and the *Comet* rolled to starboard, bearing for the A ring and the station just outside it.

"Mr. Grigsby, we're closing to firing range," Diocletia said. "Select targets and fire at will."

The Ice Wolves had other ideas, however. As the Jovian ships bore down on them, they pivoted smoothly and vanished into the whirling rock and ice of the A ring.

"Good pilots," Carlo muttered. "Shame they're traitors."

"Into the rings, just like Huff predicted," Mavry said, turning to nod at his father-in-law. "Hope Badawi doesn't fall for it."

"Admiral Badawi?" one of the Jovian captains said over the shared channel. "The insurgent vessels are—"

"I see it, *Godfrid*. Continue the pursuit and flush them out—they can run, but they can't hide."

Diocletia reached for her headset.

"They can and will hide, Admiral," she said over the shared channel. "Some of your captains have never flown through the rings. It's very difficult to maneuver in there—besides the debris, there are magnetic anomalies that will scramble your steering."

"And the same is true for the insurgents!" thundered Badawi. "You have your orders, *Comet*! Drive them out of the rings, and we'll finish them!"

Diocletia stared at the screen for a moment, then turned to nod at Carlo.

"You heard our commanding officer," she said, then tapped her finger on her chin, frowning. "Tycho, open a private channel and hail the *Ironhawk*."

"Private channel open," Tycho said as the grooved disk of the rings grew into a wall in front of them.

"I read you, Diocletia," Garrett said. "We're going in."

"We'll try to stick to your three o'clock, Captain Garrett," said Diocletia. "That's Mox's pocket cruiser in there—the *Geryon*. He has a jammer aboard. Be ready for it."

"We will be. Good hunting, *Comet*."

As the *Comet* passed into the maelstrom of particles that was the A ring, Diocletia leaned forward in the captain's chair, eyes locked on the main screen.

"The destroyers and privateers have entered the A ring," Yana said. "*Hippolyta* and *Antiope* are holding outside the perimeter."

"Stay sharp, Carlo," Diocletia said. "I know you've flown in here before, but now there are hostiles looking to take a shot at us."

Static bled out of the speakers, and Spotted Jack Almedy screeched a string of impressively horrible oaths.

"Maintain decorum and report, *Steadfast*," Admiral Badawi said with a sniff.

"Pinnaces! They're all over us!"

"*Izabella*, assist the *Steadfast*," Badawi said.

"We've lost our rudder," said the cool, cultured voice of Captain Andrade. "The magnetic drift is interfering with our instruments."

Before Badawi could reply, the captain of the *Ingvar* began shouting about enemy frigates.

And then the captain of the *Ingolfur* called out for aid.

Carlo swerved the *Comet* to port to avoid a tumbling cloud of icy rock, fighting the steering. Particles drummed against the privateer's hull.

Alarms began to blare.

"Proximity alert," Vesuvia said. "Hostile craft within firing range."

"Vesuvia, shut off that alarm!" Diocletia said. "Yana? Where are they?"

"I can't get a reading—sensors are still trying to catalog all the particles."

A deep rumble reverberated from the speakers, and

someone on the shared channel yelled out an order, his words rising into an agonized scream that was cut off.

"All craft report!" Badawi bellowed. "What's happening out there?"

"Missile launch detected," Vesuvia said with eerie calm. "Heading is—"

Carlo slewed the frigate left, diving under a scree of ice.

"Vesuvia? Heading is *what*?" he demanded.

"Heading cannot be determined," Vesuvia said. "Missile launch detected. Missile launch detected. Missile launch detected."

"Dio," Huff rumbled, "get us out of here."

"Mr. Grigsby!" Diocletia yelled into her headset. "This is a hot zone, and we are under fire—if you can see it, shoot it. Captain Garrett?"

"We can't see a thing in here," Garrett said anxiously. "And the anomalies are playing havoc with our steering."

The bright trail of a missile streaked across space in front of them, plowing through a cloud of dust fragments before changing course and carving a deadly arc toward the quarterdeck.

"Carlo!" Yana yelled.

"I see it," Carlo said. He threw the *Comet* into a hard roll to starboard, and Tycho grunted as he was thrown around in his harness, his view of the quarterdeck turning a somersault.

"Enemy frigate at three forty-five!" Garrett shouted.

The *Comet* shuddered and bounced sideways, debris pinging off her hull. Then the Hashoones were slammed forward in their seats. Tycho tasted something coppery and realized he'd bitten his tongue. He wiped his mouth on the sleeve of his jumpsuit and spit blood onto the deck. The artificial gravity failed, and he floated up a centimeter before his harness caught him, tiny red beads drifting in front of his face. Then the gravity came back, too hard, crushing him downward and turning his vision gray. He gasped for breath as the gravity lurched, then stabilized.

"—amidships," he could hear Vesuvia saying through the ringing in his ears. "Hull breach. Initiating damage assessment."

Air whistled past Tycho's face, drawn down the ladderwell behind his console and out through the hole the missile had punched somewhere in the *Comet*'s hull. Alarms rang out below, followed by the slam of bulkheads closing and the roar of the frigate's guns. The breeze fluttered uncertainly and stopped.

"Damage report?" Diocletia demanded.

"Hull breach contained," Vesuvia said. "Collating data from system diagnostics."

"*Comet*, we're taking fire from multiple angles," Garrett said. "Turn to—"

And then the jammer hit.

Tycho's board went blank. The *Comet* skidded sideways before Carlo got the frigate back on a proper heading.

"Come on, baby, quit fighting me," he muttered.

"Breach contained between portside gunnery stations nine and ten," Vesuvia said. "Both stations non-responsive."

That meant casualties, Tycho thought—just a few meters below him, men and women had died, either incinerated by the missile's fiery impact or sucked out into the void.

"Yana, countermeasures," Diocletia said.

"On it," Yana said coolly. "There's interference on all bands—same profile we saw at P/2. Don't worry, I'll have us back up in a moment."

Carlo stood the frigate on her tail and climbed to avoid a slab of striated rock—the remnant of some moon-let torn to pieces eons ago.

"Controls are really sluggish," he said through gritted teeth.

". . . totally blind!" one of the captains yelled over the shared channel, her voice eroded by static.

What, if anything, Admiral Badawi said in response was inaudible.

"Yana, tell the other captains how to break the jam-ming—maybe they'll want to listen now," Diocletia said. "Use the shared channel."

"Roger that," Yana said, activating her headset. "Task force, this is the *Shadow Comet*. Boost power on your sen-sors' PKB band and begin an oscillation within spectral harmonics six-eight point three and seven-three point six. It'll break the jamming."

"Obliged, *Comet*," someone said.

Carlo struggled to lift the *Comet* above a field of glittering ice, hands frantically pumping the control yokes as the frigate fought his efforts.

"Captains, advise on countermeasures?" Yana asked.

"It's not working!" someone yelled back through the static.

"Did you set—" Yana began, but the furious voice of Admiral Badawi broke in.

"It doesn't work!" he yelled. "Captain Hashoone, get your child off the combat channels!"

Yana stared at her monitor, face gone pale.

"Yana, why are sensors still blind?" Diocletia asked.

"I don't know," Yana said. "It's the same profile we saw at P/2! But this time the countermeasures aren't working!"

"Patience, lass," Huff said. "Give it another minute or two."

"We don't have another minute or two," Diocletia snapped. "Don't just sit there—try something else!"

Carlo dodged a flurry of spinning rocks, the *Comet*'s hull groaning at the stress of the maneuver.

"Sir, request permission to fall back," said the captain of the *Ingolfur*.

"Retreat?" Badawi asked scornfully. "We *will* break this infernal jamming. Continue with the mission."

"But sir!" one of the other captains yelled. "We're flying blind and getting torn apart!"

"CONTINUE WITH THE MISSION!"

"Missile launch detected," Vesuvia said. "Proximity alert."

"Carlo, get us out of—" Diocletia began.

A shriek of metal cut her off, and the *Comet* thrashed wildly from side to side, like a bottle of jump-pop shaken by a giant. Tycho's teeth snapped together as he was thrown violently back and forth in his harness. Then everything went black.

The first thing Tycho saw were his own hands, in his lap.

He stared at them for a moment, confused, then remembered where he was and jerked his head upright. Pain flared in his forehead above his left eye, and his fingers flew to the spot, then retreated from the lump they found there.

The quarterdeck was lit only by red emergency lighting, and it was warm. People were talking all around him, and he struggled to make sense of the noise, knowing it was important that he do so.

He forced himself to look around, the movement causing another blossom of pain in his head.

His sister was typing furiously on her console, mouth moving silently. Diocletia had one hand over her headset, staring straight ahead at the tumbling ring fragments visible through the viewscreen. Carlo was hunched over, hands on the control yokes. And Mavry was nowhere to be seen.

"Wait—I've got it!" Yana said. "Punching through the jamming now. Sensors coming back up."

"Good," Diocletia said. "Tell me what you see."

"Still establishing a scan," Yana said.

Someone muttered something behind him, and Tycho turned to see Huff on one knee, metal hand still locked to the ladder.

"Glad yer awake, lad," Huff said. "Was worried about yeh for a moment there."

"What happened?" Tycho asked groggily.

"Missile," Huff growled. "Hit the stern on the starboard quarter. Melted through half the starboard linkages to the main engine. Mavry's in the fire room, tryin' to relink 'em."

It wasn't just warm on the quarterdeck, Tycho thought blearily—it was hot. The *Comet* shuddered again, but this time the cause was her own guns—a broadside rolled from the stern to the bow, then was followed by another in the opposite direction. He realized Grigsby was ordering the crews to alternate broadsides, firing blindly into the rings around them in a desperate effort to fend off any attackers.

Huff heard it too.

"Smart lad, that Grigsby," he said approvingly.

"Tycho, if your board's working, plot a course up and out of the rings, away from the station," Diocletia said.

"Right," Tycho said. "Right, Captain."

His mother turned briefly to look back at him.

"You with us?"

"Yeah," Tycho said, forcing himself to focus on his board. He couldn't think about what enemies might be closing in on their battered stern, or how many Comets were dead or dying belowdecks. All he could do was his job. And that was to tap into Yana's sensors, determine the *Comet*'s position, and plot a course away from danger.

"I see them!" Yana said. "A frigate with a flight of pinnaces! Trying to get behind us!"

"Mr. Grigsby, sending targeting information to all gunnery stations," Tycho said.

"Aye, we got it. And we see her now."

"Mr. Grigsby, I'm cutting hard to port," Carlo said, eyeing the sensor information. "Don't miss the shot."

"Mom!" Yana said. "I see the *Ironhawk*—and she's got bandits incoming at two twenty!"

The *Comet* banked left, an ominous whine rising from somewhere deep inside the hull.

"Hope I don't blow whatever linkages are left," Carlo muttered.

Belowdecks, the guns roared, sending tremors rolling through the deck. Cheers erupted, and Tycho knew the *Comet*'s batteries had connected, ripping into one of her tormenters.

"Pinnaces are running," Grigsby growled.

"Tyke, where's my course information?" Carlo asked.

"Still calculating," Tycho said. The temperature continued to climb—sweat was running down his forehead now.

"Mom!" Yana yelped.

Tycho's eyes jumped to his monitor and the scan of the *Comet*'s surroundings. He could see the green circle that represented the *Comet*, with another green dot off to port and slightly astern. That had to be the *Ironhawk*.

And on the other side of the *Ironhawk*, three red circles were closing fast.

"Captain Garrett!" Diocletia warned. "Watch your port side! Bandits inbound!"

"Sensors are down," Garrett said through the static. "We're trying to climb out of the A ring, but we can barely steer."

"We're doing the same—I'll try to cover you. Carlo, turn to—"

Then they heard the rattle and boom of impacts over the private channel to the *Ironhawk*.

"Absalom?" Diocletia said.

A garbled snarl of voices trying to talk urgently over one another reached their ears, followed by screams. Someone was breathing raggedly into the microphone, almost panting.

"Absalom?" Diocletia asked again.

Garrett could barely whisper.

"Mox," he managed.

Then there was static.

"Vesuvia, rescan," Yana said. "I see the *Geryon*, but not the *Ironhawk*."

"Scanned object has lost structural integrity. I have an incoming message."

"Audio only," Diocletia said.

"Hashoones! I see you!" a gravelly voice said with a terrible glee.

Tycho stared at the scanner, watching helplessly as the three red dots drew closer.

Diocletia adjusted her headset.

"Admiral, this is the *Comet*," she said. "We've lost the *Ironhawk* and have hostiles inbound. Requesting assistance."

"Cannot assist, *Comet*," said Badawi. "Our mission objectives are no longer attainable. We are regrouping at the initial mustering point."

"What?" Carlo asked. "They can't just abandon us!"

"Of course they can, lad," Huff said. "We're privateers. Means we're expendable."

"Mox is closing," Yana said. "Three thousand klicks."

"With all the damage we've taken, I don't think I can outrun him," Carlo warned.

"Try," Diocletia said.

"You can't hide from me, Hashoones!" Mox said. "I'm going to catch that old tin can you call a ship! And when I do, you're going to breathe vacuum!"

Carlo mashed the throttles to the floor, and the *Comet* surged forward—but they all heard the hull groaning with the effort. Tycho wiped his sleeve across his forehead, and it came away dark with sweat.

"*Geryon* is pursuing," Yana said. "Twenty-seven hundred klicks and closing."

Carlo eyed his instruments and shook his head.

"He's going to catch us. And if I climb out of the rings, we'll get shredded."

"I know," Diocletia said. "Keep going—try to make the Keeler Gap."

"Twenty-five hundred klicks," Yana said.

"Mr. Grigsby, fire the stern chasers at the ring particles to aft," Diocletia ordered. "It might slow him down."

"I'm coming to get you, *Comet*!" Mox yelled, his voice rising to a feral roar. "I'M COMING TO KILL EVERY LAST ONE OF YOU!"

"Come on then, Thoadbone!" roared Huff.

"Twenty-two hundred," Yana said. "That's missile range. Why isn't he firing?"

"He wants the *Comet* for a prize, on account of the *Hydra*," Huff said.

"Dad, I need you and Mavry belowdecks to repel boarders," Diocletia said.

"Aye," Huff said. "If Thoadbone comes knockin', we'll give him what for."

He nodded at his daughter, who nodded back, then thumped down the passageway toward the fire room.

Tycho and Yana stared at each other through the dim red light. In a few minutes, if nothing changed, the *Geryon* would catch the *Comet*. The pocket cruiser's gunners would melt the privateer's gunports until she could offer no resistance, then attach a docking tube to her airlock. Then Mox's Ice Wolves would swarm the ship. Tycho would be able to hear the firing from the quarterdeck, hear men and women who'd spent their lives as Hashoone retainers screaming and dying below them. And then, when the Comets belowdecks could hold out no longer . . .

"Tycho, set up a communications link with your father," Diocletia said. "Keep your heads."

"Two thousand klicks," Yana said.

Carlo flung the control yokes sideways, and the *Comet* rolled sluggishly to starboard, engines sputtering, to miss a chunk of dark rock that had been hidden by a field of bright ice. But that carried them into the path of a massive blob of white. As Carlo yanked on the control yokes, it loomed ahead of them and filled the viewscreen. Yana gasped, and Tycho instinctively ducked his head as the privateer shuddered. He looked up and saw more tumbling ring particles—the *Comet* had flown right through the cosmic snowball, emerging intact on the other side.

"Ready or not, here I come!" Mox roared over the channel.

"Course calculations complete," Vesuvia said calmly amid the chaos.

Tycho looked at his display and saw that the *Comet*'s AI had obediently plotted a course out of the A ring—a course that was now useless, with Mox right behind them. He stared at the welter of objects on his screen, trying to conjure up a miracle.

"Daphnis!" he yelled. "Carlo! The Keeler Gap is dead ahead, and so is Daphnis! Remember the magnetic lee behind the moon?"

Carlo flung the control yokes left, then right, as a swirl of magnetic anomalies sent the ship spinning sickeningly, jostling the Hashoones in their harnesses.

"I have been blessed," Tycho heard Mavry say belowdecks, raising his voice above the thud of the guns. "Blessed to be born a Jovian. Blessed to seek my fortune among the stars. And most of all, blessed to serve aboard this ship, and alongside all of you. We are Comets. Thoadbone Mox has no honor, no allegiance—and no idea what a mistake he's made."

"Three cheers for Master Mavry!" the Comets cheered.

"Fifteen hundred klicks," Yana said, then cried out: "Carlo! Down!"

Carlo dipped the *Comet*'s nose, and the frigate dipped under a flurry of black boulders. Tycho could see Daphnis now—a bright hunk of frozen rock, orbiting in the gap in the rings carved out by its gravity.

"This ship is our country," Huff growled belowdecks. "An' I've got a one-way ticket to hell for anyone who dares touch a centimeter of her deck. I ain't afraid to die, boys—because I die *hard*."

"Three cheers for Captain Huff!" came the yells.

"No one strikes the colors," Diocletia ordered. "Tycho, if it comes to it, get the carbines from the equipment locker. You'll defend the aft ladderwell."

"Aye-aye," Tycho forced himself to say.

"Coming up on the Keeler Gap," Carlo said. "Hang on."

"Incoming audio message on all channels," Vesuvia said.

"Put it on," Diocletia said, grimacing as Carlo pumped the throttle, searching for speed that the battered *Comet* couldn't give him.

"This is Hodge Lazander, addressing all officers of the

Jovian Union," said a calm voice. "By mutual agreement with Admiral Badawi, we are suspending combat operations. Cease hostile action and no harm shall come to you."

"Mr. Grigsby, stop firing!" Diocletia yelled. "Carlo, keep going!"

The *Comet* shot out of the maelstrom of debris into the Keeler Gap—but Mox was right behind them, the *Geryon* now so close that the scanner showed just a tiny sliver of space between the red dot of the pocket cruiser and the green one of the *Comet*.

"Captain Mox, suspend your pursuit," Lazander ordered.

"I got a score to settle with this one first," Mox spit.

"That's an order, Mox," Lazander said.

"NO!"

Ahead, the frosty surface of Daphnis gleamed in the pale-yellow light of Saturn.

"The magnetism will intensify near the moon," Tycho yelled to his brother. "But then you'll be in the lee and get control back."

"I remember," Carlo said through gritted teeth. "Let's just hope Mox doesn't know about it."

"Mr. Grigsby, all guns forward," Diocletia said into her headset. "We'll have one chance to turn the tables on Mox. But nobody fires unless I give the order."

Daphnis loomed ahead. Then the shepherd moon's magnetic field seized the *Comet*, sending her scopes spinning wildly. Carlo yanked on the control yokes, the muscles in his forearms bulging. Shuddering, the *Comet* rolled over to port—once, twice, then three times—and the mottled, pitted surface of Daphnis flashed by the viewscreen, so close that Tycho could see shadows at the bottom of its craters.

"Come on!" Diocletia yelled, bringing one fist down on her console.

Then the ship was floating in the calm zone of the lee.

"I've got control," Carlo said, snapping the *Comet* around so that her bow—and a good percentage of her weapons—pointed at the limb of the moon they'd just cleared.

The *Geryon* tumbled around the curve of Daphnis, hopelessly out of control—and bracketed in the *Comet's* gunsights.

Diocletia lunged forward, eyes wild, one hand on her headset.

"You so much as twitch, Mox, and I'll blow you to atoms."

The *Geryon* shuddered to a halt as her pilot regained control and found his ship separated from the *Shadow Comet* by just a few hundred meters of vacuum—and helpless before the smaller craft's guns.

"Nobody fire!" Diocletia ordered. "Vesuvia, switch to video."

The video screen flickered to life. Mox glowered at them, teeth bared, the telescopic eye rammed into his skull whirring madly. He squinted at Diocletia, mouth working. Then he smiled, the expression swelling slowly until it split his face, like a terrible wound.

"Go ahead then," he said. "You can't take out all my guns—and at this range you'll be destroyed too."

"I'm willing to make that trade," Diocletia said. "Are you?"

Mox stared at Diocletia, who stared back.

"Wait!" Tycho said. "What about his share of the *Iris* cache?"

Diocletia looked back at Tycho, frowning.

"The *Iris*?" Mox demanded. "What are you accursed Hashoones blathering about? That treasure's in the hands of the Securitat!"

"You're wrong," Diocletia said. "My children found it. And we've turned it into a tidy sum at the Bank of Ceres."

"We are not paying off that plug-ugly bilge rat!" Yana objected.

"Shut that brat up!" Mox roared. "I'm entitled to my share of that treasure! You can't bargain with what ain't your property!"

"Any court that would award it to you would also arrest you for murder, piracy, and treason," Diocletia said. "You'll never see that money without us, Thoad-bone. Or, if you prefer, we can all die."

Three bells rang out on the quarterdeck of both the *Comet* and the *Geryon*. Tycho tried to wipe the sweat out of his eyes, then turned at the sound of footsteps behind him. Mavry stepped onto the deck, chrome pistols tucked into his belt. Behind him came Huff, the flesh-and-blood half of his face dark with soot.

"Are you all right, Dad?" Tycho asked.

"For now," Mavry said gravely, gazing over Diocletia's shoulder at Mox, who was screeching abuse. "But we've lost people belowdecks."

"Captain, I have three vessels inbound, following the Keeler Gap," Yana said. "Cruising speed, displaying Saturnian colors."

"So what's it going to be, Thoadbone?" Diocletia asked.

"Only one thing better than being rich," Mox said, leaning forward with his teeth bared. "And that's seeing your enemies die."

"Fire on that vessel and I'll destroy you myself, Mox," said the voice of Hodge Lazander. "*Shadow Comet*, can you prove what you say about the *Iris* cache?"

"We can contact the Bank of Ceres right now," Diocletia said.

"Very well," Lazander said. "Please do."

"Vesuvia?" Diocletia said. "Contact Mr. Hohenfauer at the Bank of Ceres. Tell him Captain Diocletia Hashoone would like to speak with him."

"Initiating transmission," Vesuvia said.

"Lazander!" Mox roared. "What's the meaning of this?"

"The meaning of this, Captain Mox, is that you are relieved of command and stripped of your commission," Lazander said as the two Ice Wolf frigates and a cruiser slowed to a halt behind the *Comet*'s stern.

"For what?" Mox demanded.

"Where to start? Dereliction of duty in launching your unauthorized operation at Europa, for one thing. To which we can now add disobeying repeated orders from a superior officer. I gave you every chance, Mox, but it's clear your only allegiance is to money—of which you owe us a considerable amount."

"Me? Owe you money?"

"For the ship you now no longer command," Lazander said. "For the crews you used for your own selfish purposes. For fuel, and expenses, and so much else. I intend to collect that money, after which our relationship will be at an end. First Mate Southard, lock down Captain Mox's console, please. You are in command now."

"Yes, sir," said a pale, bearded man over Mox's shoulder, looking more than a little unhappy.

"You useless snake! You *politician*!" Mox roared. "You stole my property! Without that there would have been no victory today. You're a thief! A double-dealing thief!"

"You will be compensated for your contributions," Lazander said.

"And after our business with Mox is concluded, what of us?" Diocletia asked Lazander.

"I give you my word that you will be accorded safe passage."

"Bank of Ceres is receiving transmission," Vesuvia said.

"Onscreen," Diocletia said.

Chimes sounded over the *Comet*'s speakers, followed by the sound of someone scrabbling at a communicator's controls. Vesuvia divided the main screen in two: Mox on the left, the Bank of Ceres's logo on the right.

"Bank of Ceres, Mr. Hohenfauer speaking." The teller appeared onscreen, eyes wide.

"Good afternoon, Mr. Hohenfauer," said Diocletia. It took a couple of seconds for the transmission to make its way to distant Ceres and back.

"Captain Hashoone," Hohenfauer said, face turning hard. "You lied to me—you're no friend of Sir Armistead-Kabila's."

"I did lie to you, Mr. Hohenfauer. Poor customer service makes a woman do crazy things. But I'm not here to talk about the past."

"We have nothing to talk about whatsoever, Captain Hashoone," Hohenfauer said.

"The balance in my family's account would indicate otherwise. Don't waste my time pretending it won't. I am authorizing a transfer of 1.68 million livres from that account to Captain Mox here. He'll be in your records as Thaddeus Moxley."

"My name is Thoadbone!" roared Mox.

"Antifraud systems verify that the man onscreen is Thaddeus Moxley," Hohenfauer said.

"THOADBONE!" Mox screeched.

"But this is highly irregular, Captain Hashoone," Hohenfauer said. "Transfers of this size between personal accounts are approved only in person. I won't authorize a remote transfer, no matter how big your balance is.

And don't try to threaten me with tall tales about Sir Armistead-Kabila either, since we both know you can't back them up."

Diocletia glanced back at the ladderwell.

"Dad, come up here for a moment?"

Huff clanked slowly across the quarterdeck until he stood by the captain's chair, glaring at the viewscreen.

"I believe you've met my father," Diocletia said.

Hohenfauer stared at the half-metal pirate, his eyes jumping from Huff's blazing artificial eye and blackened face to his pistols and cutlass. One hand went reflexively to his throat.

"Have to be there in person, eh?" Huff rumbled. "Jus' how personal do you want it? I don't know this Armistead-Kabila either. But I do know you, Hohenfauer. I know where you work. An' I can find out where you live."

"I suppose I could allow a one-time exception to our policies," Hohenfauer stammered.

"That's the spirit," Diocletia said. "You'll be employee of the month before you know it."

"An' this way, you get to stay alive," Huff said.

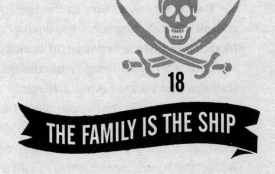

18

THE FAMILY IS THE SHIP

Attached to her long-range tanks once more, the battered *Comet* limped in the direction of Jupiter. Before she was an hour out of Saturn, the life-support systems had been restored and the damaged linkages to the engines reknit. Far more was needed— the ugly rents and melted gunports in her portside would remain isolated by bulkheads until she reached dry dock, and the damage to her propulsion systems had robbed her of much of her speed. And nothing could replace the nine retainers and crewers who had died in battle. But little by little over that first day, the ship came to feel like her old self again.

Tycho found those hours oddly comforting—all of the Hashoones were busy in the fire room and at their consoles, prioritizing repairs and performing diagnostics to check that those repairs had been successful. It was dull, but it let them delay facing the questions he knew they couldn't escape for much longer.

With the major repairs complete, Diocletia called for a meeting. Fortifying themselves with tea and coffee and a carton of jump-pop Yana had squirreled away somewhere, the Hashoones sat quietly at their consoles on the quarterdeck, waiting to hear what their captain would say.

"The important thing, to state the obvious, is that we're alive," Diocletia said, leaning on the back of the captain's chair. "We've lost people, but you kept your heads when a poor decision might have meant the end of all our lives. And that's more important than the Log, our letter of marque, or anything else."

"And what's going to happen to our letter of marque?" Yana asked. "I can't imagine the Jovian Union will be pleased when they find out how we bought our freedom."

Diocletia looked evenly at her daughter, refusing to take the bait.

"We settled a financial matter between associates in a legal business venture. Besides, I suspect the Jovian Union will be more concerned with having sent an incompetent admiral into the field, one who lost two destroyers and a privateer in a battle he was warned not to fight."

"Arrr, Badawi will be lucky if his next command is the Ganymede ferry," Huff said from his usual spot alongside the ladder.

"And what about the Ice Wolves?" Yana asked. "We didn't exactly put an end to their rebellion."

"No, we didn't," Diocletia said. "There will be a great deal of talk about that, I'm sure. And about other things as well. Apparently the Jovian Defense Force located six of Earth's secret automated deep-space listening posts while we were away. They destroyed them all. His Majesty is calling it an unwarranted provocation."

The data disk, Tycho thought. *That was the information the Securitat wanted.*

"So we're at war on two fronts?" Carlo asked.

"I wouldn't go that far. But clearly matters are worse."

"So what are we going to do?" Tycho said.

Diocletia sighed. "Well, for starters, we'll get Vesuvia's data to the Defense Force so they can figure out a better way to counteract Mox's jammer."

"About that . . . ," Yana muttered, so quietly that Tycho could barely hear her.

"About what?" Diocletia asked.

"The jamming. There's something you need to know, since you'll find out eventually."

"Is that how you decide whether or not to tell me things?" Diocletia asked.

"No . . . I mean . . . just listen, okay? I took a closer

look at my board, and my countermeasures didn't do anything. The jamming just stopped."

"What do you mean it just stopped?"

"Two minutes and thirty-seven seconds in, it stopped. So I took another look at what happened back at P/2. It was the same thing—two minutes and thirty-seven seconds of jamming, then it cleared. It had nothing to do with the PKB band or harmonic oscillations or anything else. And it had nothing to do with me."

"But that doesn't make any sense," Tycho said. "We know the jammer kept working, because the other Jovian ships were still blind."

"That's what I'm telling you," Yana said. "Some system aboard the *Comet* broke the jamming on its own."

"Vesuvia," said Diocletia, "does this make any sense? Can you analyze what Yana's talking about?"

"No analysis is necessary. The statement is correct. The countermeasures suite referenced takes one hundred fifty-seven seconds to initialize and activate."

"What countermeasures suite?" Diocletia asked, baffled.

"The one installed to counteract the technology deployed at Refueling Station Gamma earlier today."

"I've never heard of any such program. How long has it existed?"

"The program has resided in memory since September 8, 2883."

Tycho and Yana looked at each other, eyes wide.

"That's a little over a year after 624 Hektor," Yana said.

"I never loaded such a program," Diocletia said. "Who did? And on whose authority?"

And then, one by one, their eyes turned to Huff.

"Arrr," Huff said. "I did it. And on me own authority."

Diocletia looked at her father in disbelief.

"I hired someone to do the work an' loaded the program after I recovered. Did it to protect us after what happened that day."

"I was captain then, not you," Diocletia said icily. "What else have you done to my ship while no one was looking?"

"Nothin'. Nothin' 'cept that one thing, a long time ago. Which was the thing what saved our lives today."

Diocletia looked equal parts amazed and furious. "And are you going to tell me why?"

Huff raised his chin defiantly. "That's me own business. An' it'll stay that way."

And before anyone could say anything else, he turned his back and clambered up the ladder to the top deck.

"Well," Diocletia said, "that's all, then."

Tycho looked from Yana to Carlo.

"I'm sorry, Mom, but it isn't," he said. "It can't be."

"And why is that?" Diocletia asked.

The words felt like he was forcing them to his lips.

"Oshima Yakata told us Huff helped Mox distribute the program to the Jupiter pirates—the one that had been sabotaged," he said.

"Yes," Diocletia said. "He was tricked. Tricked and betrayed."

"We never knew that," Yana said. "It was our right to know that."

"Don't ask me to defend your grandfather right now."

"Nobody's asking you to," Carlo said, his face red with anger.

Diocletia shook her head.

"Maybe you deserved to know," she said. "But what does it change? Your grandfather will carry what happened that day for the rest of his life. Do you imagine he doesn't think about it during the hours he's trapped in his cabin every day? Sometimes I wonder if he thinks of anything else."

"Then why didn't he tell us?" Yana asked. "Why didn't one of you?"

Diocletia swiveled in her chair and stared out into the darkness beyond the viewports.

"Because he can barely stand to remember it," she said quietly. "Because of the guilt he feels—about having been fooled by Thoadbone Mox, about getting people killed, about having contributed to the end of the only way of life he'd ever known. Since that day, he's lived mainly for the three of you—watching you grow and learn and carry on the tradition he fears will be lost without you. If you'd known what he'd done . . . well, I don't think he could bear the idea of that."

All were quiet for a long moment. Mavry stared down at his hands in his lap.

"And what happened before 624 Hektor?" Tycho asked. "Oshima—"

"That witch again," Diocletia said, turning to glare at Mavry.

Tycho bit his lip, then pressed on. "She said you and Dad were going to join the Gibraltars—to break up the family. Is that true?"

Diocletia seemed to sag in the captain's chair.

"That's our own business."

"Grandpa just said something like that," Yana said.

"This is different—"

"Dio," Mavry said quietly, "they deserve to know this, too."

Diocletia scrubbed at her eyes with her hand.

"You tell them, then."

"No," Mavry said gently. "You're the captain."

Diocletia raised her eyes and looked at her husband, then away. Finally she nodded.

"Very well. Your grandfather always saw Carina as the perfect pirate—while I . . . well, let's just say I never met his standards. It was obvious from the day I made middie that Carina would be the next captain, and there was nothing I could do to change his mind. Not even Carina defying him and running off with Sims made a difference. He was so angry—he called Carina a traitor and accused Cassius Gibraltar of scheming to take over his ship. But he still wouldn't deny her, or consider me. Rather than accept me as captain, he was willing to see the son of his archrival on his own quarterdeck."

Diocletia looked up at the deck above their heads.

"So your father and I decided that rather than spend

the rest of our lives as dirtsiders on Callisto, we'd find another way. When we went to see him, Cassius was even madder at Sims than Dad was at Carina. But he agreed to our proposal—Sims would marry Carina and serve aboard the *Comet*, while your father and I would become part of Cassius's crew aboard the *Ghostlight*."

"But the family is the captain," Tycho said. "And—"

"And the captain is the ship, and the ship is the family," Diocletia said. "I was taught that as a child too, you know. Just like Dad, and every Hashoone back to Lodovico. But things change. You've learned that by now."

"But then why did you still teach it to us, Mom? Since you no longer believed it yourself."

"Because I still *wanted* to believe it. Because I wanted to believe I was the exception, that I was the one who'd failed to make it work."

"But it *has* worked," Yana said. "What you taught us was true. Our family didn't break apart. I mean, just look around. The family *is* the ship. It's as true as it's ever been."

"Our family didn't break apart, true," Diocletia said. "Because something terrible happened that forced us to stay together."

She sighed.

"On some level, your grandfather's never forgiven your father and me for what we tried to do then—just like I fear two of you will refuse to forgive the one who becomes captain. And maybe that's just the way it is.

But sometimes I think that tradition no longer makes sense and needs to change—just like a lot of things are changing."

It was Carlo who spoke first.

"I think our family tradition has sustained us for centuries for a reason," he said. "Maybe 624 Hektor was a blessing in disguise."

"That's quite a disguise," Mavry said sharply.

"I know. But if you'd carried out your plan, you and Mom would be Gibraltars, and our family would have been weakened."

"I don't think your aunt would see it that way," Mavry said.

"You're wrong as usual, Carlo," Yana said. "Mom and Dad would have flown with the Gibraltars, yes, but one of them would have succeeded Cassius. There'd be two Hashoone pirate ships now. We'd be stronger, not weaker."

"The Jovian Union would never have allowed that," Mavry said. "Not then, not now, not ever."

"You might be surprised," Tycho said, thinking of the title to the *Hydra* and how it would soon be in his family's possession. A lot had gone wrong recently, but they had survived. And now, perhaps, they even had a way forward—a way for him and his siblings to all keep flying.

"After today, I don't care what the Jovian Union will or won't allow," Yana said.

"And what happens when two Hashoones chase the

same prize?" Carlo asked.

"We'll do the right thing," Yana said.

"In my experience, that's not a value particularly prized by pirates," Mavry said.

"But we're not pirates anymore," Tycho said. "Which is exactly why we *should* do the right thing."

The others looked at him.

"In fact, we can start today—with the fact that Johannes Hashoone murdered Josef Unger and stole the *Iris* cache from him."

"You already told us what you and Mom discovered," Yana said. "It was a long time ago, Tyke. It's over."

"It's *not* over. Because Johannes didn't just kill Josef. He destroyed Josef's son's life too. And that ruined his grandson's life. But we can break that chain—if we do the right thing. And that starts with giving Loris his share."

"Not this again, Tyke," Yana said. "We already took it from him, fair and square."

"You know that isn't true," Tycho said. "Loris isn't one of us—he isn't a privateer, or a freight hauler, or anyone else who knows our rules. And he doesn't have tons of livres like Lord Sicyon does. We had the advantage over him, like Father Amoss said, and we used it to cheat him."

The twins glared at each other.

"Seems like every time you talk about the *Iris* cache our share gets smaller, son," Mavry said. "Maybe Yana was right and you should have let go of it under Callisto."

But his father was smiling as he said it.

"Give Loris his share," Diocletia said, sighing. "I'll answer for my latest deplorable attack of conscience. There'll still be enough to repair the *Comet*, and give us a stake for more cruises. Because we're finished with military missions. Last time the Jovian Union stole the *Hydra* from us. This time they abandoned us to Mox and his thugs. There won't be a next time. I promise you that much."

"And if they take our letter of marque?" Yana asked.

"Then we'll figure out something else," Diocletia said. "And we'll do it as a family."

19

AT SAINT MARY'S

This time, it was DeWise who contacted Tycho.

The message arrived an hour after Carlo eased the *Shadow Comet* into dry dock above Callisto. Tycho saw the message light on his mediapad while he and Yana were mustering out the Comets. He knew immediately who it was from.

"What are you smiling about?" Yana demanded.

"Just glad to be home," Tycho said.

After they reached Darklands, Tycho messaged

DeWise that he'd meet him in the morning, at the same Port Town café they'd used last time. Then, while the other Hashoones unpacked, he slipped down the steps from the homestead's lower level to the gloomy confines of the family crypt.

None of Tycho's ancestors was actually buried there—as spacers, the Hashoones found the idea of being entombed in the ground appalling. The crypt was for memories, not bodies.

A pale-green square in the darkness marked the controls for the main holographic unit. Tycho peered down at the softly lit screen until he found the name he wanted.

A moment later, a blue light filled the crypt, and Tycho stepped back to look up at a shimmering holo-gram of a man in slightly outdated clothing. Johannes Hashoone had a bald head, a sharp nose, and a slight grin that suggested he had thought of a joke that he might or might not share with the listener.

"Hello, Great-Grandfather," Tycho said. For a moment he felt foolish, talking to a dead pirate, but then he found his voice again.

"I found your treasure," he said. "Just like I figured out what you did. You murdered Josef Unger, a man who considered you his friend. You cheated your associates. And you didn't even use the money you stole—you hid it away and tried to make sure your own family would never find it. You know, Grandfather once told me you taught him everything he knows about pirating. Which means he passed that knowledge down to my mother. And she passed it down to me."

Johannes's mocking smile remained frozen in place.

"But I'm not like you, Great-Grandfather," Tycho said, suddenly shaking with anger. "And when I'm captain, I'll make sure no Hashoone is ever like you again."

Tycho stabbed at the buttons on the control unit, turned, and marched up the stairs leading out of the crypt. Behind him, the image of Johannes Hashoone flickered, lingered for a stubborn second, and then faded away.

The next morning, DeWise had a jump-pop and a nutrient square waiting on the table at the café when Tycho arrived. Tycho wondered if it was a peace offering, but the sight of DeWise's face made him think of Admiral Badawi, and the call for help that had been ignored, and everything else, and by the time he reached the table he was seething.

"We got torn up out there, you know," Tycho said, before he even sat down.

"I know you did," DeWise said. "Everybody knows. We told the JDF not to send Badawi, but they didn't listen."

"Please tell me he'll get sacked."

DeWise sighed. "He'll probably get promoted. The JDF kept imagining how impressive he'd sound making a victory speech with Earth's ministers watching. They didn't understand that we needed more skills out there than how to groom a mustache. We needed capabilities like your family's, frankly—crews that can fight, pilots that can fly, and officers who know when it's wise to do one and not the other."

"Too bad we're done fighting for you, then," Tycho said. "And anyway, what good could we do against Earth? I read about the spy stations. But I suppose you wouldn't know anything about that."

"Not officially."

"Of course not," Tycho said, disgusted. "And now I want to know something."

"Oh? Are we trading information again?"

"No," Tycho said. "This time you're just going to tell me what I want to know. It's about 624 Hektor."

"That's ancient history."

"Not to me. And not to my family."

DeWise crossed his arms. "And what do you want to know?"

"The Martian convoy that the Jupiter pirates attacked—it was carrying experimental jammers. Your . . . *employer* gave the pirates software programs that were supposed to defend against the jamming. Did my grandfather and Mox distribute them to the captains?"

"That's the story I've heard—that he was recruited by Mox."

"And the story that the program had been tampered with by Earth saboteurs? Is that one true?"

"That was a terrible day for the people I work for too,

you know," DeWise said. "Just what are you suggesting, Tycho?"

Tycho realized his fingers were mashing the nutrient square. Annoyed, he brushed them off on the leg of his jumpsuit.

"Forget it," he said. "You know what? I'm looking forward to not having to worry about you and your little games anymore."

DeWise raised an eyebrow.

"So this is good-bye, then?"

"More like good riddance. I only came to find out when we get the title to the *Hydra*."

"Ah. That."

Tycho knew instantly. He felt himself go cold.

"It can't be done, Tycho. Not after Saturn. If things go badly, we'll need every warship we can outfit with a crew."

"How many lies have you told in your life?" Tycho asked. "I'll make it easier for you—just round down to the nearest million."

"Quite a few, Tycho—though not that many. Would you believe me if I said what I told you about the *Hydra* wasn't one of them?"

"No. I don't believe a single word you say. And nobody else should either. I only wish I'd been smart enough to figure that out at the beginning."

He got to his feet, hands shaking with anger.

"We're finished, you and me. I'll find my own answers."

"I'm sure you will," DeWise said. "Just remember that can be dangerous."

Tycho started to say something but stopped at the fleeting look that crossed the Securitat agent's face—for a moment, before he became carefully expressionless again, DeWise almost looked sad.

"Every heart, Tycho, has places that are secret and doors that are shut," he said. "Think long and hard before you start opening them. They can prove difficult to close."

Tycho, still upset, got off at the wrong level for Saint Mary Star of the Spaceways, then had to retrace his steps through the chilly lower levels of Port Town.

"Come in," Father Amoss said when he met him at the door. "It's cold."

He led Tycho to his small office off the sacristy and poured him a cup of hot chocolate.

"Thank you, Father," Tycho said. "I came to talk to you about Loris. This won't be easy for me, but please give me a chance to try to say it."

Father Amoss nodded. "Go ahead, Tycho."

Tycho swallowed, then plunged ahead.

"I thought a lot about what you said, last time we were here. I've thought a lot about a bunch of things recently. We were wrong, Father—wrong to treat Loris the way we did. I tried to convince myself it was my sister and brother who were wrong, but it was me, too. I was there, just like they were, and I didn't speak up."

Tycho looked at the floor.

"We were wrong—but it's worse than that," he said. "Long ago, Father, my family did a terrible thing to Loris's. I didn't know about it when we met him, I swear I didn't. And I don't know how to fix it. I don't even know if I can fix it. But I want to try. I *need* to try. So would you tell me where he is, please?"

Father Amoss was silent for a moment. Then he put his hand on Tycho's shoulder.

"I'm sorry to be the one to tell you. But Loris died three days ago."

"Dead?" Tycho lifted his eyes and stared at the priest, stunned. "What happened?"

"A lot of things. A lot of things that had borne down on him over the years. But he was at peace at the end."

"He was at peace? What does that matter? What's a few minutes of peace worth, after a lifetime like that?"

"It's worth everything. He's at rest now, and his soul is in the hands of God."

Tycho looked away, trying to think. He had dared to imagine this morning so differently. Father Amoss would hear his admission and agree to let him help with Loris, healing the wounds his great-grandfather had inflicted on the Ungers. And then he'd return to Darklands, knowing that soon his family would get the message from the Jovian Union, telling them they now owned the *Hydra*. Things would be different—the past confronted, and the future rich with possibilities.

And now all of that was gone.

He looked back at Father Amoss and felt his cheeks flush. Loris Unger had died in the frozen tunnels of Port Town, and he'd reacted by feeling sorry for himself.

Father Amoss leaned forward.

"Tycho, listen to me," he said. "You're not responsible for the acts of those who came before you. Life will give you burdens enough of your own. You only need to answer for your own acts—which you've done today."

"But none of that will help Loris."

"No, it won't," Father Amoss said. "The past is for the Almighty to judge. It's the future that's your responsibility, Tycho."

Tycho nodded, then peered into the dim sacristy, at the cots and duffels, the stacked dishes and folded clothes.

"The other men who live here, Father—who are they?"

"Every man's story is different. But what unites them is misfortune. They lost their way somehow, through the misdeeds of others or their own weakness or simple bad luck."

Tycho reached into his jumpsuit and pulled out the currency chip that contained Loris Unger's share of the *Iris* cache. He pressed it into Father Amoss's palm.

"Please take this," Tycho said. "It was for Loris, but use it to look after them instead."

Father Amoss nodded and tucked the chip into a pocket of his cassock. He walked to the door with Tycho, then remained there as Tycho zipped his parka and picked his way around the puddles in the dim hallway.

At the corner, Tycho turned and saw the priest standing in the warm yellow light spilling from the doorway of Saint Mary's.

Father Amoss lifted his hand in farewell, and Tycho raised his own. Then he turned and waited for the elevator that would take him back to the upper levels and the grav-sled that would carry him across the frozen wastes of Callisto to Darklands, where his family was waiting.

A SPACER'S LEXICON

A

abaft. To the rear of.

able spacer. The most experienced class of crewer aboard a starship. Able spacers are more experienced than ordinary spacers, while crewers with too little experience to be considered ordinary spacers are called dirtsiders.

admiralty court. A court concerned with the laws of space, including the taking of prizes. The Jovian Union maintains several admiralty courts in the Jupiter system and abides by the decisions of the admiralty court on the neutral minor planet Ceres, with privateers and warships expected to report to the admiralty court with jurisdiction over the area of space where a prize is taken.

aft. Toward the rear of a starship; the opposite of fore.

air scrubber. A collection of filters and pumps that remove carbon dioxide and impurities from the air aboard a starship, keeping it healthy and (relatively) clean.

amidships. In the middle of a starship.

armorer. A crewer in charge of a starship's hand weapons. Most crewers on privateers and pirate ships carry their own arms.

arrrr. Originally an acknowledgment of an order ("yar"), it has become a nonspecific pirate outburst, adaptable to any situation. The more Rs, the greater the intensity of feeling.

articles. A written agreement drawn up for each cruise, setting out rules and the division of any prize money and signed by all hands aboard a privateer or pirate ship.

articles of war. The body of space law governing hostilities between spacegoing nations and their starships.

avast. Stop!

aviso. A small, speedy starship used for carrying messages across space.

aye-aye. An acknowledgment of an order.

B

bandit. An enemy starship, typically a small, maneuverable one that's likely to attack you.

bandolier. A belt slung over an arm or across the chest that holds carbines, ammunition pouches, and other nasty things.

barky. An affectionate nickname for one's own starship.

beam. The side of a ship, always identified as port or starboard.

beat to quarters. A summons to battle stations, in ancient times accomplished by beating out a rhythm on a drum, in modern times achieved by playing a recording.

belay. A ranking officer's order countermanding a just-issued order.

belowdecks. The deck of a starship below the bridge or quarterdeck, generally reserved for spacers and officers who aren't members of the bridge crew. "Belowdecks" also refers collectively to these spacers.

berth. A sleeping place aboard a starship.

bilge. In ancient seagoing ships, the lowest part of a hull, which filled with foul water also called bilge. In modern parlance, anything foul or nonsensical.

blacklist. A list of spacers to be punished for failure to properly perform their duties or for other breaches of discipline.

blackstrap. Cheap, sweet wine bought in ports.

black transponder. A transponder that identifies a starship as belonging to a pirate captain or, more commonly, transmits a blank identification.

blaster. A pistol or other handheld cannon.

boarding action. The invasion of a starship with marines or crewers.

boarding party. A group of marines or crewers whose job it is to board and take control of a starship.

bogey. A starship that has been seen on scopes but not yet identified.

bosun. A crewer whose duties include daily ship inspections. The bosun reports to the chief warrant officer.

bow. The front of a starship.

bow chaser. A gun located at a starship's bow, designed for firing at ships being pursued.

bridge. A starship's command center, generally called the quarterdeck on warships, privateers, and pirate ships. On the *Shadow Comet*, the quarterdeck is the middle deck and is reserved for the bridge crew.

bridge crew. The officers who serve aboard the quarterdeck or bridge. On many privateers, the bridge crew is limited to the family that owns the ship or their close associates.

bridle port. A port in a ship's bow through which the bow chasers extend.

brig. A room used as a jail aboard a starship.

broadside. A volley of shots aimed at the side of an enemy ship and delivered at close range.

bulk freighter. A large merchant ship, typically corporate owned.

bulkhead. A vertical partition dividing parts of a starship. In the event of a breach, bulkheads seal to isolate damage and prevent the atmosphere from escaping.

buoy. A marker defining a spacelane. In the modern age, buoys send electronic signals to starships and maintain their positions through small, efficient engines.

burdened vessel. A starship that doesn't have the right-of-way; not the privileged vessel.

burgoo. A gruel made from shipboard rations, not particularly liked by crewers.

C

cabin. An enclosed room on a starship. Generally refers to an officer's personal quarters.

cannon. A general term for a starship's hull-mounted weapons. Cannons can fire laser beams or missiles and are designed for different intensities of fire and ranges.

captain. The commander of a starship. Traditionally, a former captain is still addressed as Captain.

carbine. A pistol.

cargo. Goods carried by a merchant starship.

cargo hauler. A no-frills class of freighter, typically corporate owned.

carronade. A powerful short-range projectile cannon used in combat.

cartel ship. A starship transporting prisoners to an agreed-upon port. Cartel ships are exempt from capture or recapture while on their voyages, provided they don't engage in commerce or warlike acts.

cashier. To discharge a crewer.

caulk. Thick rubber used to plug holes and seams in a starship's hull.

centaur. A celestial body with an unstable orbit and a lifetime of several million years, with characteristics of both asteroids and comets.

chaff. Scraps of metal released by a starship to confuse the sensors of an enemy ship or guided missile.

chamade. A signal requesting a cessation of hostilities and negotiations.

chandler. A merchant who sells goods to starships in port.

cheroot. A cheap, often smelly cigar.

chronometer. A timepiece.

coaster. A starship that operates close to a planet or within a system of moons, as opposed to starships that make interplanetary voyages.

cold pack. Flexible packet kept cold and used to numb minor injuries.

condemn. To seize a ship for auction or sale under prize law.

container ship. A large merchant ship that typically carries cheap bulk goods.

convoy. A group of merchant ships traveling together for mutual protection, often with armed starships as escorts.

corvette. A small, fast, lightly armed warship.

crewer. A member of a starship's crew; the equivalent of sailors on ancient ships. "Crewer" technically refers to all members of a starship's crew, but members of the bridge crew are rarely if ever called crewers.

crimp. A person who captures spacers in port and sells them to starships as crewers, usually by working with a press gang. Navy officers who lead authorized press gangs are never called crimps—at least, not to their faces.

crowdy. A thick porridge. More edible than burgoo, but not by much.

cruise. A starship's voyage.

cruiser. A fast, heavily armed warship.

cuddy. A cabin in which officers gather to eat their meals.

cutter. A scout ship.

D

dead lights. Eyes.

derelict. Cargo left behind after a shipwreck with no expectation of recovery. Any claimant may legally salvage derelict.

destroyer. A small warship with the speed to hunt down small, nimble attackers.

dirtside. A spacer's term for being off one's ship on a planet or moon. Said with faint derision and distress.

dirtsider. A spacer with minimal training and experience, limited to simple tasks aboard a starship. A hardworking dirtsider may eventually be rated as an ordinary spacer.

dog watch. Either of the two short watches between 1600 and 2000. At two hours, a dog watch is half the duration of a normal watch.

down the ladder. Tradition in which a midshipman spends a year or more belowdecks, learning the spacer's trade from an experienced crewer.

dreadnought. A large, well-armed, but slow warship.

dromond. A very large merchant ship, often one that carries expensive goods.

dry dock. A facility where starships are taken out of service for substantial repairs or refitting.

duff. A kind of pudding served as a treat aboard starships.

E

engineer. The crewer or officer responsible for keeping a starship operating properly.

engine room. The control room for a starship's engines. Sometimes the same as the fire room.

ensign. A flag indicating a starship's allegiance.

escort. A starship providing protection for another vessel, typically one that is unarmed.

F

fanlight. A portal over the door of an officer's cabin, providing light and air while maintaining privacy.

fenders. Bumpers on the sides of a starship, used to protect against damage in crowded shipyards, on landing fields, or in parking orbits.

fire room. The control room for a starship's reactor. Sometimes the same as the engine room.

fireship. A starship loaded with munitions and exploded among enemy ships to damage them.

first mate. A starship's second-in-command.

flagship. The starship commanded by the ranking officer in a task force or fleet.

flip. A strong beer favored by crewers.

flotsam. Debris and objects left floating in space after a starship is damaged or destroyed.

flummery. A shipboard dessert.

fore. Toward the front of a starship; the opposite of aft.

forefoot. The foremost part of a starship's lower hull.

freighter. A general term for a merchant vessel.

frigate. A fast warship used for scouting and intercepts, well armed but relying more on speed than weapons. The *Shadow Comet*, the *Ironhawk*, and the *Hydra* are heavily modified frigates.

G

galleon. A large merchant ship, particularly one that carries expensive cargoes.

galley. The kitchen on a starship.

gangway. The ramp leading into a ship, lowered when a ship is on a landing field.

gibbet. A post with a protruding arm from which criminals sentenced to death are hanged.

gig. A small, unarmed ship used for short trips between nearby moons or between ports and starships in orbit. An armed gig is generally called a launch.

grav-sled. A small wheeled vehicle used for trips on the surface of a minor planet, moon, or asteroid. Not a luxurious ride.

green. When referring to a system or process, an indication that all is ready or working normally.

gripe. A malfunction or problem with a system aboard a starship.

grog. A mix of alcohol and water, beloved by starship crewers. Also refers to alcoholic drinks imbibed in port, which shouldn't be mixed with water but often are.

gunboat. A small but heavily armed warship. Often found patrolling ports or spacelanes.

H

hail. An opening communication from one party to another.

hammock. A length of canvas or netting strung between beams below-decks, in which crewers sleep.

hand. A crewer. Use generally limited to discussions of "all hands."

hang a leg. Do something too slowly.

hardtack. Bland starship rations that don't spoil over long cruises but aren't particularly tasty. Unlike in ancient times, hardtack is rarely actually hard.

hatchway. An opening in a ship's hull for transferring cargo to and from the hold.

head. A bathroom aboard a starship.

heading. A starship's current course.

head money. A reward for prisoners recovered.

heave to. A command for a starship to stop its motion.

heel. To lean to one side.

helm. Originally the controls for piloting a starship, but now generally a term indicating an officer is in command of a starship.

HMS. His (or Her, depending on who is the monarch) Majesty's Ship, a prefix for a warship from Earth.

hold. The area of a starship in which cargo is held. Hatchways or bay doors generally open to allow direct access to the hold.

hominy. Ground corn boiled with milk.

hoy. A small merchant coaster.

I

idler. A crewer who isn't required to keep night watches.

impression. Forced service aboard a starship during wartime.

in a clove hitch. Dealing with a dilemma.

in extremis. Unable to maneuver safely due to malfunction, damage, or some other condition. Privileged vessels must yield the right-of-way to starships in extremis.

in ordinary. Out of commission; said of a starship. Also applies to the crew of a starship while she is laid up in ordinary.

in soundings. Sufficiently close to a celestial body that its gravity must be taken into account during maneuvers.

intercept. The process of examining a starship for possible boarding, often followed by a boarding action.

interrogatories. Reports prepared about an intercept and boarding action, detailing events with evidence from the ships' records. Interrogatories are submitted as part of a claim in admiralty court.

invalid. A spacer on the sick list because of illness or injury.

J

jetsam. Objects jettisoned from a starship in distress.

job captain. A captain given temporary command of a starship while the regular captain is away or indisposed.

jolly boat. A small craft used for inspections or repairs of starships in orbit.

jump-pop. A sugary, caffeinated drink loved by children and crewers alike. Bad for you.

Jupiter Trojans. Two groups of asteroids that share an orbit with Jupiter, lying ahead of and behind the giant planet in its orbit. The group ahead of Jupiter is called the Greek node, while the trailing group is called the Trojan node. That naming convention developed after individual asteroids were named, resulting in an asteroid named after a Greek hero (617 Patroclus) residing in the Trojan camp, and an asteroid named after a Trojan hero (624 Hektor) residing in the Greek camp.

K

keel. A long girder laid down between a starship's bow and stern, giving her structural integrity.

keelhaul. To abuse someone. Derived from the ancient practice of hauling a disobedient sailor under a ship's keel.

keep the matter dark. Keep something confidential.

ketch. A short-range merchant starship.

kip. A cheap lodging house in a port.

klick. A kilometer.

L

ladderwell. A ladder connecting decks on a starship.

lagan. Cargo left behind after a shipwreck and marked by a buoy for reclamation. Lagan can be legally salvaged under certain conditions.

LaGrange point. A stable point in space where the gravitational interaction of various large bodies allows a small body to remain at rest. Space stations, roadsteads, and clumps of asteroids are often built or found at planets' LaGrange points.

landing field. An area of a port where starships land. Typically, only small starships actually use landing fields, with larger vessels remaining in orbit.

larder. A room aboard a starship in which provisions are stored.

lash up and stow. A command, typically piped, for crewers to roll up their hammocks, clearing space for shipboard operations.

launch. A small, lightly armed craft kept aboard a starship, used for short outings and errands between ships. An unarmed launch is generally called a gig.

lee. An area where magnetism or some other measurable hazard drops to zero or close to it. A term borrowed from ancient ocean sailors.

letter of marque. A document giving a civilian starship the right to seize ships loyal to another nation, an action that otherwise would be considered piracy.

liberty. Permission to leave a ship for a time in port.

lighter. A starship used for ferrying cargo between ships and to and from ships in orbit above a port.

loblolly boy. A surgeon's assistant.

log. A record of a starship's operations.

longboat. A small starship primarily used for provisioning bigger starships.

long nine. A cannon designed to hit targets at very long range.

lumper. A laborer hired to load and unload a merchant ship in orbit or in port.

M

magazine. A section of a starship used for storing missiles and other ordnance.

marine. A soldier aboard a warship who splits his or her duties between gunnery and boarding actions. The term is typically reserved for formal military ships, though it is sometimes extended to soldiers serving for pay to defend merchant starships. Crewers who perform this role aboard civilian ships are never called marines.

mast. A pole attached to a starship's hull to maximize the capabilities of sensors and/or antennae.

master. A member of the bridge crew who is not the captain or first mate. A female crew member holding this rank is sometimes but not always called mistress.

master-at-arms. A crewer responsible for discipline belowdecks. On some ships the warrant officer or bosun serves as the master-at-arms, but wise captains avoid such an arrangement, as many crewers regard it as unfair.

matey. An affectionate word for a shipmate.

mess. Where meals are served belowdecks.

midshipman. A crewer training to be an officer. Midshipmen typically begin as children and spend years as apprentices belowdecks before being appointed to a starship's bridge crew. Low-ranking masters who are new to the bridge crew are often still called midshipmen.

moor. To secure a starship during a period of inactivity, whether in orbit or on a landing field.

musketoon. A pistol with a broad, bell-like muzzle.

"my starship." A declaration of a captain or ranking officer indicating that he or she is assuming command. Command can be assigned through the order "your starship," etc.

O

off soundings. Sufficiently far from a celestial body that its gravity can be ignored during maneuvers.

ordinary spacer. A spacer capable of performing most activities aboard a starship, but not an expert. With work, an ordinary spacer may rate as an able spacer.

ordnance. A starship's offensive weapons and materials, from cannons to missiles.

ore boat. A starship hauling ore, typically owned by a prospector.

P

packet. A small passenger boat that carries mail and personal goods between ports.

parley. A negotiation, often informal, between enemies.

parole. A prisoner's pledge of good behavior while in captivity, or conditions agreed to if released.

pass. A document indicating a starship's allegiance, good for safe-conduct from privateers aligned with a given nation. The validity of a pass is ensured by transmitting the proper recognition code.

passageway. A corridor aboard a starship.

peg. To figure, as in "I didn't peg you for a lawyer/pirate/etc."

performance bond. A financial guarantee that a privateer will abide by the terms of its letter of marque. Fines can be levied against a performance bond by an admiralty court or by the government issuing the letter of marque.

persuader. Slang for a carbine, large knife, or other weapon that can sway the less well-armed participant in a dispute.

pinnace. A small, fast, highly maneuverable ship used for offensive and defensive operations by warships and other starships, and typically operated by either a single pilot or a pilot and a gunner.

pipe. A whistle used by the bosun to issue orders to a crew. Any spacer quickly learns to identify the unique tune for each order.

pirate. A civilian starship (or crewer aboard such a starship) that seizes or attacks other ships without authorization from a government. Piracy is punishable by death. A civilian ship with authorization for such seizures or attacks is a privateer.

pitch. A starship moving up or down through the horizontal axis. Sometimes an involuntary motion if a starship is damaged, malfunctioning, or being piloted poorly.

port. The left side of a ship, if a crewer is looking toward the bow from the stern. A starship's port hull is marked by red lights. Also, a planet, moon, or asteroid where a starship crew takes on supplies, offloads cargo, or has other business.

porthole. A small, generally round window in the hull of a starship.

press gang. A group of spacers that prowls ports, looking for men or women to impress into the navy, merchant marine, or crew of a starship. Press gangs are now rare in most ports.

privateer. A civilian starship authorized to take offensive action against another nation, typically by seizing merchant ships belonging to that nation. Unlike pirates, privateers possess a letter of marque, which requires them to abide by the laws of war and all other laws of space.

privileged vessel. A starship that has the right-of-way while navigating.

prize. An enemy vessel, crew, and cargo captured in space by a warship or privateer. The claiming of a prize is declared legal or illegal through a hearing in admiralty court. A legally taken prize is either condemned, and sold to a nation or on its behalf, or released for ransom and allowed to continue on its way. Either way, the proceeds (prize money) are divided among the ship's crew.

prize agent. An agent who sells prizes on behalf of a nation, pocketing a fee for his or her efforts.

prize court. A court that decides claims on captured starships.

prize law. The interplanetary laws governing the taking of prizes.

prize money. The proceeds from the sale of a prize and the ransom of its crew, shared out among the bridge crew and crewers at the end of a cruise.

protection. A certificate attesting that a spacer is a member of a starship's crew. Designed to thwart press gangs, though not always effective in doing so.

purser. A crewer responsible for keeping a starship's financial records and distributing provisions to crewers. Typically a role assigned by the warrant officer to a trusted veteran spacer.

put in irons. To imprison.

Q

quarterdeck. A starship's command center, often known as the bridge on civilian ships. Typically reserved for the officers of the bridge crew.

quittance. A release from a debt.

R

ransom. Money paid to pirates or privateers for the safe return of a ship and/or its crew. Also, money paid to privateers to allow a captured starship to proceed along its course without being taken to prize court for claiming and condemnation.

reactor. The power source of a starship, housed near the engines and heavily armored for protection and to prevent radiation from leaking and poisoning the crew.

recall. An order to return to a starship and prepare for liftoff.

red. In reference to a system or situation, an indication that things are not ready or functioning normally.

rescue. The recapture of a prize by a friendly ship before it can be claimed in prize court and condemned. A rescue restores the starship to her prior owners.

retainer. A crewer whose family has served aboard a starship or for a specific family or shipping company for multiple generations. Many privateers and merchants are crewed in large part by retainers.

right-of-way. An indication that a starship has priority for navigating over other starships in the area. The starship with the right-of-way is the privileged vessel; other starships are burdened vessels.

roadstead. A safe anchorage outside a port or a port's orbit, often at a space station or isolated asteroid.

roll. A starship moving to port or starboard of the horizontal axis while changing its vertical orientation. Sometimes an involuntary motion if a starship is damaged, malfunctioning, or being piloted poorly.

rudder. The device used by the pilot to steer a starship. A physical object in ancient times, but now a series of software commands.

S

salvage. Abandoned or lost cargo (or a starship) that has been legally claimed or been claimed subject to a legal ruling.

scope. A screen showing the result of sensor scans or providing diagnostics about other starship functions.

scow. A dirty, poorly run starship.

scurvy. Originally a disease to which sailors were susceptible; now a term of contempt.

scuttle. To intentionally render a starship or an important system aboard a starship inoperable, so as to deny it to an enemy.

Securitat. The intelligence service of the Jovian Union.

settle one's hash. To subdue or silence someone, often violently.

shindy. A dance favored by boisterous crewers. Also: a good time had by same. A night of hijinks while at liberty in a port would be remembered as "a fine shindy."

ship of the line. A warship big and capable enough to take part in a major battle.

shoals. The area of space near a celestial body, within which particular care must be taken by a pilot. A term borrowed from ancient sailing.

shore leave. Free time in port granted to a starship's crew.

short commons. Thin rations.

sick list. The roster of crew members ill and unable to perform their duties aboard a starship.

silent running. Operating a starship with as few systems engaged as possible in an effort to avoid detection.

slew. A maneuver by which a starship turns around on her own axis.

sloop. A small, fast starship with weapons. Sloops are smaller than corvettes and typically used for interplanetary voyages.

slop book. A register of items given to crewers by the purser. The cost of these items is subtracted from their pay or share of prize money.

soft tack. Bread or cake, a treat during long cruises.

space. To expose someone deliberately to a vacuum, with fatal results.

spacelane. A corridor through space near a planet, a moon, or an asteroid, typically marked by buoys.

spike. To render a cannon inoperable.

squadron. A division of a fleet.

starship. Technically a starship is a spacegoing vessel capable of operating between planets or other distant points in space. In practice, any spacegoing vessel. Starships are called "she" and "her," with the exception of some commercial craft and small starships such as gigs, gunboats, and pinnaces. Military ships serving nations are usually called warships.

starshipwright. A designer or maker of starships.

stand. To hold a course for a destination.

starboard. The right side of a starship, as seen from a crewer at the stern looking toward the bow. The starboard side of a starship is marked by green lights on the hull.

stateroom. The cabin of a starship captain, another high-ranking officer, or an important person on board.

stern. The rear of a starship.

sternboard. A method of turning a starship when the pilot cannot maneuver forward. A real test of a pilot's ability.

stern chaser. A gun mounted at a starship's stern, used for firing at pursuing vessels.

sternpost. A thick beam rising from a starship's keel at the stern and helping to support her engines and reactor.

straggler. A crewer absent from his or her ship.

summat. Something.

supercargo. A crewer in charge of a merchant vessel's cargo. A supercargo is typically not a regular member of the crew, but a representative of the shipping line or starship's owner. Not all merchant vessels have supercargoes aboard.

surgeon. A doctor aboard a starship, whose responsibilities include treating everything from common illnesses to wounds suffered in battle. Such medical care is often rudimentary.

T

tender. A vessel that carries supplies, provisions, and personal deliveries to a warship in port.

ticket. A written document promising payment of wages or other compensation at a later date.

top deck. The uppermost deck of a starship. Often living quarters for the starship's officers and reserved for them.

transom. The aft wall of a ship at her stern. The transom is strong and heavily reinforced, helping to support the engines and often the reactor.

transponder. An electronic system that automatically broadcasts a starship's name, operating number, home port, and nationality. Many civilian ships travel with their transponders disabled, and some broadcast false identities to confuse pirates and privateers.

tub. A slow, ungainly starship.

V

victualing yard. A part of a port where the stores of many victuallers, chandlers, and other merchants are found. Typically, purchased items are delivered later.

victualler. A starship that sells provisions to other starships in orbit above a port. Also: the owner of such a starship or his or her store in a port.

viewport. A large window in a starship, typically found on the bridge/quarterdeck.

W

wardroom. The cabin belowdecks reserved for the warrant officer and spacers assigned significant roles by him or her.

warrant officer. The ranking officer belowdecks, typically a spacer who has worked his or her way up through the ranks, but sometimes one drawn from the bridge crew.

wash. The ion exhaust of a starship's engines.

watch. A period of time during which an officer, a crewer, or a group of crewers is responsible for certain operations aboard a starship. The day is divided into seven watches: the first watch lasts from 2000 to midnight, the middle watch from midnight to 0400 hours, the morning watch from 0400 to 0800, the forenoon watch from 0800 to 1200, the afternoon watch from 1200 to 1600, the first dog watch from 1600 to 1800, and the second dog watch from 1800 to 2000.

watch officer. The ranking officer during a given watch. The watch officer retains command in the event of an emergency during his or her watch unless relieved by the captain or sometimes the first mate.

Y

yaw. A starship's motion to port or starboard of the vertical axis but maintaining the same horizontal bearing. Yaw refers only to an involuntary motion, as when a starship is damaged, malfunctioning, or being piloted poorly. A deliberate move to port or starboard of the vertical axis is simply a turn.

Turn the page for a sneak peek at
the third thrilling book in the
Jupiter Pirates series, *The Rise of Earth*.

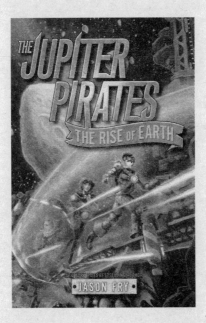

1

THE RELUCTANT CAPTAIN

"Your fuel-efficiency calculations for the simulated journey from Callisto to Neptune are incorrect . . . again," Vesuvia said in her cool, dispassionate electronic voice.

It was the "again"—combined with the brief pause preceding it—that made Yana Hashoone angry.

The computer program that the *Shadow Comet* used to communicate with her crew was a stern taskmaster. Vesuvia had insisted it was an ideal time to test sixteen-year-old Yana, despite the fact that it was only an hour into the morning watch, with the rest of the bridge crew asleep in their cabins on the top deck and most of the crewers snoring in their hammocks one deck below.

Yana was the only member of her family who actually enjoyed the solitude of the middle and morning watches. Her twin brother, Tycho, and their older brother, Carlo, spent that time doing homework, but Yana preferred to tackle her studies in her cabin after dinner. While everyone else was sleeping, she'd read old tales of Earth on her mediapad or run battle simulations in which she tried to turn famous commanders' historical defeats into successes. A silent quarterdeck was perfect for such pursuits, with no lights except those of her crew station and the main screen displaying a readout of anything the ship's sensors might scan.

"Let me point out—*again*—that doing these calculations by hand is pointless," Yana said, tapping at her keyboard. "See my screen? That sensor indicator displays the fuel efficiency. It's currently ninety-four point one percent, resulting in a lovely shade of emerald green. Exercise successfully concluded. Now leave me alone."

"Since you prefer a real-world exercise, the *Comet* is currently cruising in the Hildas, four days, nine hours, and eleven minutes out of Ceres on its way to Jupiter," Vesuvia said. "Based on this—"

"Is it possible you think I've sustained a head injury? First you think I can't read a sensor indicator, and now you think I don't know where we are."

"Please do not interrupt," Vesuvia sniffed. "Since you indicate you are aware of the *Shadow Comet*'s position, and are presumably also aware that the *Shadow Comet* has followed this course before, please tell me what level of fuel efficiency is the historical norm for this heading."

Yana sighed and tapped at her keys, but Vesuvia wasn't finished. "You appear to be determining fuel efficiency for the current heading. The request was for the historical norm."

"Which is why I was *querying the Log*," Yana said, hastily switching over to that input screen. Some parts of the Log were captain's eyes only, but most of its records were available to any member of the bridge crew, and summarized thousands of voyages made over hundreds of years.

As Yana typed, the access prompt for the Log flickered and vanished, replaced by an error message.

"It seems the Log is unavailable," Vesuvia said. "Perhaps battle damage has severed linkages somewhere."

"That's a dirty trick, even for you."

"Severed information linkages are a known hazard of combat situations," Vesuvia said, sounding pleased with herself. "As are interrupted fuel lines, damage to engine baffles, and other perils. An officer faced with such a situation must be able to do more than read a sensor indicator—she must also be able to verify that a sensor indicator is providing accurate information."

Yana sighed and folded her arms, glaring at the main screen.

3

"All right, have it your way," she grumbled, then reached for her keyboard. "But first let me run a quick sensor scan."

"Sensor scans run automatically every ninety seconds," Vesuvia objected. "Anomalies are reported to the watch officer immediately."

"And what if *you're* the one who isn't providing accurate information?" Yana asked. "Shouldn't an officer verify that you're performing those automatic scans correctly and communicating them properly?"

"Your stalling tactics are—" Vesuvia said, then stopped. "Sensor contact."

"That isn't funny."

"The sensor contact is not simulated. It has just entered the long-range sensor cone. Initial readings positive for metallic signature and ion emissions."

Yana leaned forward to stare at her scopes. This wasn't an exercise—it was real.

"The heading is for Saturn," Yana said. "Distance to sensor contact?"

"Eighteen thousand kilometers and closing."

Not so long ago, a heading for Saturn wouldn't have meant anything. The ringed planet's moons were officially members of the Jovian Union, whose government the Hashoones served as privateers. But two years ago, a group known as the Ice Wolves had proclaimed Saturn's independence, then backed up their claim by defeating a hastily assembled task force of Jovian warships—a task force that had included the *Comet*.

Some called the Ice Wolves revolutionaries, because they were seeking freedom from the Jovian Union just as the Jovian Union had once sought freedom from the government of Earth. Others called them pirates, and charged that they were part of a plot hatched by Earth to regain control of her former colonies.

Yana liked arguing about such things—it made family dinners more entertaining. But this wasn't the time for it. The ship out there could be loyal to Earth, registered with the Jovian Union, or pledging allegiance to the Ice Wolves.

If she was Earth's, the *Shadow Comet* could seize her as a prize, with the possibility of a big payday. If she was Jovian, Yana would have to let her pass—under the terms of the Hashoones' letter of marque, only enemy ships could be attacked.

And if the ship out there was loyal to the Ice Wolves? Well, that was the kind of question that led to arguments at dinner.

"Seventeen thousand kilometers," Vesuvia said.

"Tactical readout on the main screen," Yana said. "Sensor and communications data on my monitor. And shut off the autopilot—I'll take the sticks."

"Acknowledged," Vesuvia said as lights began flashing on Yana's station.

A U-shaped control yoke whined and rose from beneath her console. Yana closed her hands around it and pressed her feet against the pedals below the console. The *Comet* could be steered from any of the five stations on her quarterdeck. Normally, that job belonged to Carlo—just as communications was generally Tycho's job. But both of them were still asleep on the top deck.

Yana twitched the control yokes to port and the *Comet* rolled obediently in that direction.

"Controls green," Yana said. "Charge up the communications mast. Don't display colors—black transponders."

"Acknowledged."

Every starship had transponders that identified her allegiance to other ships. But unless on a heavily patrolled spacelane or near port, starships rarely broadcast that allegiance openly, for fear of attracting enemy privateers—or, worse, pirates who'd attack any vessel, without regard for the law. So civilian starships typically hid their true loyalties, showing no allegiance or claiming a false one.

"Query the bogey's transponders," Yana said. "And do you have a sensor profile yet?"

"No response to transponder query. Still building sensor profile. Shall I beat to quarters?"

"I'm thinking."

If that was a hostile ship out there, the *Comet* would need all hands, including crewers manning the gun emplacements below and a full complement on the quarterdeck. Beating to quarters now would ensure everyone was decently awake if the *Comet* had to fight. On the other hand, it would be humiliating to rouse the entire ship just to make small talk with a Jovian freighter. Tycho would yawn theatrically all day, while Carlo would mock her mercilessly until they reached Jupiter.

"Fifteen thousand kilometers," Vesuvia asked. "Have you reached a decision?"

"I have. Detach from the long-range tanks, plot an intercept course, and open communications channels. But that will do for now. I want to take a look first."

"Acknowledged. Disconnecting fuel lines. Stabilizers disengaged."

Yana felt a bump, and then the *Comet* shook slightly as Vesuvia broke the connection between the sixty-meter frigate and the massive, bulbous fuel tanks she used for long-distance travel. With the *Comet* now free to maneuver, Yana pushed down on the control yokes and the privateer dipped her nose and accelerated away from her tanks.

"This is the *Shadow Comet*, operating under let-ter of marque of the Jovian Union," Yana announced, the sensor masts broadcasting her message into space. "Unidentified craft, activate transponders and respond at once."

There was no response but the hiss of static.

"Fourteen thousand kilometers," Vesuvia said. "Sensor calculations complete. Profile fits modified Galicia-class caravel, confidence eighty-four point three three percent."

A caravel was a small freighter, perhaps thirty or forty meters larger than the *Comet* and relatively speedy. But the Hashoones' ship was faster, Yana thought with a grin.

"Unidentified caravel, we are on an intercept course," she said. "Activate transponders immediately."

The *Comet*'s bells rang out—a *clang-clang*, followed by a brief pause and a single clang. Three bells meant it was 0530. The bells struck every half hour, whether the privateer was sitting peaceably in port or trading broadsides with an enemy in deep space.

As the bells died away, Yana heard footsteps behind her. She turned and saw Diocletia Hashoone—her mother and the *Comet*'s captain—descending the forward ladderwell. Her eyes were puffy with sleep. Right behind her came Yana's father, Mavry Malone.

Yana started to ask what her parents were doing on the quarterdeck, then stopped herself—no self-respecting officer could sleep through the familiar rattle and bump of a starship detaching from her long-range tanks.

"Modified Galicia-class—she's ignoring my hails," Yana said as Diocletia studied the tactical screen with a practiced eye.

"Well, that's rude," Mavry said, flopping into his chair at the first mate's station, then putting one foot on the console and yawning.

"She's heading for Saturn?" Diocletia asked.

Yana nodded, automatically rechecking her sensor scans.

"That could mean anything these days," Mavry said as they heard new footsteps behind them.

"Hang on—transmission's coming through," Yana said. "She's flying Jovian colors."

"Of course she is," said twenty-year-old Carlo, peering over his sister's shoulder. "Ask for the current Jovian recognition code."

"*Thank you*, Carlo," Yana said. "I've handled an intercept before, you know. Would you also like to remind me about the difference between port and starboard?"

"Well, Yana, take your left hand—"

"Behave yourselves," Diocletia said as Carlo settled into his chair and began buckling his harness. "Where's Tycho?"

"Right here," Tycho said sleepily, his footsteps a bit tentative on the ladder.

"Nice of you to join us, little brother," Carlo said, his grin causing the pale scar on his right cheek to flex.

Tycho grunted, refusing to be baited, but Yana saw spots flare in his cheeks, beneath his haystack of dark hair. Tycho was frequently the last to the quarterdeck except for their grandfather, Huff. And Huff had an excuse—he needed to attach his cybernetic limbs and power up his systems.

"Vesuvia, I'll take the controls," Carlo said.

"Belay that," Yana snapped. "My starship."

"Don't be ridiculous—"

"Members of the bridge crew will obey the officer of the watch or return to quarters," Diocletia said without taking her eyes off the tactical screen.

"Twelve thousand kilometers," Vesuvia said.

"Tyke, monitor communications—let me know if she tries to call for help," Yana said. "Unidentified caravel, acknowledge transmissions before I start knocking pieces off of you."

"Hold yer fire, *Comet*," a voice grumbled over the speakers. "Our commo board's slow to warm up. This be the *Lampos* out of Ganymede, runnin' freight from Ceres. We're bound fer Titan—an' we're on a tight schedule."

"We won't keep you, *Lampos*," Yana said. "Transmit the current Jovian recognition code and we'll be on our way."

Silence.

"Eleven thousand kilometers," Vesuvia said.

Yana looked at Tycho, who shook his head.

"*Lampos*, transmit the recognition code," Yana said.

"We just did, missy," the caravel's captain growled.

Yana covered her microphone as Huff Hashoone descended the ladderwell, his metal feet clanging as they struck the rungs. Nearly half of Huff's body was metal—the rest of him had been blasted away in a terrible battle when Yana and Tycho were babies. One side of his face was a mass of scarred flesh, while the other side was a bare skull of gleaming chrome. The old pirate's artificial eye blazed white as he stared at the screen, and the wicked-looking blaster cannon screwed into his metal forearm twitched in response to its master's thoughts.

"*Lampos*, we are not receiving your code," Yana said. "Retransmit immediately."

"We *are* transmittin'. P'raps yer sensor mast is faulty, missy."

"Call me missy one more time and I'll turn your ship into a debris field," Yana said, then shut off her microphone. "Vesuvia, diagnostics on all sensor masts."

"I already checked," Tycho said. "Our gear is functioning normally."

"Ten thousand kilometers," Vesuvia said.

Yana reactivated her microphone. "*Lampos*, we claim your vessel under the articles of war governing interplanetary commerce. Heave to and prepare for boarding. Vesuvia? *Now* you can beat to quarters."